RESCUED BY THE WOLF

OTHER WORLD SERIES BOOK FOUR

RAMONA GRAY

EK PUBLISHING INC.

RESCUED BY THE WOLF

OTHER WORLD SERIES BOOK FOUR

Radek has no use for humans. As a wolf shifter, he values loyalty and courage - something humans lack. As far as he's concerned, the only thing worse than a human is a shifter who falls in love with one.

When he stumbles upon a human woman deep within the forest that surrounds his home, he's tempted to leave her to her fate. A human means trouble - especially one who speaks of a glowing orb and strange creatures who drink blood. He would be wise to ignore her intoxicating scent and the way her soft body fits so perfectly against his.

Sara isn't sure what's happening or how she ended up in the forest. She's desperate to find her friends, and is relieved when the large wolf shifter saves her life. Despite Radek's coldness toward her, she knows he's her only chance of survival. When he reluctantly agrees to help her, she is puzzled by his hatred toward her. She's even more astonished when she discovers that his hatred is hiding a sizzling, uncontrollable desire for her.

Note: This is Book Four in the Other World Series. Although it tells a stand-alone story, you will have a better understanding of the characters if you read Books One to Three BEFORE reading Book Four.

CHAPTER 1

Sara groaned and touched her head without opening her eyes. She felt sick to her stomach and she wasn't surprised by the wetness on her fingertips. She opened her eyes and squinted at her fingers. They were red with blood and she groaned again before sitting up cautiously.

The world spun crazily for a moment and she dropped her head and waited to see if she was going to throw up or pass out. After a moment, the dizziness passed, and she lifted her head again. She studied her surroundings. She was in a forest with thick trees that rose high into the night sky, and she staggered to her feet.

"Abby?" She called. "Abby, are you there?"

There was no reply and she pinched back her moan of dismay and cleared her throat.

"Abigail? Can you hear me? Abigail!" She shouted this time and cringed when something in the dark answered with a loud and raucous cry.

"Okay, it's all right," she murmured to herself as she wrapped her arms around her thin body. The night air was cold, and she was soaking wet and already beginning to shiver uncontrollably. "Don't panic. They probably aren't far."

You don't know that. You don't even know where you are. For all you know, Darius and his men could be closing in on you right now. You need to get moving before they find you.

She squinted at the trees. They didn't look particularly familiar to her but until Darius had raided their village, she had never really been outside of it before. Besides, the last thing she remembered was stepping into the light with the man Abby had called Michael. She didn't have a clue how she could be in the arena one moment and then in the middle of the forest the next, but what was important was finding Abby and the others before Darius found her.

Gathering her courage, she moved away from the tree she was leaning against and stared up at the sky. She could just see the moon filtering through the trees and she sighed. At least it had stopped raining, she was grateful for -

There was a soft rustling behind her and she swung around, her heart beating fiercely and the coppery taste of fear flooding her mouth.

"Wh-who's there?" She whispered.

There was no response and she took a step backward as her heart began to slow to its normal pace. It was nothing. Just the wind perhaps.

What wind?

Never mind that, she really needed to –

The rustling happened again, and she gave a soft shriek of surprise when a large bird emerged from behind a tree. It was huge, well over nine feet tall, and its plumage was a rich, dark, green. Its head was a lighter shade of green and its red eyes stared curiously at her.

She blew her breath out in a relieved little rush as the bird shook itself and spread its short wings. It didn't look like it could fly at all with such short wings, but its legs were long and powerful looking and ended in thick, sharp talons. It tapped one talon against the ground as it cocked its head and studied her silently.

"Go on, bird. Shoo!" She waved her arms weakly at it and it took a step backward, shaking its body in a disgruntled manner. Feathers floated to the ground and she clapped her hands over her ears when the bird opened its beak wide and let loose with an eardrum shattering cry.

"Stop!" She shrieked. "Stop it!"

The bird continued and, feeling like her ears were bleeding, Sara groped on the ground for something to throw. Her fingers swept past a large stone and she gripped it and threw it at the bird. The stone hit the bird dead center in the chest, and it gave a startled squawk and closed its beak.

"Get lost!" She shouted at it.

Her eyes widened when the bird lowered its head and scratched at the ground again with one large talon. It looked like it was getting ready to charge and she backed away as it made a high-pitched humming noise.

"Get out of here," she whispered.

The bird scratched twice more and then, with a quickness that surprised her, charged. She screamed and sprinted through the trees. She could hear the bird closing in on her. She dodged around the trees and thick bushes, looking desperately for a hiding spot as she forced herself to run faster.

She risked one terrified glance over her shoulder and screamed again in sudden terror. The bird was nearly upon her, and its large and ridiculously sharp beak was opening and snapping with deadly force.

Her foot hit an exposed root and she went sprawling, landing on her belly with a hard thud. The breath was knocked out of her and she stared mutely at the bird standing over her. It made another screeching cry and then it was pecking at her, its beak tearing through the soft flesh of her side.

She gasped in air and shrieked. She beat at its feathery body with her fists before trying to crawl away. The bird clamped one talon around her calf and dragged her back as easily as a mouse, before pecking viciously at her once more.

She curled into a ball and covered her head with her arms as the bird pecked at her exposed back. Each peck of its beak was like a hot needle in her flesh and she screamed again, the sound muffled by her arms.

She was going to die. She was going to be pecked to death by some weird giant bird and no one would ever know that she –

There was a loud growling and the bird suddenly made its own terrified squeal before it was ripped away from her. It hung on grimly to her leg with its talons, and she screamed in pain when its sharp nails dug into her skin and tore it open.

There was more growling and snarling and she lowered her arms and sat up, staring in numb shock at the giant, black wolf that was ripping and tearing into the bird's belly. The bird squirmed and twisted but the wolf held it down easily. It tore a large chunk of intestine from the bird's stomach and the bird made one final scream of pain before collapsing.

The wolf leaped from the bird's body, raised its snout to the sky and howled deafeningly. Sara moaned and scooted backward on her butt as the wolf lowered its head and stared at her.

"No, please, no," she whispered, holding her hands out pleadingly in front of her as the wolf stalked toward her on stiff legs.

She closed her eyes in defeat as the wolf bent its head and

sniffed at her face. If she was lucky the wolf would end her life more quickly than the bird would have. She jerked in fear when the wolf chuffed and his warm breath washed over her face.

There was a moment of silence and she opened her eyes warily. The wolf had moved away from her and her eyes widened in surprise when it abruptly shifted into a man. He was the biggest man she'd ever seen, his shoulders broad and his arms thick and powerful. His hair was short and a slightly darker shade of blond than hers, and his eyes were dark brown.

His skin was tanned and the muscles in his abdomen rippled as he walked toward her. He looked like he was chiseled out of granite and he was, she thought dimly, the most beautiful man she'd ever laid eyes on.

He was also completely naked.

She blushed furiously as her gaze dropped to his penis. She had never seen one before and her eyes widened at the size of it. How on earth would that ever fit into a woman? She wasn't naïve, she knew how sex worked, but there was no way something that size could fit into –

He crouched in front of her and she raised her eyes to his face. He was frowning and she gave a soft whimper of fear when he leaned forward and inhaled again. A brief look of distaste crossed his face. "You are human."

"Y-yes," she said. "My name is Sara. What's yours?"

"How did you travel so deep into the woods, human?" He asked.

For some odd reason his low voice sent shivers down her spine.

"I – I was with some friends and we got separated," she said.

He continued to stare at her, and she gave him a weak

smile. "Thank you for saving me from that bird. Wh-what was that?"

He frowned again. "How do you not know what a floran is? Have you been living under a rock?"

"A floran?" She gave him a puzzled look. "I've never seen one before."

He grunted in annoyance before standing and walking away. She staggered to her feet and yelped as pain coursed down her leg. She could see the blood flowing from the deep scratches left by the bird's talons and her entire back felt like it was on fire.

"Hey, don't leave!" She called. "Please!"

He sighed and turned back around. "Go and find your friends, human."

"I don't know where they are, and I don't even know what part of the forest I'm in. Could you – do you think you could help me find them?"

He hesitated, and she gave him a pleading look as she balanced carefully on one leg. "Please? I'm sorry. I hate to ask you for help but I'm -"

"No." He interrupted. "I have helped you enough."

WHEN HE REFUSED TO HELP THE HUMAN, THE SHIFTER expected her to beg, perhaps to start crying and wailing like so many humans were prone to doing. But she only nodded and gave him an oddly gut-wrenching look of resignation. "All right. Thank you for your help."

He frowned when she turned and limped deeper into the woods. She should have been heading for the edge of the forest, not deeper into it. A floran would be the least of her worries if she continued on.

"Human!" He shouted.

She flinched and gave him a tentative smile. "Yes?"

"Do not go that way. Go in that direction." He pointed behind him and she nodded before limping toward him.

"Right, okay. Thank you."

He frowned again as she moved slowly past him. Her face was unbelievably pale, even for a human, and he could see the blood flowing steadily from her leg. She was dressed in an astonishingly tiny skirt and odd-looking shirt that barely covered her small breasts. Her skin was covered in goose bumps, and he winced when she passed by him and he saw the multiple puncture wounds from the floran's beak on her back. All of them were bleeding freely and he couldn't imagine how much pain she was in. The way she was bleeding she was lucky she hadn't passed out.

As if she heard his thoughts, she stopped and swayed alarmingly before reaching for a tree with one shaking hand. She gripped the bark and dropped her head forward, taking a few deep breaths before coughing.

"You're okay, Sara," she whispered to herself. "You're okay, just

She swayed again and, as she crumpled to the ground, he ran forward and caught her before she could hit the hard floor of the forest.

She stared up at him with hazy eyes. "What's your name?" She whispered.

"Radek," he grunted.

"Radek," she breathed before her eyes rolled up in her head and she fainted.

He studied her pale face before cursing and lifting her into his arms. With a soft grunt, he carried her deeper into the forest.

CHAPTER 2

"Reese!" Raina came hurtling into the cabin and Reese sat up in the bed and gave her a startled look.

"Raina? What's wrong?"

"Kane and the others are back! You will not believe what they brought back!"

Reese laughed. "I'm sure it'll be something I've never seen before. I swear, there are more creatures living in this forest than -"

"They're not creatures! Well, two of them might be, they smell very odd but the woman! The woman smells like you, Reese!" Raina crowed excitedly.

"What are you talking about, Raina?" She slid out of the bed as Raina grabbed her hand and began to yank her toward the door.

"Come quickly! You must see them!"

Reese pulled on her pants and threw a sweater over her thin top before hurrying after Raina. She followed the young shifter to the campfire in the middle of the clearing. It was close to dawn and the entire pack had gathered in the clearing. Raina, holding her hand, pushed her way through them.

"Move, Teagan! Daven – get off my foot!" She finally reached the front and grinned triumphantly at Reese. "Look, human!"

Reese stared at the humans standing next to the fire. There were seven of them, three women and four men and she studied them silently as Kane joined her.

"Hello, my love." He squeezed her waist and kissed her on the mouth.

"Hi."

He pulled her close to him before bending his head to her ear. "We found them in the forest after the storm. The blond male spoke of a ball of light bringing them here."

She stiffened and stared at him in shock as he rubbed her back with his warm hand. "The blond male and the long-haired male are not human."

"What are they?" She asked in a low voice.

"I do not know. But the woman who wears a collar around her neck smells like you."

"Are you certain?"

"Aye."

He raised his head and stared at the strangers. "This is my mate, Reese."

The woman wearing the collar gave the lightening sky an oddly nervous look before smiling at Reese. "Hello, I'm Abigail. This is Val, Michael, Neil, Maria, Sienna and Faren. It's nice to meet you."

The shifters stared silently at them and Abby glanced at Val. The vampire was studying the largest shifter thoughtfully and she took his hand and squeezed it. His gaze shifted to hers and she shook her head. She knew exactly what he was thinking, and she squeezed his hand again. He was fast, he might even be able to take down the big one, but there were too many of the shifters. They would kill him if he killed their leader.

"Tell us what type of creature you are," the big shifter said suddenly.

"I'd rather not," Val said coldly.

"I do not care. You will tell us what we want to know."

Val laughed. "And if I do not?"

"I will kill you," the shifter replied.

Faren rolled his eyes. "If he only knew how many of his kind we have killed, Val. Remember, those wolf shifters that attacked us in Tolina? Their leader was bigger than this idiot. Do you remember?"

"I remember," Val said.

"We took his head and we'll take yours." Faren smiled at Kane.

The shifter growled and both Val and Faren hissed in reply. The crowd of shifters made a loud noise of surprise at the sight of their fangs. Abby groaned when nearly all of them began to swell and thick hair sprouted on their faces.

"Oh fuck," Neil said. "We're fucking dead."

As the shifters growling grew louder, their leader's mate wormed free of his grip and took a step toward Abigail. As Kane reached for her, she said, "Abigail – what's your favourite Starbucks drink?"

"Caramel macchiato," Abby replied automatically.

A large grin crossed the woman's face and she glanced excitedly at her mate before glaring at the other shifters. "Enough, all of you!"

To Abby's surprise, they quieted immediately, and the woman tugged on Kane's arm. "Let me go, Kane."

He frowned but did as she asked, and the woman took a few steps closer to Abigail. Val hissed at her and Abby squeezed his hand. "Don't, Val."

She took her own cautious steps forward and studied the woman carefully. She was very tall, Abigail guessed her to be close to six feet, and she was on the chubby side with long dark hair and dark eyes. She was dressed in loose cotton pants and a heavy sweater.

"Did you – did you just ask me about Starbucks?" Abigail asked.

Reese nodded. "What kind of car did you drive?"

"A Honda Civic. It was a piece of crap."

"I drove a Toyota Corolla. Where are you from?"

"California. You?"

"Montana." Reese's face was flushed with excitement and she moved even closer. "What's your favourite movie?"

"Wizard of Oz. Yours?"

"The Princess Bride." Reese reached out and touched Abby's face. "We're from the same world."

Abby swallowed heavily. She was trying hard not to cry, and she could see the glint of tears in Reese's eyes. "Yes, I think so."

She had a ridiculous urge to hug the woman in front of her and she laughed out loud when Reese suddenly threw her arms around her and hugged her. She returned her hug and Val and Kane watched in confusion as they both burst into tears.

"WILL THIS BE ENOUGH?" REESE ASKED. OUTSIDE THE CABIN, Teagan and Borek placed the last board across the window and hammered it into place. There were small beams of light streaming in between the boards and Val navigated around them as Abigail nodded.

"Yes, I think so."

"Good. We put Faren in a cabin just across from this one." Reese paused. "You might want to speak to him later. He was already trying to convince one of the female shifters to join him so he could feed from her. Kane will allow you to stay but only if you do not feed from any of us."

Val, tiredness seeping through every bone in his body, studied the woman. He suspected that the only reason the alpha shifter had allowed them to stay was because Abigail and Reese came from the same world. He yawned hugely and sat down on the bed as Abigail joined him.

She stroked his long hair and grinned at Reese's gasp of surprise when Violet came zipping out of his hair and flew around the room. She hovered in front of Reese and studied her carefully as Reese reached out her hand.

"What is she?"

"She's a pixie. Her name is Violet and she cannot speak."

"Hello, Violet. My name's Reese." Reese continued to hold out her hand and after a moment Violet landed on it.

"Do you need to feed before you go to your daysleep, Val?" Abigail asked.

He shook his head. "No, but I would feel better if you stayed in the cabin with me, little dove."

She smiled. "I want to visit with Reese, honey. I'll be fine."

He gave her a weary look. "I do not trust them."

"You don't trust anyone." She kissed him and pushed him onto his back on the bed. "Don't worry, I can take care of myself. I'll come back later this afternoon and join you."

"WAIT — SO THEY'RE NOT THE UNDEAD?" REESE ASKED.

"Not like they are on our world, anyway," Abigail replied.

"Val has a heartbeat and a soul but he needs blood to survive."

"Weird," Reese said.

They were in Reese and Kane's cabin, it was the largest one in the group, and Reese poured Abigail more tea before sitting down at the table again.

Abigail smiled tentatively at her. "The last year and a half have been nothing but a giant ball of weirdness."

Reese nodded, "I can imagine. I've been here less than six months, but I've seen things I never thought were possible. I mean, I'm in love with a guy who can change into a wolf whenever he feels like it."

"I'm with a guy who drinks my blood on a daily basis," Abigail said.

They sat in silence for a moment before Reese said, "I've never been happier. How about you?"

"The same," Abigail said. "I miss our world so much but the thought of being without Val…"

She trailed off and Reese squeezed her hand. "What do you miss the most?"

"Coffee," Abigail said immediately. "I used to work at Starbucks. You?"

"A hot shower."

"Oh God, that would be amazing," Abby sighed.

"I think," Reese said slowly, "what I really miss the most is just having someone else who – well – understands things like electricity and cars and giant shopping malls. Kane tries, he really does, but it's hard for him to imagine those things."

Abby squeezed her hand. "Well, now you have me. We can talk about our old lives whenever we want."

"Yes, I suppose we can," Reese said. "Do you ever think about trying to get back to our world?"

"At first, yes. Even though I knew it would probably be

impossible. What are the odds of even finding another glowing light ball that serves as a portal to another world?"

"You found one," Reese said.

"Yeah, and it didn't return me to our world," Abigail said. "It doesn't matter. I won't leave Val and I'm not sure that being in our world would be the best thing for him. Do you want to return?"

Reese shook her head. "No, I love Kane and would never leave him. But," she smiled ruefully, "I really do miss hot showers."

Abigail yawned tiredly and Reese gave her a hesitant look. "Can I ask you something, Abigail?"

"Yes."

"How can you be sure that you are in love with Val? You told me that once they bite you there's an obsession for them. How do you know that what you're feeling isn't just the obsession from being bitten by him?"

Abby smiled at her. "After Val found me again, I wouldn't let him bite me. I swore I would never be under his control again. When he was nearly killed by Darius, I healed him with my blood because I loved him. I had been foolishly denying it for weeks, but I loved him, Reese. There was no more denying it."

She yawned again. "I need to get some sleep. Once it's dark, Val and I will search the forest for Sara."

"Kane sent a few members of our pack to search for her," Reese said. "If she's out there, they'll find her."

"Unless she's hiding from them. She'll be frightened."

"How do you know that she's even on this world?" Reese asked delicately. "What if she was sent to another world?"

A look of dismay crossed Abby's face. "I guess I don't, but I have to search for her. She's all alone and she's – well – she's fragile. I need to find her before something else does."

"You can't go into the forest alone," Reese said, "I will ask Kane to send more of our pack with you."

"Thank you, Reese," Abby said. "I can't tell you how much I appreciate that."

She stood and moved to the door of the cabin. A cold wind was blowing and with a final smile at Reese, she ran across the clearing and disappeared into the cabin she had left Val in.

MARIA SANK TO THE GROUND AND LEANED AGAINST THE large pine tree. A bitterly cold wind was blowing and flakes of snow were starting to fall from the sky. She wrapped her arms around her knees and stared blankly at the ground.

She was safe. She wasn't going to die. At least not in some arena surrounded by thousands of jeering, taunting vampires. Her hand drifted up and touched her short hair. She had cut it herself using the blade of a dull knife, after her first fight in the arena. The woman was older and smaller than her, but she had fought bitterly for her life. She had grabbed Maria by her long hair and nearly cut her throat. If she hadn't stabbed her before the woman could slice her throat…

She took a deep breath as hot tears leaked down her face. She had killed two people and although she had killed them in self-defence, she was still a murderer. She had resigned herself to dying and her sudden freedom still felt like a dream. Any moment she would wake up in her cell and know that today could be the day she died.

Stop, Maria. You're safe. You'll never go back to that arena again. Have you forgotten that you're on a different world?

More tears coursed down her cheeks. As happy as she

was to be alive and away from the vampires, the thought that she would never again see her world filled her with a horrible depression. How had her husband lived with the knowledge that he would never set foot on his world again? How had he –

He didn't, remember? He killed himself because you didn't love him enough to help him forget his own world and live in yours. It's your fault he's dead.

"Shut up," she moaned softly. "Just shut up. It's not your fault."

There was a low growling and she froze with her hands gripping her knees as a grey wolf appeared in front of her. Her eyes widened and she leaned back against the tree. There was no escape for her. The wolf would hunt her down and rip her apart.

She sighed with relief when the wolf shifted to his human form. The man, he was older with grey hair and a beard and a stupidly good body for his age, squatted in front of her. She avoided looking below his waist as he studied her carefully.

"You should not be in the woods alone, human." His voice was gravelly and low.

"I'm not far from your home," she said.

"Too far to survive if a creature of the forest caught your scent."

"I'm fine," she said shortly. She wished he would leave her alone. It was getting increasingly difficult not to stare at his naked body – the guy had to be pushing sixty, how the hell did he have a six pack? – and she wanted to wallow in her self-pity.

"Why are you out here?" He asked.

"I wanted to be alone." She gave him a pointed look.

He ignored her look and moved closer to her. She looked

away as he reached out and touched her short hair. "You have strange hair for a female. It is so short."

"Please don't do that," she said as she moved her head away from his hand.

He leaned closer and inhaled. "I like your scent, human. It's pretty."

"Thank you," she stared into his dark brown eyes as he inhaled again.

"Um, could you move back please?" She asked when he actually stuck his face into her neck. His beard tickled and she squirmed away from him.

He studied her for a moment, "Why are you crying, human?"

"Because I spent the last few months thinking I was going to die every day," she snapped.

She rubbed at her forehead wearily. It wasn't the shifter's fault that she was feeling this way. "I'm sorry, I shouldn't have -"

"Why were you going to die?" He interrupted.

"I was captured by vampires and they made us fight to the death for their amusement."

His gaze dropped to her chubby body and she crossed her arms nervously over her chest. "What? Why are you looking at me like that?"

"They used you for fighting?" He gave her a skeptical look before reaching out and stroking one thigh. "You're very soft and weak, even for a female. It would not be much of a fight."

"I killed two people," she said angrily as she pushed his hand away from her leg. "I'm not as weak as you think me to be."

"How did you kill them?" He asked curiously.

"I don't want to talk about it," she said. "Just leave me

alone, please."

The tears were leaking back down her face and she rested her forehead on her upraised knees as the shifter stared at her.

"You're safe now, human. Stop your crying - it is foolish and pointless."

She glared at him. "My name is Maria and I'll cry if I fucking feel like crying."

He blinked at her sudden anger. "I am Asher."

She made a soft squeak of surprise when he put one hard hand under her arm and lifted her to her feet. "Come, human. It is not safe in the woods. I will escort you back to my pack."

He shifted to his wolf form and growled when she started to sink back to the ground. She glared at him and had to restrain herself from swatting him on his haunches when he used his large body to push her forward.

"Fine! I'm going," she said irritably.

He growled again in reply and wiping the tears from her cheeks, she followed him toward the cabins.

"IT IS TOO DANGEROUS," KANE SAID.

"We're not asking you to send your pack members with us," Abigail replied. "Val and I will go on our own."

"I will go as well," Michael said.

Abby smiled gratefully at him. "Thank you, Michael."

"It is my fault she is lost," he said.

She shook her head. "No, it isn't."

"It sort of is," Val said.

Abigail glared at him and he shrugged. "He let go of her hand, little dove."

"It was an accident," she snapped at him.

"The leech is right," Michael said. "I lost my grip on her hand and it's my fault."

"Michael -"

"Who fucking cares who is to blame!" Faren interrupted irritably. "The girl is lost. And we all know that if she is on this world, she's dead. Even if she has managed not to be eaten by something, she'll never survive this storm. She was wearing very little and there are no wolf shifters to give her warmer clothing."

Abby glared at him before pulling the sweater she wore closer to her body. "All the more reason for us to leave right now. We need to find her before she freezes to death."

"You cannot," Kane said.

"Kane," Reese placed her hand on his arm, "We have to -"

"No." Kane shook his head. "I am sorry for your friend but they will not survive if they go out in this storm. It is only going to grow worse, and the humans and the creature will freeze to death."

"We can't just sit here and do nothing," Abigail protested.

The wind howled and Neil, holding Sienna's hand, said, "He's right, Abby. If you go out there looking for her, you'll die."

Val took Abby's hand as Violet flew out from his hair and landed on Abby's shoulder. She patted her neck anxiously as Abigail chewed on her bottom lip.

"You cannot go out there, little dove."

"Val, she'll die."

"Yes, she may," he said. "And you will die searching for her."

"When the storm ends, I will take you out in the forest myself in search for her," Kane said. "I promise."

"Search for her body, you mean," Abby said.

The crowded cabin was silent, and Abby pulled away from Val and went to the window. She peered outside into the blowing snow as Faren sighed. "I don't suppose there's any point in trying to find something to eat in the woods tonight?"

Kane shook his head. "No creatures or humans will be out in this storm."

"Fuck," Faren snapped. "I'm going to fucking starve to death."

"It's been two days, Faren," Val said. "Must you be so dramatic?"

"I get dramatic when I'm hungry," Faren said sulkily. He eyed Sienna thoughtfully. "Perhaps you would care to join me in my cabin, sweet girl?"

Neil yanked Sienna behind him and glared at Faren. "Go anywhere near her and I'll cut off your head, leech."

Faren laughed. "She found my touch pleasing enough before, human. I suspect that her yearning for me has not quite dissipated. Why should you let her suffer? Give her to me. I will ease her need far better than you ever will."

"I'm going to fucking kill you!" Neil roared. He charged forward and bellowed angrily when Val and Kane stepped in front of him. The shifter and the vampire held him back easily as Faren grinned tauntingly at him.

"What's the matter, human? Does it bother you that your girlfriend desires me?"

"Shut up!" Sienna snapped as she placed a hand on Neil's back. "I don't desire you."

"We both know that isn't true," Faren said.

Neil surged forward, trying to break free of Kane and Val, and Val glared at Faren. "Leave, Faren! Go back to your cabin!"

"I am not your pet, Val," Faren replied. "Why should I do as you command?"

"Because I'll rip off your damn arm if you don't," Val said shortly. "Go, Faren."

With a small grin, Faren turned to leave. A woman, tall and blonde with warm brown eyes, was standing behind him. She stared unblinkingly at him as he inhaled. A strange look flickered across his face and he inhaled again before leaning forward and pressing his face into her neck.

"Adina," Reese said nervously, "get away from him."

Adina ignored her and closed her eyes. She bit her bottom lip when Faren licked her throat delicately.

"Adina," Reese repeated before moving toward them. Kane immediately stepped in front of her, blocking her from Faren, and shoved the vampire to the side before taking Adina's arm.

"Go to Reese," he said.

Adina stared blankly at him and Kane gave her a small shake. "Go, Adina. Your alpha commands it."

She nodded and with a final glance at Faren, hurried to Reese's side. Reese put her arm around her and said in a low voice, "Adina? What were you thinking?"

Adina didn't reply as Faren, his hands shaking, straightened his shirt before walking to the door.

"Well, this has been fun," he said with a forced cheerfulness. "But I think it's best if I go." His gaze flickered to Adina before he opened the door and disappeared into the blowing snow.

"Neil?" Sienna said. "I don't want him, I don't."

"I know." Neil kissed her on the mouth before nodding to Val. "I'm going to take Sienna back to our cabin."

"Everyone should return to their cabins," Kane said. "There is nothing we can do about the girl until the storm ends."

The door opened and Raina appeared in a swirl of cold air

and snow. She shook the snow from her hair and stomped her feet. "Reese? Can I sleep in yours and Kane's cabin tonight? Radek is still not home and I -"

She stopped and stared at the people in the cabin. "I'm sorry, I didn't mean to interrupt."

"You didn't," Reese smiled at her and Raina put her arms around her waist, "and yes, you may sleep in our cabin tonight."

"Thank you, Reese," Raina said before hugging her.

Kane snorted irritably and Reese grinned at him before kissing Raina's forehead. "The bed is made up in the second bedroom. Go and climb under the covers and I'll be in to say goodnight in a few minutes, all right?"

"All right," Raina agreed happily.

She went into the second bedroom as Kane muttered into Reese's ear, "You will regret letting the girl stay the night when you have to be quiet while I'm fucking you."

She blushed and whacked him on the arm before turning to Abby. "Abby, I'm sorry. Really I am."

Abby didn't reply and Val put his arm around her waist and led her to the door. "Come with me, little dove."

"What do you want?" Faren said rudely.

The woman pushed past him, and he shut the door of his cabin as she tugged back the hood of her cloak. Her pale cheeks were flushed with the cold and she was covered in snow. She shook her cloak out and clasped her hands nervously in front of her.

"Adina? Is that your name?" Faren asked.

She nodded and he paced back and forth in front of her as she watched him carefully.

"What are you doing here?" Faren said softly.

"You know why I am here," she said.

"I want to hear you say it."

She took a deep breath. "I want you to feed from me."

He stopped pacing. "Do you? And why is that?"

"Does it matter?" She asked. "You're hungry and I have what you need."

She shrieked in surprise when he moved across the room in a blur. One strong arm wrapped around her waist and pinned her body against his, while his hand tangled in her hair and drew back her head. He stared at the pulse beating in her neck and licked his lips.

"I am very hungry," he muttered.

She was trembling against him and he could see the fear on her face, but she tilted her head to the side. "Do it. Bite me."

He bent his head to her throat, and she stiffened against him in anticipation. She made a sharp cry of disappointment when he pressed a light kiss against her cold skin.

"Wh-what are you doing?" She whispered when he kissed his way up her throat. He licked behind her earlobe, making her entire body tingle. She jerked against him helplessly when he cupped one full breast.

"You smell good, Adina," he muttered into her ear before taking her mouth in a hard kiss. She moaned and returned his kiss, touching his fangs with the tip of her tongue as he pressed his erection against her belly. He wormed his hand under her shirt and cupped her naked breast. He traced circles around her nipple with his thumb as she moaned again.

"Do you want me, Adina?" He whispered.

"Yes," she whimpered. "Please."

A shudder of desire went through him. The woman was unbelievably soft, and he suddenly, desperately wanted to strip her naked and bury himself within her. Her blood was singing sweetly to him and his fangs lengthened as he lowered his face to her throat.

Bite her. Take her blood and her warm body and she'll be yours forever.

He hesitated. If he bit her, she would want him and the thought of having her in his bed every night was oddly pleasurable. The woman was a stranger but fuck, he wanted her badly. She would be his, drawn to him by her obsession to be bitten repeatedly but it would be a false need.

He stared down at her flushed face. She wanted him right now – an honest and true desire. He could take her to his bed without biting her and the pleasure she would feel from his touch would be real. He could make her feel good. When she sought him out again, it would not be the compulsion from being bitten that would be leading her to him but rather the pleasure he brought to her with his mouth and his tongue and his cock.

Bite her!

He pressed his fangs against her smooth skin and her body immediately stiffened. She was frightened. She wanted him to bite her, for whatever reason, but it also scared the hell out of her. He squeezed her breast but instead of a soft moan of pleasure, he could hear her panting harshly as the scent of her fear bloomed between them.

He pushed away from her so suddenly she stumbled and nearly fell. "What is wrong?"

"Nothing," he said hoarsely. "Leave me."

"What? I – you need to eat," she said in confusion.

"You need to leave," he said.

"But you need blood, do you not? I am offering mine," she said. "Why aren't you -"

"Go!" Faren suddenly shouted at her. "Get out of my cabin before I change my mind and drain you dry, human!"

She staggered back with a white face and huge eyes before fleeing from the cabin. He slammed the door behind her, blocking out the wind and the snow. He made a harsh noise of anger before picking up the small table and throwing it across the cabin. It crashed into the wall and broke into pieces as he clenched his fists and paced restlessly back and forth.

CHAPTER 3

R adek shifted the human in his arms. He had been walking for nearly two hours and as light as the human was, his arms were growing tired. The wind was blowing, and he glanced at the dark storm clouds. It was going to storm but whether it would be rain or snow, he couldn't tell. Either way he needed to find shelter that was large enough for the both of them.

He stared down at the woman in his arms and muttered a curse. His time around Kane's human mate had made him soft toward the humans. He should have left her to her fate. The three humans they had in their pack was already too many.

He bent his head and sniffed at the female. Her scent wasn't completely unpleasant. In fact, she had a light almost flowery scent that his wolf found oddly intriguing. It urged him to sniff her again and he lifted her a little higher and buried his nose in her hair. He had never seen such curly hair, and his wolf made a soft growl of happiness at the smell and softness of it.

He thought briefly about what it would be like to sink his

hands into that mass of soft hair. How she would look as he guided her mouth to his cock and her hair draped across his thighs. It would –

He suddenly growled and shook himself all over. What the hell was he thinking? The woman was a human and while he may no longer have such a deep hatred for them, he had no interest in them. Humans were weak and this woman in his arms was obviously no exception.

He checked her leg. He had found some liptus leaves and wrapped them around the deep scratches in her leg and plastered them to the wounds on her back. The liptus plant had large broad leaves that were used by healers. At least he thought they were. He had seen the blonde woman, Adina, using them on Theran's human mate when she was badly scratched by a poison tree. No blood oozed from beneath the leaves and he breathed a sigh of relief. Not that he cared if the human bled to death, but he did care about leaving a trail of blood that would lead predators right to them.

He snorted to himself. How humans even survived to outnumber them, he would never know. They must fuck and breed like bunnies to make up for their losses to injury and sickness. Based on the woman's outfit she obviously had no problem with fucking. Her skirt barely covered her ass and he could easily see her nipples through the thin material of the odd-looking shirt she wore. He studied the thin leather collar she wore around her neck. What kind of human would allow herself to be collared like a dog? His eyes dropped to her small chest again. Thanks to the cold air, her nipples were hard and pressing against the thin material. Without thinking about it, he rolled her in his arms until her chest was pressed against his. The human was freezing cold and if he didn't find shelter soon, she would -

His wolf made a warning growl and he froze and lifted his

head. He sniffed the air and his eyes widened. Holding the woman, he turned and slipped into the thick brush. He scanned the area desperately, the slow burn of panic beginning in his belly as he moved quietly through the thick bushes. Branches scratched his naked body and he grunted impatiently when one got caught in the woman's blonde hair. He pulled it out roughly and continued on, his eyes darting back and forth and his nose sniffing the air constantly.

He stopped and turned to his left, his eyes gleaming in the darkness. There was a dark shadow against a large dead tree about twenty feet away. Praying he was right, he strode quickly toward it. The tree was, in fact, hollow and he released his breath harshly. The bugs were drawing closer and with no time to check if there was anything else living in the dead tree, he turned sideways and squirmed into the tight opening.

There wasn't enough room for him to stand. He sunk to the ground and moved the woman until she was straddling him. He grunted at the feel of her naked center pressing against his cock. The woman wore no underwear under her short skirt. He ignored the feel of her damp, warm skin as he shoved her face into his thick neck and pressed himself as far back in the tree as he could.

He cocked his head, listening for the faint flapping of wings. After a moment, he heard it and his wolf growled. By the sounds of it, there were at least five of the mantorians and he couldn't slow the rapid thump of his heart.

As the sound of the wings grew louder, he groaned inwardly when he realized the woman was stirring on his lap. She moaned and he threaded one hand through her thick mass of hair and clamped the other one over her mouth. She made a muffled noise of fear and he placed his mouth to her ear.

"Make not a sound, human. Our lives depend on it."

She froze and then nodded in understanding. He released her, dropping his hands to his side and she sat up. It was dark in the tree, but he could see the fear in her eyes. Her body was already beginning to vibrate but to his surprise, she kept her mouth shut and allowed no whimpers of fear to escape.

The flapping grew louder, and the tree creaked alarmingly above them. He groaned to himself again. It sounded like the damn mantorians were roosting on the fucking tree. A thousand trees in the forest and they had to choose this one. The buzzing began, a sound felt more than heard. Although he had heard it a hundred times before, his teeth began to ache and he could feel the adrenaline surging through his body. It was a sound meant to disarm an enemy and he watched as the woman's shaking intensified. She bit her bottom lip and stared wild-eyed at him. He put his finger to his lips, and she nodded but he could see the fear growing in her eyes. The buzzing grew louder, and the woman clapped her hands over her ears. He watched in alarm as she swayed back and forth, and he yanked her against his chest. She buried her face in his throat, keeping her hands over her ears, and he stroked her thin thighs. She was freezing cold and her teeth were chattering so loudly he worried the mantorians would hear it.

"Be quiet!" He hissed into her ear.

She nodded and with a snort of disgust, he put his arms around her in a desperate bid to warm her. The buzzing continued and after nearly ten minutes, even he wanted to bolt from the tree. The buzzing of one mantorian was bad enough but the sound of five was excruciating. His wolf howled miserably, the woman moaned, and he squeezed her so tightly she made a low gasp of pain. Loud flapping of wings signalled the mantorians' descent from the tree to the ground. The woman stared at the long white legs of the bugs, her eyes growing rounder and rounder. He gripped the back of her neck and forced her face back into his throat.

The buzzing grew and his wolf howled madly. As suddenly as they appeared, the mantorians rose into the air and flew away. The buzzing faded and then disappeared completely, and he released the harsh breath he was holding as the woman made a soft whimper. They waited silently for nearly fifteen minutes and when he shifted beneath her, she sat up and stared at him.

"What was that?" She whispered.

"Mantorians," he muttered. How the hell the woman knew nothing of mantorians or florans he didn't know

"What was that horrible noise?"

She was almost crying, and he realized that he was stroking her upper back, trying to soothe her.

He dropped his hands and scowled at her. "It's how they communicate."

"It was so awful," she whispered before shuddering all over.

He didn't reply and she gave him a tentative smile. "Thank you for helping me."

"Aye," he muttered.

"Your name is Radek, right?"

"Aye." He wished she'd stop talking. Her low voice was doing weird things to his insides.

"Is it – can we leave now?" She asked him.

He frowned at her and she licked her lips nervously. "Is it safe to go out? I need to find my friends."

"It's late. We will spend the night here," he said gruffly.

She looked like she might argue, and he glared at her. She gave him a frightened look and bowed her head immediately, cupping her elbows as her thin body trembled. Her lips were turning blue. The only part of her that was warm was resting against his cock, and he studied her mouth as she gave him another timid look.

"Do you have any food?" She asked suddenly.

He scowled at her. "Does it look like I have food, human?"

She stared at his naked chest and blushed miserably. "Sorry, that was foolish of me to ask. I didn't even think that you were naked and -"

She stopped, her eyes widening, and he almost laughed as it finally sunk in that her pussy was resting against his cock. She tried to scramble back, making a soft cry of pain when her head and injured back scraped across the tree.

He gritted his teeth as her pussy rubbed against him, and he willed his cock to behave as he grabbed her arms and shook her. "There is no room for you to move, human. Stop it!"

"Please, I'm not wearing any underclothes," she whimpered and tried to squirm away again.

With a soft snarl, he gripped the back of her neck and pulled her forward. "I am well aware of that, human. Lucky for you I am disgusted by humans in general and have no interest in what you have to offer."

She flushed and he gave her a predatory grin. "But if you keep squirming the way you are, I may be persuaded to change my mind. My cock cares not that the warm pussy rubbing against it belongs to a human."

Her eyes widened and she froze on his lap. He grinned again at her. "Unless that's what you want. Is it, human? Do you want my cock deep in your naked little pussy? Do you want to be fucked?"

"No," she whispered.

"No what?"

"No, I don't want to be fucked."

Tears were sliding down her cheeks to drip onto his naked chest and self-loathing flooded through him. The woman was injured, freezing, and clearly frightened of him and he was suddenly deeply ashamed of his treatment of her. If his mother was alive and saw how he was acting she would be angry and, even worse, disappointed in him.

"Do not cry, human." He made his voice gentle and wiped the tears from her cheeks with a rough swipe of his thumbs. "I will not harm you, I promise."

She nodded and he didn't stop her when she rose up on her knees so that her pussy was no longer touching him. She balanced stiffly on her knees, trying to keep as much of her thin body from touching him as possible. She would not be able to hold that position all night and even if she could, the cold air would soon send her back to the warmth of his body.

He leaned his head back until it rested against the tree and closed his eyes. "I'm going to sleep, human."

"All right, I'll keep watch," she said anxiously.

He cracked open one eye. "Keep watch?"

"For the mantory things or the giant birds," she replied.

He snorted. "Even asleep I will hear them before you do."

"Oh. You have good hearing, huh?"

"Aye, human. I have good hearing," he said sarcastically. "Now quiet your tongue, I want to sleep."

"Okay. Good night, Radek."

He grunted in reply and closed his eyes.

She lasted longer than he thought she would. For an hour and a half, she balanced above him on her knees but eventually the cold and the pain drove her back into his lap. As she settled against him, he kept his body still and his breathing even. She rested her head on his broad chest and he kept his arms at his sides even when he felt the warm tears dripping onto his skin. She cried silently for nearly half an hour before she fell asleep. Her cold body went limp as she drifted into sleep. When she slid sideways, he caught her before she could smack her head against the tree.

He pressed her against his chest, and she made a soft sigh and wrapped her thin arms around his waist. He rubbed her thighs and her upper back until her cold skin was warmer and then closed his eyes and waited for sleep.

IN HER DREAM SHE WAS AS NAKED AS THE WOLF SHIFTER. SHE was lying on her back in a soft bed and a large fire was crackling loudly and sending delicious waves of heat over her naked body. Radek was lying beside her and she moaned when he traced the tip of his finger across her breast. Her nipple hardened immediately, and she arched her back when he dipped his head and sucked on the dark pink bud.

"You're so beautiful, Sara." Instead of his usual anger, his voice was filled with a hoarse desire that heated her insides into an aching need.

"Please touch me, Radek," she whispered.

"Whatever you want." He smiled at her and traced her flat abdomen before making tiny circles in the soft, blonde curls between her legs.

"Open your legs," he murmured.

She spread her legs immediately and made a soft cry of excitement when he stroked the lips of her pussy. She moaned his name as he slid his finger between her wet lips and rubbed her clit. The roughness of his fingers felt amazing and she couldn't stop the rise and fall of her hips.

"Harder, Radek," she moaned.

He kept the same gentle pressure. Feeling desperate and needy she wrapped her arms around his body and rubbed herself against his fingers. She was going to come. She could feel it starting, a warmth in her belly that was rapidly turning into a blazing burn.

He groaned and her eyes popped open. She blinked in confusion. The bed and fire were gone and she could feel the cold air blowing against her back. Radek's hand was in her hair and he gripped it tightly as she looked up at him. His eyes were closed and he made a low moan as his hand tightened in her hair. She realized with a mixture of shame and desire that she was rubbing her naked crotch against Radek's very erect cock.

Stop, Sara! Her inner voice said anxiously. *He's going to be so angry with you.*

Yes, he would be. He'd made it very clear that she disgusted him but oh God, she was so very close to coming and her body didn't seem to care that he would be angry. Her body wanted the orgasm and it was determined to have it. She rubbed harder, her breath coming in harsh pants as another wave of pleasure rolled through her belly.

A moan slipped from between her lips and Radek's eyes opened. His formerly dark eyes were glowing a bright green. She stared in fascination at them even as her traitorous hips rocked and pressed and rubbed against his cock.

She was so close. Just a few more seconds and she would have the relief she so desperately craved and damn the consequences. His cock slid exquisitely along her clit. A brief part of her was surprised at how smooth and hard it was, and she moaned again. One more stroke, just one more touch and –

She yelped in surprise when he pushed her out the opening of the tree. She landed on her side, her body screaming in protest when it felt the cold, wet blanket of snow. He squirmed out of the tree and she caught a glimpse of his cock, slick and wet with her juices and unbelievably big. She had thought it to be big before but seeing it erect dampened her desire almost immediately. He would split her in half if he tried to take her.

He hurried away from her, standing a few feet away and leaning against a tree as he breathed heavily of the cold air. The snow that had collected on the ground didn't seem to bother him nor did the heavy flakes that were falling from the grey sky.

She could feel shame flooding through her. She had practically tried to rape the wolf shifter – a complete stranger - and her face burned hot as she remembered the way she had rubbed herself against him. What was she thinking? She staggered to her feet as the cold snow burned like fire, and stumbled toward him.

She gathered the tattered remnants of her pride and cleared her throat. "Radek, I'm so sorry. I – I shouldn't have done that."

He didn't reply and she touched his naked back hesitantly. He jerked away from her, his breath hissing out between his teeth and snarled, "Do not touch me, human!"

She backed away, fear making her throat close up, as he turned his head and pinned her with his angry, glittering glare. "Go back into the tree."

When she hesitated he bared his fangs at her. "Now!"

She fled back to the tree, slipping inside of it as Radek turned away from her and stared blindly into the trees. His cock throbbed and pulsed, and his wolf was howling at him to take the small, soft human. When he had woken to find her rubbing her pussy against him, her heat and wetness surrounding his cock, he had very nearly lifted her tiny body and thrust himself inside of her. He knew without a doubt that she would be wet and tight. He groaned when an image flashed through his mind of him pushing her onto her hands and knees, lifting that ridiculously short skirt and sliding his cock deep into her pulsing warmth. He would fuck her hard and rough until she was begging him to make her come and when he felt her coming around him, he would sink himself deep within and fill her with his seed.

His cock pulsed again at the thought and with a muttered curse he reached down and gripped it. He jerked once, twice, and then threw his head back and tamped down his howl of release as he came in large spurts. He leaned against the tree, his breath coming in harsh pants as he rubbed his cock and the last of his seed spilled onto the cold snow.

He waited nearly ten minutes for his legs to stop shaking and his breathing to return to normal. He stared at the hollow tree, sorely tempted to just shift to his wolf form and abandon the human to her fate. His wolf made an odd angry snarl at the thought and he frowned before returning to the tree. He bent and peered inside. The woman was huddled in a small ball inside the tree. When he held his hand out to her, she moaned and shook violently.

"Please don't kill me," she whispered. "I'll leave. If you let me live, I'll walk away and you'll never see me again. Please."

Another unexpected feeling of shame went through him. He had frightened her so badly she thought he would kill her simply for rubbing against him. He crouched and smoothed the anger from his face.

"I'm not going to kill you, human."

She continued to stare wide-eyed at him and he held his hand a little closer to her. She sank back against the tree. He saw her wince of pain when her injured back pressed against the rough wood and he tried to smile reassuringly at her.

She tensed even more and her eyes widened. "Are you going to rape me?"

His stomach clenched at the thought and he shook his head immediately. "No, of course not. I won't hurt you. I promise."

When she continued to hesitate, he moved back a little and smiled again at her. "Come, human. The storm is only going to grow worse. We must find better shelter or you'll freeze to death."

She nodded and he moved away as she slid out from the tree. She tugged down her short skirt nervously and crossed her arms over her chest when his gaze dropped to her breasts. Her eyes skittered to his naked cock. He thought he saw a look of disappointment mixed with relief, before she dropped her gaze to the ground.

"Come. We must hurry." He turned and walked away without looking to see if she would follow.

He could hear her stumbling after him and, already, the sound of her teeth chattering. It would be faster if he shifted to his wolf form and allowed her to ride on his back but his wolf growled angrily at the thought. He was not a horse and the human would simply have to hurry. If she froze to death before they found shelter, well, that would not be his fault. Besides, it would be better for her. How she had survived this long as weak and soft as she was, he had no idea.

She's very soft. And warm and wet. We should take her. She wants us to.

He ignored his wolf and scanned the woods. They were at least a day's journey from his pack. If they didn't find shelter soon, the woman really would die.

CHAPTER 4

"I'm sorry. Could we stop, please? Just for a moment," the woman said.

They were only walking for half an hour and he sighed in annoyance before turning to face her. "The storm is growing worse, human. If we do not find shelter, you will die. Do you understand that?"

She nodded, her face pale and her body trembling. "I just need a moment to warm my feet."

He cursed to himself as she leaned against a fallen log and lifted her leg. Her feet were pale, and she winced as she wrapped her hand around one and rubbed briskly. The cold snow didn't bother him, but he had forgotten the human was barefoot.

He strode toward her, his stomach sinking a little at the way she shrunk back, and lifted her onto the log. He took her feet and tucked them under his arms. They were like blocks of ice and he scowled at her. "Why did you not remind me of your bare feet?"

"I'm sorry," she whispered.

"You will be sorry if they blacken and fall off," he said gruffly.

She gave him a frightened look and he waited five minutes before examining her feet. "They do not look like they are bitten by frost. Are they warmer?"

"Yes, thank you." She smiled tentatively before pulling her feet away from him. "I can walk now."

He shook his head and turned until his back was to her. "Climb on."

"I – what?" She said.

"Climb on." He gave her an impatient look and pressing her lips together nervously, she stood on the log and draped her small body across his back. He hooked his hands around her thin thighs and pulled them around his hips. He groaned at the feel of her warm core rubbing against his back and she tried to squirm free.

"I can walk, really. I was just being a baby and -"

"Be quiet, human."

He started to walk, and she made a frightened squeak and clung to his broad shoulders. They walked in silence for nearly an hour. He needed to find shelter. The female on his back would not survive the storm even clinging to him.

"Am I too heavy?" She asked.

He snorted. The woman weighed less than Raina and he used to carry his baby sister around on his back for hours. "No, human. I carry my sister on my back all the time and you are half her size."

"You have a sister. That's nice," she said. "I have – had – a brother. His name was Garen. What's your sister's name?"

"Raina."

"What a pretty name. Is she older or younger?"

"Younger."

"Do you have any other siblings?"

"Do you always ask this many questions?" He grumbled.

"I'm sorry."

"You say sorry too much."

"I – I'm sorry?"

He laughed, he couldn't help it, and she patted his shoulder nervously. "I do need to apologize for uh, what happened in the tree. I was having a dream and that's not an excuse but I should not have, uh, touched you like I did. I know I disgust you."

"Aye, you do," he lied.

She flinched and he could practically feel the heat of her embarrassment rolling off of her. "I know. I'm very sorry, Radek. I'm not usually like that."

"Are you not?"

"No." She sounded like she was going to cry and feeling unsettled, he hurried to change the topic.

"What happened to your brother?"

"Darius and the other vampires attacked our village. He was killed trying to protect me."

"What is a vampire?"

She jerked in surprise and he pulled her closer against him until he could feel the soft curls between her legs nestled against his back. He ignored his wolf's soft growl of happiness.

I hold her closer only to keep her warm. I have no interest in mating with the human, he snarled inwardly to his wolf. The damn thing had scented the female and didn't care that she was human. It wanted her badly.

He realized the human was speaking to him and he craned his head to stare at her. "What did you say?"

"You really don't know what a vampire is?"

He could feel heat rising in his cheeks and he scowled at her. "Tell me what it is and be quick about it."

"Well, it's a – a blood sucker. They need blood, human blood, to live. They have sharp fangs and they bite their victims and drink their blood."

He stopped and stared silently at her. Her blonde curls were covered in snow and the flakes were catching on her eyelashes. Her lips were still blue despite his body heat.

"There is no such creature."

"There is." She frowned at him. "I was captured by Darius. He's a very cruel vampire who was using humans for sport. He made them fight to the death in front of an audience of vampires."

"You were going to be used in a fight to the death? Someone as little as you? It does not seem like much of a sport."

She flushed. "No, I – I was going to be used for something else."

"What?"

"Well, I – you know…"

She trailed off. Her face was very pale except for the bright red spots high on her cheeks.

"No, human. I do not know. Tell me before I lose my patience."

"Some vampires keep humans as pets. I was captured by Darius to be used for feeding from and for, uh, sex."

His hands tightened around her thighs. "They forced you to fuck them?"

She shook her head. "No. A few days after Darius killed my brother and brought me to his home, I was given to a nice vampire as a present. At least I think he is nice, Abigail says he is, and he didn't want me for food or sex."

"Why not?"

"Well, he has Abby. He feeds from her and I think he loves her."

He was silent and she cleared her throat. "It's why I'm dressed the way I am. The vampires took my clothes and made me wear this outfit. I normally wear, um, underclothes."

"How did you escape the vampires?"

"I don't really know. I mean, they were about to kill us because they discovered that Joven was not who he said he was and -"

"Who is Joven?"

"He's the nice vampire, only I think his name is Val. I'm not sure. It was very confusing."

"Go on."

"They were about to kill us and then there was this big ball of light and Michael had my hand and we -"

"Who is Michael?" He interrupted. "Is he your mate?"

His hands tightened on her thighs and she squirmed against him.

"Radek, my legs – please, you're squeezing too tight," she whimpered.

He relaxed his hands and gave her a guilty look. "Is Michael your mate?"

"No, I don't have a – a mate. I don't even really know who Michael is."

His wolf had surged forward at the mention of this Michael and the question about her mate had spilled out before he could stop it.

She has no mate! Are you happy? Will you stop this ridiculous behaviour now?

His wolf growled happily, not the least bit ashamed of his behaviour, and he rolled his eyes as the woman continued.

"Anyway, Michael took my hand and he dragged me into

the ball of light and the last thing I remember is his hand slipping from mine. Then I woke up in the middle of the forest and that bird thing attacked me and then you saved me."

The shifter didn't reply, and she touched his shoulder. "Radek, what's wrong?"

"You are not on your world any longer, human," he said suddenly.

"What?"

"That light, it brought you to a different world. My world."

Sara stared at the back of Radek's head before whispering, "That's impossible."

She wondered if the shifter had gone mad and she unconsciously eased her upper body away from his as she glanced around them. If she got away from him, she could slip away in the storm. Maybe he couldn't smell her in the snowstorm.

If you leave him, he won't even bother searching for you. He doesn't care if you live or die.

That was true. Of course, if she did leave him, she really would die. She knew that perfectly well. Even if the shifter was mad, she needed him to find Abigail and the others.

"It is true."

"No, it can't be."

"It is," he insisted. "I know of another who was brought to my world."

"Someone else from my world?" She asked.

He shook his head. "No, I do not think so. You don't have the same scent as her."

She was silent and he gave her a quick look. Hot tears

were flooding her cheeks and he frowned at her. "Why are you crying?"

"Why am I crying?" She glared at him. "You just told me that I'm on some – some different world and you wonder why I'm crying?" She smacked him on the back. "Put me down."

"No."

"Put me down! I have to use the bathroom!" She punched him on the shoulder. She imagined he barely felt the blow, but he slid her to the ground.

She pushed down her skirt and scowled at him before marching into the bushes.

"Do not go far, human!" He called after her.

She turned and gave him another glare. "I know!"

———

"HUMAN, DO NOT FALL ASLEEP!" RADEK HAD TO SHOUT TO be heard above the howling wind.

"I'm so tired," she muttered.

"Stay awake!" He shook her and she moaned as she slumped against his back.

He squinted through the blowing snow. Three hours had passed, and the storm had grown steadily worse. It was almost impossible to see, and he realized that if he did not find shelter soon, the human really would die. Even his heat was being leeched from his body by the wind and she was like a frozen piece of meat against him.

He walked blindly forward. Perhaps he could shift to his wolf form and wrap himself around her. It might work better to –

He grunted when he ran into the wall. He touched the wood with his hand and walked beside it until his fingers traced the seam of a door. He fumbled for the door handle and wrenched open the door. He placed the human on the floor and slammed the door shut against the fierce wind. The sound of the storm quieted to a dull roar and he shook the snow from his thick hair before glancing around.

They were in a small shack and he wrinkled his nose at the horrific smell. The smell was strongest from the pile of pelts in the corner. He approached it and kicked at it gingerly before clapping his hand over his nose. The scent of human stench along with urine and semen was thick in the air and he cursed under his breath. There was no way he was using any of those pelts to wrap Sara in.

There was no fireplace and no furniture other than a chair and an old table shoved against the far wall. Other than the pile of pelts in the corner and a pair of worn boots by the door, the room was utterly empty. The woman made a soft groan and he hurried over and sat her up.

"Wake up, human." He shook her until the snow fell from her mass of curly hair and frowned when she didn't respond.

"Wake up, human!" He patted her on the face.

When she still didn't respond, he hesitated and then returned her to the floor before covering her small body with his. The shack was cold but being out of the wind and the snow had helped and he was already warmer.

She moaned at the feel of his warmth and he touched her face. "Open your eyes, Sara."

Her eyelids fluttered open and she stared blearily at him. "Radek? Where are we?"

"We're out of the storm."

"Why does it smell so bad?" She wrinkled her nose and he smoothed back a strand of her curly hair.

"You will get used to it. I'm going to shift to my wolf form. It will be warmer for you if I do. All right?"

She nodded. Already her eyes were drifting shut and he didn't like the paleness of her skin. He stood up and shifted abruptly before curling his massive body around hers. He chuffed at her, nudging her face with his nose and she squinted at him before touching the fur on his face with a trembling hand.

"So warm," she whispered before she turned on her side and pressed her body into his. She dug her toes into his abdomen and burrowed her face into the thick fur on his chest. He covered her legs with his long tail. She was so tiny that she was nearly completely covered by him and she sighed happily before slipping into slumber.

Radek rested his chin on his paws and closed his eyes wearily.

———

SARA STRETCHED CONTENTLY AND BURROWED DEEPER INTO the pelt. Her bed was incredibly warm and soft and there was a steady and oddly comforting thumping noise coming from it. She pressed her ear against the noise and smiled happily. Her brother would be coming soon to wake her. Dova, their cow, was a stubborn beast and Sara was the only one she would allow to milk her. She shivered a little at the thought of leaving her warm bed. Normally she didn't mind but her bed was not usually this comfortable.

She frowned and rubbed her cheek against the soft fur. The fur was softer than the bear pelt that was on her bed. Where did this one come from? She buried her fingers in the soft fur and stroked. Her bed made a rumble of contentment and she smiled and stretched her hands higher. She rubbed and the bed lifted its head so she could stroke the thick fur on its throat. It chuffed happily, its hot breath washing over her, and she scratched harder. When the warm and wet tongue licked her forehead she giggled. It was –

Her eyes flew open and she stared at the wolf beneath her. She was lying completely on top of his warm body, her tiny one nestled against him. Her eyes widened when his eyes opened and his light green eyes glowed brightly. The confusion in them turned to outrage and she squeaked in alarm when the wolf shifted and soft fur turned to warm, hard flesh.

"Get off me!" Radek shoved her away and she landed on the floor with a thud as he scrambled to his feet and backed away from her.

RADEK SHOOK HIMSELF ALL OVER AND GLARED AT HER. HE had licked the woman, licked her like he was nothing more than a common dog and she his mistress. And why? Because she had scratched his throat? He growled angrily as Sara climbed to her feet.

She gave him a cautious look as she backed away. "I'm sorry, Radek."

He glared at her and she cleared her throat nervously before looking around. "Wh-where are we?"

He shrugged dismissively. "I do not know. I stumbled onto it in the storm."

"What is that smell?" She covered her mouth and nose with her hand and he glared again at her.

"If this place is not to your liking, human, you are more than welcome to go out into the storm and find another."

"No." She shook her head and wrapped her arms around her thin torso. "This is good, Radek. Thank you."

He stalked to the door and opened it. Cold wind and snow

blew in and she shivered and took a step back as he peered into the gloom.

"Stay here," he ordered curtly.

"Where are you going?"

Without answering he disappeared into the storm, slamming the door shut behind him.

CHAPTER 5

He returned an hour later, his arms filled with wide
green leaves, wet plants and green pods. He dumped
them on the table and she examined them curiously.

"What are these?"

"Food," he said gruffly. "Eat only the stalks of these ones,
"he pointed to a pile of limp plants, "and the leaves of those."

She nodded and smiled tentatively at him. "Thank you."

"Aye." He picked up one of the green pods. "These are
called charkas. You peel them like this and eat the center."

He peeled away the green skin and scooped out the white
meat-like substance within it before holding it out to her. She
took it from him gingerly, being careful not to touch his
fingers, and ate a small piece of it. It was good and her
stomach rumbled as she quickly ate the rest of it.

"They're really good. Thank you."

He nodded and ate a few of the charkas himself. He'd had
to dig through the snow to find them and the plants but the
girl had looked like she was going to pass out. He needed to
get something into her belly.

She ate a few of the plants and another charka before stepping away from the table. He frowned at her. "Eat more."

"I'm full," she said. "You eat the rest."

"You are not full."

"I am," she insisted. "I don't eat very much."

He stared at her flat abdomen and she blushed a little.

"You eat less than a bird," he said grumpily as he ate another charka.

"A regular bird or one of those floran things?" She gave him a small smile and he rolled his eyes before picking up the liptus leaves.

"Come here, human."

"Why?" She asked nervously.

"I want to check your wounds."

Her hands reached around and touched the leaves that were still plastered to her back. "I think they're okay."

"Stop arguing with me."

She licked her lips nervously before approaching him and turning around. He peeled the leaves from her back and examined the puncture wounds. He thought they looked all right. They weren't swollen or dripping blood anymore and he quickly peeled the leaves from the back of her leg. She hissed as it stuck to the deep scratches and he scowled when trickles of blood dripped down her leg.

"Stay there," he said curtly.

He stepped outside and gathered a handful of snow. He rubbed the snow on her leg, cleaning off the dried blood and washing away the fresh as she flinched and tried to move away.

"Hold still," he muttered. He curved one hard hand around her thigh and held her steady as he wiped at the scratches.

"How bad does it hurt?" He asked.

"Not as bad as it did but more than my back does," she replied in a soft voice.

"The scratches are deep but they should heal with time." He wrapped her leg with two of the wet liptus leaves. She cringed at the cold but stayed where she was as he went outside and gathered another handful of snow.

"Bend over the table."

"What?" She gave him a startled look and he rolled his eyes.

"Relax, human. I just want to wash your back of the dried blood."

She bent over the table gingerly, her arms resting on the top of it as he stepped behind her and studied her. Her short skirt had ridden up and he could see the bottom of her small ass. His cock stirred and he had to stop the ridiculous urge to reach out and caress her pale flesh.

She suddenly yanked at the bottom of her skirt and gave him a look of embarrassment. "Radek, are you going to wash my back or…"

"Aye," he snapped. He tore his gaze from her ass and washed her back quickly with the cold snow. He was rougher than he intended, and she flinched but didn't say anything.

"Sorry," he muttered.

"That's all right."

He picked up the last liptus leaf and carefully pressed it over the puncture wounds on her lower back.

"They tingle," she said suddenly.

"Aye. They have healing properties." He took one final look at her ass before stepping away from her.

She straightened and smiled sweetly at him. "Thank you for helping me, Radek."

He nodded and she clasped her hands nervously together

before boosting herself up and sitting on the table. "So, how long do you think the storm will last?"

He didn't reply. She cocked her head as her entire body shivered, and she listened to the wind howl. "Are the storms always this bad here? On my world, we get snowstorms but they rarely last more than a few hours."

When he continued to stay silent, she rubbed her hands together. "This place is really great, huh? I mean, it smells pretty bad. I was going to use those pelts to keep warm but," she shuddered, "I couldn't do it, but at least we're out of the wind. Did you smell those pelts? They smell like a dead horse. I'd rather freeze to death. Too bad this place doesn't have a fireplace. That's strange, right? Why would you build a cabin in the woods and not have a fireplace? Wouldn't you want -"

Sara stopped talking as Radek suddenly shifted to his wolf form and walked away. He laid down in the corner farthest from her and closed his eyes.

"Don't feel like talking, huh?" Sara said with forced cheerfulness. "I understand. My brother doesn't – didn't – talk much either. He always said I talked enough for both of us. He was right, I suppose. I do talk a lot. I guess I just have a -"

The wolf opened his eyes and growled at her. She shut her mouth with a snap and gave him a weak smile. "Right, I'll just be quiet now."

The wolf stood and circled three times before collapsing on the floor with his back to her. He sighed and she wiped at the tears that were starting to slide down her cheeks. She was scared and cold, her leg was throbbing, and she was suddenly incredibly homesick. She took a deep breath and wiped away the tears. She had cried enough. If she was going to survive in this new world, she had to become tough. She was all alone and stuck in a smelly shack with a very large wolf shifter who hated her. She was certain that when the storm ended, he would abandon her. Her only chance was to figure out a way to make the wolf shifter like her.

She stared at his sleeping body and considered offering herself to him. If she pleased him in bed and gave him sex whenever he wanted, perhaps he would be more inclined to keep protecting her until she found other humans. He was handsome and it's not like she had anyone special to give her virginity to. Perhaps she would tell him she was a virgin and that she would give it to him in exchange for his protection.

Yes, she decided suddenly, that's what she would do. Her friend Tora had told her that men liked virgins. They liked being the first to introduce a woman to sex, she said it made them feel more like men. The shifter might not be a conventional man but, no doubt, he would have the same reaction.

Have you gone mad, Sara? You've seen the size of his cock. It will hurt so bad.

Yes, it probably would but if she asked him nicely maybe he would be gentle with her.

He won't be, her mind moaned. *You know he will not.*

She studied her short fingernails. No, he wouldn't be, but she would just close her eyes and wait for it to be over. Tora said that once the man was inside a woman, it only lasted a few moments. She could handle a few moments of pain.

He finds you disgusting. Remember?

She flinched. He had said that humans disgusted him but, in the tree, he was hard, and he had moaned like he enjoyed her touch. Besides, he had admitted that his cock didn't care that she was a human.

She slid off the table and moved the chair to the small window near the door. It was grimy with dirt and she scrubbed a small clean spot with her fingers before sitting on the chair and peering at the whirling snow. She glanced at the shifter. He hadn't moved and she shivered delicately as she rubbed her arms. She would wait until he woke from his nap. He would be in a better mood and she could use the time to figure out what she was going to say to him.

———

RADEK STARED THROUGH HALF-LIDDED EYES AT THE HUMAN. He had stayed in his wolf form all afternoon. The female had not tried to speak to him again, although she had taken quick, nervous peeks at him for the first few hours. Eventually she had stopped staring and alternated between limping the length of the small room, swinging her arms and stomping her feet to warm up, and sitting on the chair at the window. Every once in a while, she would sing softly to herself. They were words and a tune he didn't recognize, and he hated to admit that he liked the sound of her singing.

He sat up when she stood and walked to the door. As she slipped the boots sitting by the door onto her feet, he barked. She flinched and gave him a nervous look. "I just have to use the bathroom."

He stood and stretched, yawning hugely before padding to the door. She opened it and he slipped outside. The snow was still falling heavily and it was so dark he knew the human couldn't see a thing.

She hesitated by the cabin and gasped when he took her hand in his mouth. He guided her to the large bushes that were to the left of the shack and she muttered a soft thank you before disappearing into them.

He waited patiently until she reappeared and then guided her back inside. She was shivering violently, and she shook the snow from her hair before reaching down and brushing the snow from his back.

He growled at her and she gave him a cheerful smile. "You're covered in snow. Just let me wipe it off so you're not cold."

He shook his large body and the snow flew from his fur and hit her in the face and body. She sputtered and wiped the snow away before grinning at him. "You did that on purpose."

He chuffed, his gaze sliding down to her small breasts. The cold air had hardened her nipples and he watched the flush rising on her chest. He lifted his hot gaze to hers and uncertainty flickered in her eyes before she straightened her back. She thrust her small chest out and gave him a slow smile. "Radek, would you change to your human form? I would speak to you about something important."

He growled and moved away from her.

"Please, Radek," she called.

He ignored her completely and lay down with his back to her.

———

SARA SCOWLED AND WALKED BACK AND FORTH IN THE SHACK. Her plan to seduce Radek and to offer her virginity in exchange for his protection would not work if he stayed in his wolf form the entire time. Unfortunately, she couldn't force him to shift. She rubbed her arms briskly before eyeing the pelts in the corner. She was cold but she wasn't that cold. She yawned and with a soft groan, stretched out on the hard floor. She could feel the cold air seeping through the floorboards and she stared at the table. Perhaps she could lie on the table.

It would be just as hard as the floor, but it wouldn't be as cold.

She was about to stand when Radek, still in his wolf form, lay down beside her. She turned to face him and gave him a small smile. "Thank you, Radek."

He chuffed and she curled into his warm body. She stroked the thick fur on his side, thinking perhaps it would tempt him to shift but he twitched and bared his teeth at her in a silent snarl. She immediately tucked her hands between her thighs and smiled apologetically.

"I'm sorry."

He glared at her before closing his eyes. Her plan was falling apart before it even got going.

IT WASN'T HALF AN HOUR AFTER THE HUMAN FELL ASLEEP before she was squirming on top of him like he was a bed. She sighed, sinking her fingers into the fur around his neck and rubbing before she relaxed against him.

He waited another half hour and then shifted to his human form. He caught her before she could roll off his body. She muttered before straddling his large thigh and resting her head on his chest. Her hands traced the hair on his chest as she raised her head and blinked sleepily at him.

"Radek?" She murmured.

"Go to sleep, Sara." He pressed her head against his chest and rubbed her upper back.

She moaned happily and hugged him before slipping back into slumber.

He traced the soft skin on her back then touched her hair. He tugged on a strand, straightening the curly lock before letting it go. It sprang back into a tight curl and he grinned before doing it again. He had never seen hair like hers before and he was fascinated by it. He eased his hands into her hair until his fingers pressed against her scalp. He was suddenly helpless to stop the image of Sara on her knees in front of him. Of his hands buried in her thick hair and guiding her mouth to his cock.

No doubt she had plenty of experience pleasuring a man with her mouth, and he shuddered with need as he pictured her pink tongue licking his shaft. His cock hardened and his wolf made a low growl of lust. It would be so easy to turn the female onto her back, to ease up her skirt and bury his face in her pussy. He wondered what she sounded like when she came, wondered what she tasted like.

She would taste sweet like honey, he decided, and he would make her come multiple times before he fucked her. He would make her say his name while he fucked her. He liked how it sounded when she said his name and he could only imagine how much better it would sound when she was on her hands and knees as he slid his cock into her. She would –

He jerked beneath her. She muttered something he didn't understand and tightened her slender arms around his waist, and he stared wide-eyed at the ceiling. What the fuck was wrong with him? The woman was a human. Her kind had tortured him. They had burned him and choked him and nearly drowned him, and he was imagining what it would be like to fuck one of them.

He rolled to his side and released the human. She tried to snuggle closer and he backed away until she gave up and curled into herself. He stared silently at her for nearly an hour and when goose bumps appeared on her skin and she began to shiver in her sleep, he sighed angrily and pulled her back into his embrace before rolling onto his back. She made a noise of contentment and relaxed against his warm body, her hands stroking his chest and sides. He stared at the ceiling and tried to ignore how perfectly her slender body fit against his as the wind howled and moaned.

WHEN HE WOKE IN THE MORNING, SHE WAS STILL IN HIS ARMS and she had her thin thighs wrapped around one of his large ones. She was rubbing herself against him once more and he could feel the wetness from her pussy sliding down his leg.

The human was insatiable. His wolf howled happily and without thinking about it, he flipped her to her back, keeping his thigh wedged between hers. Her eyes popped open and she stared at him in a sleepy daze before glancing down at her body.

"Oh no," she moaned as she halted the motion of her hips. "I'm sorry! I didn't mean -"

"Aye, you keep saying you don't mean to but I believe you to be lying," he said.

She shook her head and tried to squirm free, gasping when he took her thin wrists and pushed them above her head and pinned them to the floor. He stared at her small breasts in their thin top before tugging it up around her throat and baring her breasts.

"Perhaps I should give you what you so desperately need."

She flushed miserably even as her nipples hardened. "Radek, I -"

He dipped his head and licked the tip of one nipple. Her reaction was hot and immediate. His cock throbbed when she arched her back and made a soft mewling noise of need.

"Do you like that, human?"

"Yes, oh yes!" She cried out.

He grinned and bent his head to her breasts once more. He licked and sucked at her nipples. They swelled in his mouth and he bit them gently as he moved from breast to breast. The human was writhing beneath him and he sucked on her right nipple. He had never seen such a reaction before and he grinned fiercely. Her nipples seemed to be more sensitive than most and precum dripped from his cock as he thought of all the ways he could tease her. He circled his tongue around one hard nipple and then swiped across the tip of it.

"Oh please, Radek!"

"Please what, human?"

"Please suck on them!"

She turned bright red at her needy cry but continued to arch her back. She was pulling helplessly at his hand, trying to free herself, and he growled before giving her what she wanted.

She made a loud cry of pleasure at the feel of his hot, wet mouth surrounding her swollen nipple and rubbed her pussy furiously against his leg. He sucked hard as her entire body stiffened. He realized with a mixture of shock and red-hot desire that the woman was coming. Her body shook under his, desperate cries of pleasure spilled from her lips and wetness flooded his thigh.

She collapsed, panting harshly, and he nuzzled her breast before licking her collarbone. His cock was throbbing and he rolled her onto her stomach before lifting her to her hands and knees and kneeling behind her. He reached under her skirt and stroked her bare ass as she moaned. He would take the human. There was no harm in it – she wanted him and his wolf, at least, wanted her. He would need to go slowly and carefully. She was so incredibly small compared to female shifters but he was confident he could take her without hurting her. He buried his hands in that gloriously soft mass of hair and pushed it to the side as he leaned over her to nuzzle her throat. He stared at the collar around her neck and stiffened, his head flooded with the memory of the humans who had collared him and choked him.

With a harsh gasp, he pushed away from the human. He buried his face in his hands and breathed deeply. When she touched his back, he snarled and jerked away from her.

"Radek, what's wrong?" She asked. "Did I do something to upset you?"

"Leave me be, human."

"No, tell me what's wrong," she said with unexpected bravery. "Obviously I did or said something and I -"

"I gave you what you wanted! Now leave me be!" He shouted. He staggered to his feet and nearly ran from the shack, slamming the door behind him.

CHAPTER 6

Sara was sitting on the chair by the window when Radek returned with an armful of plants and charkas, and a dead rabbit in one large fist. She jumped up and approached him nervously.

"Radek, I'm so sorry. I didn't mean to upset you."

"You didn't," he grunted as he dropped the plants on the table. They were wet with snow and he peeled a charka and ate it as she returned to the chair.

"Eat, human," he snapped.

"I'm not hungry."

"You need to eat." He skinned the rabbit and tossed the fur outside before tearing into the bloody meat.

Sara, her stomach queasy, looked out the window at the blowing snow. She tried to ignore the smell of the blood in the air.

"Eat, human."

"You can't tell me what to do," she said.

He growled angrily, "I can make you eat."

"Go ahead and try!" She gave him a defiant look and he growled again.

"Fine! Don't eat! It matters not to me if you starve to death!"

"I'm sure it doesn't!" She shouted.

"It doesn't!" He shouted back before shifting into his wolf form. He picked up the bloody body of the dead rabbit and stalked to the corner. He ate it quickly, his large teeth crunching through the bones as she stuck her fingers in her ears and stared out the window.

After a few minutes, she unplugged her ears and glanced at Radek. He had finished the rabbit and she muttered, 'ugh' under her breath when he licked the blood from his mouth.

He snarled under his breath and she scowled at him. "If shifters hate humans so much why did you even save me from that stupid bird thing?"

To her surprise he shifted to his human form and glared at her. "You could try being grateful that I saved you."

"I am!" She snapped. "I told you thank you."

He folded his arms across his chest and she sighed. "Radek, I – I don't want to fight with you, all right? I just want to know why your kind hates humans."

"We don't all hate humans," he said. "My alpha's mate is human."

"What?" She sat up straight and stared at him. "You have a human in your pack?"

"We have three human females," he said.

"Why?"

"What does it matter?"

"I'm just curious."

"Our former alpha wanted a human as a mate. My cousin and two others in our pack bought three female humans from the slavers and brought them back."

"Slavers," she whispered. "You bought slaves?"

Her hand reached up and she touched the collar around

her neck as he scowled at her. "We don't treat them as slaves."

"What happened to your former alpha?"

"My cousin killed him."

Her eyes widened. "Why would he do that?"

"Because he fell in love with one of the humans," there was a note of distaste in his voice, "and our alpha wanted her for himself. Kane killed him and took his place as alpha."

"Did the woman want – I mean, is she in love with your cousin?"

"Aye," he said impatiently. "Of course she is. Do you think Kane would take her as his mate if she was not?"

"How would I know?" She asked. "I've never even met a shifter before you. I don't know anything about you. For all I know you could have saved me from the bird just so you could take me back to your pack and allow them to hunt and torture me for fun."

"We don't kill for sport like humans or those creatures you spoke of. Kane had no interest in being alpha but was left with no choice. Besides, our alpha had gone mad and he deserved to die."

"How long has your cousin been alpha?"

"Not long," he replied.

They sat in silence for a few minutes before Radek sighed. "I want you to eat something, human."

"What do you care if I eat or not?"

"If you are to find your friends after the storm ends, you need food in your belly. You will not get far if you are weak from hunger."

"Fine." She stood and walked to the table, peeling a charka and eating it slowly before eating a few of the plants.

"Eat more," he said.

"I told you, I don't eat very much," she argued.

65

"One more charka," he said.

She rolled her eyes and quickly peeled a charka before popping the meat into her mouth and chewing in exaggerated fashion. She swallowed and then opened her mouth and stuck her tongue out. "Happy?"

"Aye," he grunted.

She wiped her hands on her tiny skirt and marched back to the chair. She stared out the window as he studied the lean length of her thighs. She wondered if he could see the goosebumps on the pale skin as he made a harsh grunt.

"What?" She scowled at him.

"Come over here. I will warm you."

"No, thank you," she said before turning her gaze back to the window. "I'm not cold."

"I can see you shivering from here, human."

"I'm fine."

He growled and stomped across the small shack before scooping her up.

"Put me down!" She smacked him in the chest and he made another warning growl before sitting down and leaning against the wall.

"Stop squirming, human."

"I don't want you to hold me. I'm not cold!" She said angrily.

"Your skin is like ice. Stop being so stubborn," he said. He folded his arms around her and tucked her against his chest.

"Shift to your wolf form," she demanded.

"Why?"

"You're warmer in your wolf form."

For some reason, Sara not wanting him to touch her while he was in his human form, sent a trickle of hurt through him.

"I am just as warm in my human form," he lied. "Now stop your wiggling and stay still." He tightened his arms around her until she could barely breathe and with an angry squeak, she gave up her struggling and relaxed against him.

He should have been shifting to his wolf form but for some ridiculous reason he wanted to feel her bare skin against his. It was so soft and despite his dislike for her, it had been a long time since he had mated.

Not that he wanted to mate with the human, he told himself hastily. His wolf might have scented her but his momentary lapse of judgement this morning was just that. Hell, any shifter in his place would have fucked the human. She had just come all over his leg for God's sake and she had obviously wanted him to fuck her.

His cock stirred at the memory of her soft voice moaning in pleasure and he made an angry growl. She stiffened against him and tried to lift her head but he threaded his hand through her hair and kept it against his chest.

"What's wrong?"

"Nothing," he muttered. "Be quiet."

"I don't feel like being quiet," she said. "Tell me about your pack."

When he didn't reply she pinched him on the side. "If you don't tell me about your pack, I'll start telling you my entire life story. I swear it."

She would too. The little human talked more than Kane's mate. He shifted on the floor and pulled her a bit closer. "My pack is large. There are more than thirty of us, most of them male, and -"

"Is that unusual?" She interrupted.

"Yes, a little. Most packs have more females than males."

"Why do you have more males?"

"Many of the females mated with shifters from other packs and joined their packs."

"Why?"

"I don't know," he lied.

Once Dagon had become alpha and his cruelty to his mates became known, many of the families in his pack had urged their daughters and sisters to leave the pack as quickly as possible. He had, in fact, been planning on finding a suitable male from another pack for Raina in the next year or so to keep her away from Dagon's cruelty.

"Why are you lying to me?" She asked.

He jerked against her. "Why do you think I'm lying?"

She stared up at him as best she could with his hand holding her head. "I can see it on your face, Radek. You're not a very good liar."

He growled at her and she shrugged. "Don't be angry with me just because you can't lie. Tell me why the female shifters left the pack."

"Dagon, our former alpha, had four mates before he bought the humans from the slavers. All of the mates died suspiciously."

"Did he kill them?" She asked.

He hesitated before nodding. "Aye, we believe so."

"So, the female shifters were afraid and that's why they left," she said.

"Aye."

"Your kind doesn't seem very nice."

"You shouldn't judge us based on the action of one," he snapped at her.

"You do," she replied. "I've never done anything to you,

and you hate me just because a human has hurt you in the past."

"I haven't been hurt by a human."

"You're lying again," she said calmly.

He looked away from her and studied his arms. Although he had been young and his healing abilities were not as strong as they would be once he hit puberty, there was enough to heal him from the wounds inflicted on him by the humans. It had taken longer and he suffered in agony while they healed but no scars or marks were left on his body to remind him of the pain. Still, he could remember it easily enough. How it felt when the flame from the candle had licked at his skin. How it reddened and blistered, and how he had finally given in and screamed as the humans laughed.

"Radek," Sara whimpered.

He twitched guiltily. He had tightened his hold on the fragile human until his biceps bulged and he relaxed his grip as she made another soft whimper of discomfort.

"I'm sorry," he said gruffly.

"That's all right. Will you tell me what humans did to you to make you hate us so much?" She asked.

He shook his head. "I will not."

"I won't ever hurt you, Radek. I promise," she said suddenly.

He barked harsh laughter. "As if you could hurt me, human."

"I'm tougher than I look." She scowled at him and then shivered when he ran one rough hand over her flat abdomen.

"You weigh next to nothing, human. A strong wind would blow you over. Do you even know how to fight?"

"I – no, but I'm going to learn."

"And who will teach you?"

"Will you please stop doing that," she said.

69

He realized he was still rubbing her stomach and that his hand was, in fact, inching higher toward her small breasts. He pulled his hand away as the smell of her desire drifted to him.

"Do you have no shame, human?"

"What do you mean?"

"I can smell your need for me," he said.

She blushed to the roots of her hair and tried to struggle out of his arms. He growled and held her more tightly until she collapsed against him.

"You were the one touching me," she said defensively. "And you were mistaken, I don't want you."

He laughed, this one full of genuine amusement, and she gave him a dirty look. "I was having a dream, that's the only reason I…"

"Came all over my leg?" He suggested when she trailed off.

She blushed again and shifted uncomfortably on his lap. "You don't need to be so rude."

He grinned and let one hand drift down to her smooth thigh. "You were the one who marked me with your sweet cream and yet I am the rude one?"

She pushed his hand away. "I told you – it was because I was dreaming."

"Right." His hand moved up to her head and as though it had a will of its own, tangled itself into her soft, utterly intoxicating mass of curls. He tugged until she was staring up at him.

"Did you know that a male shifter bites his female to mark her as his mate?"

She shook her head, staring wide-eyed at him as his gaze drifted down her slender neck to the tops of her breasts. "They bite them to show other shifters that the woman

70

belongs to them. No other male will touch her when they see the claiming mark."

"That's – that's barbaric," she muttered.

"Female shifters are not allowed to bite their mates," he continued as if she hadn't spoken. "A male shifter would be seen as weak if he allowed his female to bite him. But our females are clever and have their own way of claiming us."

"Wh-what do they do?" She whispered. He knew his eyes were changing colour to a brilliant jade and his beard was thickening. She stared fascinated at him as his gaze dropped to her crotch.

"They do what you have done to me, human. They mark them with their scent. When I return to my pack, the females will smell your sweet cream and know that you have taken me for your own."

His hand tightened in her hair. "They will be displeased with you, little human."

He wondered if she would see this lie on his face. He had no particular interest in any of the females in his pack and they had no interest in him.

Not true. Kavine has been trying to mate with you for months.

A thread of irritation went through him. The female shifter would not accept his lack of interest in her and it was a daily annoyance to him.

When she smells the human's scent on you, she will leave you alone.

Aye, or perhaps she would try and injure the little human. The girl had a mean streak. When Kavine had discovered that Mia, his little sister's best friend, had a crush on him, she had been particularly cruel to her and Kane was forced to reprimand her.

"I – I'm sorry," Sara whispered. "I didn't know."

He didn't reply and she shifted again on his lap. He gritted his teeth. If she didn't stop moving, he would have to release her. His cock was already half-hard and any minute she would feel it.

"The females in my pack may not believe you," he said.

She swallowed nervously before suddenly giving him a strange look. "It doesn't matter, Radek. I won't be meeting anyone in your pack. Once the storm ends, we will say our goodbyes and I'll never see you again."

"It will be difficult to find your friends in a forest this size," he said.

She shrugged. "What do you care if I find them? You will just be happy to be away from me."

"That is true," he replied. "But how do you know that your friends were even brought to this world? Perhaps when this Michael let go of you, you were separated by more than just a few miles. My alpha's mate is not from this world or yours – who is to say how many different worlds there are."

"They have to be on this world. I can't be all alone, I…"

She trailed off and he felt a trickle of guilt as her face paled and tears began to gather in her eyes.

"I never thought of that," she whispered dejectedly. "You're right – they may not even be on this world."

"What will you do then?" He asked as she slumped against him.

He waited patiently and when she didn't reply, prompted her again. "Human, what will you do if you cannot find your friends?"

She wiped at the tears dripping down her face and took a deep breath. "Find my way out of this stupid forest and look for other humans, I guess."

He sighed but didn't say anything. Winter had arrived and the human wore little clothing and no shoes. She would freeze to death within hours of leaving this disgusting shack, even once the storm had ended. If, that is, she was not killed first by one of the many creatures that lived in the forest.

His stomach tightened oddly at the thought of the human being torn apart by a bear shifter. Or what if she was discovered by a tagen? Their lust for humans was well known and they often raided human villages and stole their females. If one found Sara, she would not last ten minutes in his bed.

"Radek, you're squeezing me too tightly," she whispered. "I cannot breathe."

"You will freeze to death even when the storm ends, human," he said as he relaxed his hold on her.

She glanced at the pile of pelts in the corner before shrugging. "I'll think of something."

"Will you?"

"Yes. Can you let me go, please? I'm much warmer now."

He hesitated before releasing his grip on her. She wormed her way out of his lap and he watched as she moved to the pile of pelts. Holding one hand over her mouth and nose, she used her other hand to drag the first few pelts from the top before grabbing a pelt from the middle. She dragged it to the door and slipped her feet into the boots.

"What are you doing?" He asked curiously as she opened the door and the cold air and snow blew in.

"I'm going to try and clean this one with some snow," she said before stepping out into the storm.

———

"It does not smell any better, human."

It was nearly twenty minutes later and Sara, her hair covered with snow and her lips blue, was spreading the wet pelt out on the floor.

"I-i-it smells a little b-b-better," she stuttered. "Wh-when the st-torm ends, I'll use it to w-wrap myself in."

He touched her cold skin. "You are freezing again."

"Y-y-yes."

Without speaking he shifted to his wolf form and stretched out on the hard, cold floor. She gave him a grateful look and nearly flattened her shaking body against him. He curled his large body around hers, using his tail to cover her thighs, and growled when she dug her cold toes into his belly.

"S-s-sorry," she stuttered but didn't move her feet. She buried her face into the thick fur of his throat and he closed his eyes as she made a soft noise of contentment.

CHAPTER 7

They were coming. He could smell their foul human scent and hear their footsteps. A whimper escaped from his throat before he could stop it, and he backed into the corner of the stall as the barn door opened.

They stared at him as his hackles rose and he growled. He yanked futilely at the collar around his neck but the chain that was attached to it was thick and heavy and fastened securely to the wall. He gagged and choked, saliva dripping from his mouth, as the hateful human male grinned.

"Papa, make him shift to his human form."

The boy holding the man's hand was only a little older than Radek but there was an adult-like cruelty on his face that made another whine want to slip from Radek's throat. He held it back fiercely as the human stepped into the stall.

"Shift, dog."

He growled and bared his teeth at him in reply, and the man crouched down. The stink of human was nearly overwhelming in the small space but Radek refused to back away. Showing fear just made the human crueler.

"Shift now, or I'll cut yer little pecker off," the man said.

With an angry snarl, Radek shifted to his human form. The man made a satisfied grunt as the little boy moved closer and studied Radek carefully.

"His wounds are gone, papa."

"Aye, I told you he would heal eventually. If he was older it would have happened much sooner," the man replied.

"Let's hurt him again," the boy said gleefully. "It's fun."

"What this time, then?" The man asked. "Water or fire?"

"Fire," the boy decided. "It's funny to hear him scream so loudly."

The man ruffled the boy's hair before ducking out of the stall. He returned with a candle and crouched in front of Radek again.

"You know the drill, dog. If you shift or try to fight me, I'll slit your throat again. Only this time, I'll cut it deep enough that there won't be no healing for you."

Radek stared at the flickering flame as the man held out his hand.

"Your arm, dog. Give it to me."

He didn't want to. It would hurt so bad and he was so tired and hungry. He wanted to cry. He wanted his mother. He took a deep breath and blinked back the tears. He didn't know how long he had been here, chained to the wall of the filthy human's barn, but he could not give up hope that his father would find him.

"Now, dog. Before I lose my patience," the man said.

Steeling himself but unable to keep his hand from trembling, he stretched out his arm. His father would find him and when he did he would kill the humans for what they had done to him, he told himself repeatedly.

He watched with horrified fascination as the flames licked at his skin. The flesh was reddening and already the pain was unbearable. As the smell of his own burning flesh drifted to him, he fought bitterly against the scream building in his chest. He began to squirm, harsh barks bursting from his throat as the man's hand tightened around his wrist and held him. He wouldn't scream, he wouldn't beg for mercy. Not this time, this time he would be strong and –

"Radek, wake up. Open your eyes."

Her voice was full of worry and fear and it tore him up and out of his dream. He staggered upright, shuddering all over as he shifted to his human form. She was sitting up beside him and confused and afraid, he howled and slammed her back to the floor. He pinned her body down with his and yanked her hands above her head.

"It's okay," she said. "You were barking in your sleep." She made no attempt to wiggle free from his harsh grip. "And crying."

He stared wildly at her, still not quite sure where he was or what was happening. The dream was so vivid and so frightening. He was shaking and his heart was thudding in his chest.

"You're hurting me, Radek."

He realized he was squeezing her wrists and he let go of them, giving her a look of shame.

"It's all right," she whispered.

He knew he should be rolling off of her, knew he should be allowing her to get up but he continued to stare at her. He was afraid. He didn't want to be afraid but here in the dark with the wind howling and the memory of his dream clinging to him, he found the softness and warmth of her body comforting in a way he didn't understand. He wanted to bury his face in her throat and feel her arms around him as she soothed away the nightmare.

As if she read his mind, she wrapped her arms and then

her legs around his body and squeezed him. He pressed his face into her neck, wiping away the dampness on his cheeks on her soft skin as she made a quiet cooing noise and rubbed his back. Afraid he was crushing her, he rolled to his side and brought her with him. He tightened his arms around her slender body and kept his face buried in her throat.

"It's all right, Radek. You're safe," she murmured.

"I'm sorry, Sara."

She squeezed him even tighter. "It's okay. Everyone has bad dreams. Do you want to talk about it?"

He shook his head immediately and when he spoke there was panic in his voice. "No, I don't. I won't talk about it."

"Shh. That's fine," she said soothingly. "You don't have to talk."

They lay together in silence for nearly half an hour. She rocked and soothed him like he was a small child until his shaking stopped and then pressed a light kiss to the top of his head. "Better?"

"Aye. Thank you, Sara."

She shivered all over. "You're welcome, Radek."

He lifted his head and studied her face. She smiled hesitantly at him and he cupped her face, rubbing his thumb over her bottom lip. He could smell her desire almost instantly and his cock responded. It pushed against her hip and he groaned when her small pink tongue licked at her upper lip.

He pushed his thumb into her mouth and when she didn't do anything, whispered, "Suck, Sara."

She blushed but closed her lips around his thumb and sucked obediently. He pressed the pad of his thumb against her wet tongue and she sucked harder. He moaned and pulled his thumb free before tugging her head toward his and kissing her. She made a soft squeak of surprise and he frowned when she didn't respond to his kisses.

"Kiss me, Sara," he muttered against her mouth.

She took a trembling breath and pressed her lips awkwardly against his. He frowned again at her odd movements and pulled his head back to stare at her.

"I'm sorry," she said breathlessly. "I've never kissed someone before."

He stared at her in shock. "You have never kissed a man?"

"No," she whispered.

He eased away from her, ignoring her small sigh of dismay and studied her carefully. "But you have mated before, have you not, Sara?"

She blushed furiously and he swore and pushed away from her. The girl was a virgin. He had never deflowered a woman in his life and he certainly wasn't going to do so with the fragile human before him. She scrambled closer to him and placed a hand on his chest.

"Please don't stop, Radek." She gave him a pleading look. "I want you to have it, okay?"

He stared at her. "You barely know me, human. Why would you offer this gift to me?"

She stared at the floor. "Well, I – I'm attracted to you and is it not better to give it away then to have it taken from me?"

She gave him an oddly defiant look. "You're right, you know. I am weak and soon I won't be around people or – or shifters who can defend me. My brother is the only one who cared for me and now he is dead and, according to you, I am on another world. I will be lucky if I don't die in the next month and we both know it. What good will my virginity be then?"

"That does not mean you should give your virginity to the first person who is kind to you."

Her voice was rising, her chest heaving with each angry

breath she took. "Kind? You haven't been kind to me, Radek."

He winced but she carried on without noticing. "You keep saying you find me disgusting but your – your," she flushed more brightly, "dick doesn't seem to find me so disgusting. Why should I not take advantage of that?"

She gave him a dark look of desperation. "I wish to make a bargain with you, Radek."

"What type of bargain?"

"I know that when the storm ends you will abandon me to my fate and I – I don't blame you for that. I've been nothing but a nuisance to you, and you would have been home with your pack by now if it was not for me."

"Aye, that's true," he said gruffly.

She flushed but carried on grimly. "I will make you a deal. If you stay with me, if you protect me until we find my friends or other humans, I will give you my virginity."

"Your virginity," he repeated.

"Yes. You can have it tonight, right now, if you will protect me."

"You only offer this gift to me as payment for my protection?" He was oddly upset by the thought.

"I have no money and nothing else of value," she said.

"What makes you think I won't fuck you tonight and then abandon you anyway?"

"I – I trust you to be a man of your word, Radek."

"You don't even know me."

"I know you will keep your word," she said steadily but there was doubt in her voice. "Do we have a deal?"

He was tempted. His wolf was howling at him to take the female and he was tired of ignoring it. He was, in fact, nearly desperate to be deep inside of Sara. Her attempt to bargain away her virginity to him would give him the perfect excuse for fucking her.

She only offers it to you because she is desperate.

His stomach churned at the thought. He didn't know why it bothered him so much that Sara offered him her innocence not because she wanted him but because she was looking for protection, but it angered and upset him. What did he care why she did it? His wolf wanted her and this was the way to quiet the beast's incessant howling.

He stared silently at her and she gave him a nervous smile. "Radek? Do we have a bargain?"

"No, we do not. Shifters prefer their mates to have experience," he lied. "I have no interest in fucking someone who has no idea what she is doing."

Her face paled and she gave him a sick look of embarrassment before turning away and curling into a small ball on the hard floor. "Fine. Goodnight, Radek."

"It is too cold for you to sleep alone. Come back over here and I will keep you warm."

"I'm fine."

"Human!" He growled angrily. "You will freeze to death. Come over here now before I -"

"Before you what?" She turned and glared at him. When he didn't reply she snorted derisively. "I won't freeze to death and if I do, think of how much easier it will be for you. You'll be able to leave this disgusting place and return to your pack."

"Do not be ridiculous. I know you're upset because I won't fuck you but -"

"Be quiet!" She snapped. "I'd rather freeze to death than ever touch you again!"

"Fine!" He shouted before shifting to his wolf form. He

padded to the far end of the shack and lay down with his back to her.

———

"MAYBE YOU SHOULD TAKE THERAN OR HANIF WITH YOU," Reese said worriedly as she stared at the clear night sky.

"We will be fine, Reese," Kane replied.

"Be careful, please?" Reese put her arm around his narrow waist, and he leaned down and kissed her.

"Aye, I will be."

"Michael?" Abby reached out and touched Michael's forehead. He was burning up and he gave her a faint smile.

"I'm fine."

"You're not. You have a fever."

"It's just a cold," he said as he shifted unsteadily. "Let's go."

He flinched when Adina pressed her hand against his forehead. "Your friend is right – you have a fever. You need to lie down."

"I'm fine," he protested. "I want to help you find Sara."

"You'll slow us down," Abby said. She glanced at Val and Kane. "The three of us will move faster without you."

He gave her a stubborn look and Val rolled his eyes. "I will keep Abigail safe, human. There is no need for you to join us."

"Abby doesn't need me or you to keep her safe," Michael said. "She can handle herself and you should know that by now. She isn't the same person she -"

He broke off in a fit of coughing and Abby rubbed his back. "Go back to your cabin and lie down, Michael."

He frowned at her and she squeezed his arm. "Please."

He nodded as Adina patted his back. "I have a tea that will help with the fever. Come."

He shuffled after her as Abigail studied Val's hair. "Violet, come out."

The pixie stuck her head out of Val's hair and stared innocently at her. "I want you to say here, little one. It's too dangerous."

Violet shook her head and made a rude gesture with her hand. Abigail grinned at her. "Please, Violet. Stay with Reese. We will return shortly, all right?"

"Go on, bug," Val said.

Pouting, Violet flew from Val's hair and tangled herself in Reese's. She stared moodily at the three of them as Reese patted one tiny thigh with the tip of her finger.

"We will return soon, Violet," Abby said.

Kane leaned down and kissed Reese a final time before nodding to Theran. "You are in charge until I return."

"Aye, my alpha," Theran replied.

Reese, worry gnawing at her belly, watched as Kane, Abby and Val disappeared into the woods.

SARA WRAPPED THE DISGUSTING-SMELLING PELT A LITTLE closer around her and shuffled through the snow. The boots were too big and she could feel little piles of snow falling into them to melt against her bare feet. Her breath puffed out like smoke in front of her and she squinted into the dim light. The storm had finally ended and soft moonlight was filtering through the trees.

She wondered briefly what time it was. The sun couldn't have set too long ago, she decided, the moon wasn't that high in the sky. A few hours after her fight with Radek, the howling of the wind had abated. Cold and miserable on the hard floor, she had crept to the window and peeked outside. The snow had stopped and she had made a sudden decision. One that she wasn't regretting now, she told herself grimly.

There was no point in staying any longer with the shifter. He had made it clear that he would leave her once the storm ended, and she would not make a fool of herself by begging and pleading him again to help her.

Is that it? Or are you just humiliated that he wouldn't take what you were offering?

No that most certainly was not the reason she had crept from the shack like a thief in the night while he slept. She had left because he would have left her in the morning anyway, and the sooner she found her friends, the better.

And you think wandering around a dark forest at night is the smart thing to do? Fool. You're going to die out here.

She shut out her inner voice and concentrated on picking her way through the trees. Hopefully she was headed for the edge of the forest and not deeper into it. She thought she was but certainly couldn't tell by the trees.

A soft whine broke the stillness of the air and she froze for a moment before scurrying behind a tree. She clutched at the bark with her heart beating too loudly in her chest, as there was another louder whine.

She waited a few minutes before creeping forward silently. It was only a few minutes before she stumbled onto the massive body of a gold-coloured beast. Blood stained its mouth and chest and she winced when she saw the arrow sticking from its chest. It whined again, a sound of pain and fear, and she moved a little closer as the beast took a final shuddering breath and died.

She studied it carefully. She had never seen an animal like it before and she reached out and touched the gold fur on its shoulder. It was massive, even bigger than Radek in his wolf form, and its body was thick with muscle. It had a long tail with a tuft of dark gold hair at the end of it and its paws were three times the size of her hand. If she had stretched out beside it, her feet would barely reach its ribs. Its mouth was lined with teeth and two thick fangs protruded from either side of its mouth.

She felt a moment of pity for the beast. It was magnificent looking and to come to such a cruel end – alone in a dark forest in the cold – made her heart ache.

Too bad you didn't have a knife, you could skin it for its pelt.

She was a little shocked by the coldness of her inner voice.

Do you want to die out here? Her inner voice said impatiently. *Stop feeling sorry for the beast and figure out a way to use it. Look for a rock, anything, that will help you break a fang from its mouth. They're bigger than your wrist and will work well as a weapon.*

That was true. The fangs were large and sharp, and she would need some kind of weapon if she wanted to have even a chance of making it out of the forest alive. She crouched and began to dig through the deep snow. There had to be a rock under here somewhere, it was a forest for god's sake.

A soft mew made her stiffen and she glanced upward. The tiny baby, the spitting image of its dead mother, had crept out from the bushes and was sniffing at the blood around its mother's mouth. As she watched, it backed away and made a loud cry of misery that broke Sara's heart.

She stood and without thinking of the consequences,

scooped up the tiny baby. It hissed and swatted at her with its sharp claws. She winced as it drew blood across the back of her hand but tucked the shivering baby under the pelt.

"There, there, little one. It's all right," she crooned as it bared its small fangs at her.

"Shh, it's okay. I'll take care of you." She petted the top of its head and it stopped struggling and stared up at her with its bright blue eyes.

"Don't cry, little baby," Sara said as she rubbed under its chin. "You're safe with me."

A smile curved her lips when the creature began to purr and relaxed against her. "That's right. Sara's going to take care of you. I won't let anyone hurt you, I prom –

"Well, what do we have here?"

Sara jerked her head up and stared wide-eyed at the man standing in front of her. He was dressed in a few layers of furs and a long, thick beard hung to his chest. A bow and a quiver of arrows was strapped across his back and she watched as he glanced down at the dead beast and made a grunt of satisfaction. He yanked the arrow from its chest as the baby in Sara's arms hissed.

"What's a sweet little girl like you doing all alone in the forest?" He cocked his head at her as Sara took a stumbling step backward.

"Stay away from me," she warned shakily when the man stepped around the dead beast.

He looked her up and down before squinting at her feet. "Is that – why are you wearing my boots, little girl? And is that one of my pelts?"

"Stay away from me," she repeated as he drifted closer. "I'm not alone. I'm with a wolf shifter and he'll kill you if you touch me."

The man glanced around the empty forest. "I don't see a

wolf shifter. All I see is a sweet little thing wearing my boots and my pelt. Are you wearing anything underneath it? Why don't you give me a little look?"

He reached out with surprising quickness and snatched the pelt from her body.

"Ooh, you're even prettier than I thought. A bit small for my tastes but beggars can't be choosers, now can they?" He grinned at her and the coldness in his smile made her turn and flee.

He chased after her. The too-big boots made it nearly impossible to run and he caught up to her quickly and wrapped one large hand in her hair. He yanked her to a stop. She cried out at the pain in her scalp as the baby tumbled from her arms and landed in the soft snow.

"Let go of me!" She screamed and kicked at him.

He laughed and knocked her to the ground. He pulled the boots from her feet as he pinned her down with a hard knee to her stomach and tossed them aside. "I don't remember giving you permission to borrow a pelt or wear my boots."

She swung at him and he dodged her fists easily as he eyed the collar around her neck. "A slave are you? Did you escape from the slaver house? If so, how on earth did a little thing like you make it this far into the woods?"

"Get off of me!" She wheezed as the man's knee dug painfully into her ribs.

"Oh, I don't think so. It gets awfully lonely out here, you know," the man said as he straddled her. "I've been looking for a girl like you to keep me company."

Her blood turned cold and she stared wide-eyed at him as he stroked her stomach. "The question is - do I take you right here or do I take you back to my cabin first?"

He grunted with pain when the golden-coloured baby

attacked his leg, snarling and biting at the flesh through the thin pants he wore under the furs.

"Fucking koran!" The man shouted before grabbing it by the scruff of the neck and throwing it into the bushes.

"The mother's pelt will make a fine coat and the baby's will be useful as a hat, don't you think?"

"Stay away from it!" Sara shouted. "Don't you go anywhere near that baby or I'll kill you!"

He laughed and leaned over her. "Aren't you a brave one? It shouldn't take you too long to learn to keep your mouth shut, I suppose."

His hand closed around the collar and panic gnawed at her belly when he pulled it and her breath was cut off. She struggled against him as he yanked the collar tighter and stared at her red face and bulging eyes.

"Now, you've obviously been to my cabin, the stolen boots on your feet give it away, so what do you think, girl? Should we fuck right here or should I take you back to my place? It ain't much but maybe it's better than the cold snow, am I right?"

She clawed at his hand and he loosened the collar enough for her to take a gasping, wheezing breath. She mouthed something at him and he frowned and put his ear to her mouth. "What was that, girl?"

He screamed, an oddly girlish sound, when she sank her teeth into his earlobe and bit it off with a viciousness that surprised the both of them. She spat the chunk of flesh out and heaved her body upwards. The man tumbled from her body with one hand clapped to his bleeding head, and he cursed as she shot to her feet. She ran toward the baby koran that had slunk out from the bushes and snatched it up with one hand before fleeing. The man chased after her and she forced herself to run faster through the deep snow. Her feet were burning with cold and she was slipping and sliding in the snow.

"I'll kill you for that, you stupid little bitch!" The man's voice was very close and she made a sharp cry of fear as his hand slipped across her back.

She screamed and twisted away, nearly falling on her ass but somehow keeping her balance as the man tripped over his own feet and fell. He cursed again and she put on a desperate burst of speed as he staggered to his feet.

"Running just makes it worse, bitch!" He spat at her as he ran after her. Already he was catching up to her. She could almost feel his hot breath on the back of her neck and she screamed again as he snarled at her.

"I'll catch you and when I do, you'll wish that you were -"

The loud growl blocked out the sound of his voice and Sara's head snapped up. She stared wide-eyed at the black wolf that was running straight toward her. As it began its leap she instinctively dropped to her knees and threw her body backwards. She slid through the snow on her back, staring at the dark fur on the wolf's belly as he sailed over her and landed on the man behind her.

The man screamed and Sara stared at the glimpses of sky through the dark trees, clutching the koran to her chest. The wolf growled again and the man's scream ended abruptly. She continued to lie on her back in the snow, her mouth trembling and hot tears spilling down her cheeks as she blocked out the sound of teeth ripping into soft flesh. She closed her eyes and jerked compulsively when a hand dropped onto her arm.

"Sara? Are you all right? Look at me." Radek's voice, oddly tinged with worry, demanded obedience and she opened her eyes.

He was crouched beside her and she stared mutely at him

as he gave her a worried look. "Sara? Are you hurt? Answer me."

She shook her head and a look of relief crossed his face. He scooped her up, she was still clutching the koran to her chest, and she pushed her face into his neck and closed her eyes as he carried her through the forest.

CHAPTER 8

Radek carried Sara into the shack and set her on the table. He wanted to be angry with her, wanted to shake her and tell her how foolish and dangerous her actions were, but she was trembling wildly. The look of fear in her eyes made his anger dissipate. She was holding the koran tightly and she whimpered when he tried to take it from her.

"I won't hurt it, Sara," he said.

She relinquished her hold on the animal and he set it down on the floor. It stretched and began to move about the room, sniffing at the floor curiously as she stared numbly at the floor.

"Why did you leave the cabin?" He asked.

She didn't reply and he grasped her chin and lifted her gaze to his. "Why did you leave, human?"

"What was the point in staying?" She asked in defeat. "You would not accept my bargain and the storm had ended. You were going to abandon me in the morning and I – I told myself to accept it, that there was no reason you should help me, but I knew I would beg and cry for your help. I decided to leave before you thought me more pathetic than you already do."

"I don't think you're pathetic, human."

"You do. And you should – I am pathetic."

He thought she would start crying but she stared dry-eyed at him. He reached for the buckle on the collar, ignoring the way she cringed when he reached for her neck. He removed the collar and threw it to the floor before tracing the red mark on her throat.

"You never have to wear a collar again, Sara. Do you understand?"

"You might as well leave it on me. I will never be anything more than a slave to someone – human, shifter, vampire – what does it matter?" She said bitterly.

"Don't say that. It isn't true." He scowled at her.

"It is and we both know it. I am weak. Weak and pathetic."

He cupped the back of her neck. "You will be fine. You just need to find a mate who will protect you."

She stared silently at him and he took a deep breath. "I will take you to my pack, Sara. The other human females are nice, and you will like them, I promise. You will have your choice of mates from the males in my pack and whoever you choose will keep you safe."

She laughed bitterly. "Shifters like their mates with experience, remember? Who among your pack will take me as their mate when they find out that I am a virgin? That I don't even know how to kiss or how to please them? Hmm? You might as well leave me in the morning, Radek. There is no safety for me within your pack."

He cupped her face and rubbed his thumb across her bottom lip as he pushed her thighs apart and stood between them. He rubbed her damp back with his other hand, tracing the soft skin with the tips of his fingers, as she stared up at him. He smiled to himself when the scent of her despair disappeared, and desire took its place. The female was unbelievably responsive to his touch and it made his wolf growl happily.

"I will teach you to kiss, human." He threaded his hand through her hair and tugged her head back.

"I don't want you to touch me," she muttered.

"Do you not? Your scent says differently." He leaned down and inhaled. "Your scent is begging for my touch."

"No, it isn't," she lied. It was ridiculous, ten minutes ago she had almost died in the forest and now she was feeling desperate and needy for Radek's touch. She was going mad, she decided.

He grinned at her and lowered his mouth to hers. He pressed a light kiss on her lips and smiled again when she moaned and opened her mouth.

"That's right, Sara. Open your mouth for me," he whispered.

Her lips parted further, and he slipped his tongue between her lips and stroked hers. Her hands clutched at his biceps and she gasped when he sucked on her bottom lip before whispering, "Now you."

Swallowing nervously, she pressed her mouth against his and slid her tongue timidly into his mouth. He immediately sucked hard on it, liking the way her hips arched against him when he did so, and her nails dug into his arms. She sucked on his upper lip before tracing it with the tip of her tongue. He groaned and she pulled back to give him a timid look.

"Am I – is this right?"

"Aye, so right," he muttered. He pulled her closer, held her head steady and devoured her lips. He sucked and nibbled and feasted on them for long moments. When he finally lifted his head, her lips were red and swollen and she was staring at him with a hazy look of desire.

"Please don't stop," she moaned.

"Do you like my kisses, Sara?" He whispered into her ear before nipping at her earlobe.

"Yes, I want more, Radek."

She tried to kiss him again, pouting when he pulled his head back. He grinned at her. "There are so many other places to kiss you, Sara."

"Wh-what do you mean?" She gave him a nervous look.

"You know what I mean."

She tried to close her legs, but they were blocked by his narrow hips and her eyes widened when he pressed her onto her back and hovered over her. "I want to taste your sweet pussy, Sara."

She blushed furiously and his grin widened. "I think you want that too."

"I – no, I don't."

"Why not?"

"Well, I – that won't help me find a mate in your pack."

He wanted to laugh but he could smell her desire fading so he leaned in and kissed her. She moaned and he cupped her breast, rubbing his thumb over her nipple. "I promise you that it will."

"How?" She muttered. "It doesn't bring pleasure to you."

He kissed her again. "You're wrong, Sara."

She continued to hesitate, and he pulled on her nipple. "It will feel so good, sweet one. If you don't like it, I'll stop."

"Do – do you promise?"

"Aye. I promise."

"All right."

He kissed her on the mouth before kissing his way down her neck. He stopped to tease her nipples through her shirt, and she grabbed his hair and tried to force him to stay when he moved lower.

"It's your sweet pussy I'm kissing. Remember, Sara?"

"Yes," she moaned.

He placed her hands on her breasts. "Touch them, sweet one."

More embarrassment coloured her face, but she couldn't resist pulling on her nipples as Radek licked a slow path down her flat abdomen. He stopped to nuzzle her belly button, smiling at her soft giggle, before placing a kiss just above the waistband of her skirt. He reached for the bottom of her skirt and tugged.

"Lift your hips."

She raised her hips and he quickly swept her skirt up around her waist. He stared at her pussy. Her lips were already wet and slightly swollen and he pressed a kiss against the soft blonde curls above them before briefly kissing her wet lips. She jerked and cleared her throat nervously.

"You're right. That, uh, does feel good," she said politely. "Thank you, Radek."

He hid his wide grin from her. "You're welcome, Sara."

"Will you come up here and kiss my breasts?" She asked.

"In a moment, sweet one."

"But it feels so good. Please, Radek."

"This will feel better."

As he bent his head between her legs, he heard her mutter, "Nothing feels as good as that."

He licked the lips of her pussy and gripped her thighs when she jerked again.

"Oh!"

Using his thumbs, he parted her lips and stared hungrily at her clit. Small and pink and perfect, it glistened wetly. He licked it slowly, relishing the taste of her.

"Radek!"

He raised his head and feigned a look of concern. "Did you want me to stop?"

She shook her head quickly. "No."

"Are you sure? I can stop if you'd like. I know you want me to suck on those beautiful nipples."

She flushed and her hands squeezed her breasts in a tight grip. "Uh, no. I wouldn't mind maybe one more kiss, just to see which I like more. If you don't mind."

"It would be my pleasure, Sara," he said. "Spread your thighs wider for me, sweet one."

She widened her thighs, exposing her clit fully, and he dipped his head and licked it repeatedly. When her thighs clamped around his head and one hand dug into his scalp, he stopped and pried her thighs apart before raising his head.

She was giving him a look of desperate need and he smiled at her. "Shall I continue?"

"Please!" She shouted.

This time he sucked her clit into his mouth and laved his tongue over it repeatedly. When her thighs clamped around his head again, he used his hands to push them apart. He held them open as she moaned and panted and pumped her pelvis against his face.

***

SARA STARED WIDE-EYED AT THE CEILING AS RADEK MADE A soft growl and sucked on her clit again. She gasped and moaned repeatedly. It felt like every single nerve ending was on fire and she couldn't stop pushing her hips into his face. She had never felt anything remotely as good as Radek's tongue between her legs, and she made a loud squeal of pleasure when he pinched her clit with his fingers.

He licked her again and she shouted his name. She was going to come, hell, she was going to explode, and she arched her back off the table as Radek sucked her clit back into his mouth.

"What the hell?"

Sara shrieked as Radek lifted his head and growled. She scrambled off the table, shoving her skirt down and staring in disbelief at Abigail and Val standing in the doorway.

"Sara?"

"Abby!"

<hr />

RADEK, HIS BODY SWELLING AND A THICK DARK BEARD growing on his face, snarled at the strangers in the doorway. His wolf was howling at him to protect Sara and he shoved her behind him and blocked her from the strangers with his large body. The man standing in the doorway hissed and bared his fangs. Radek howled. He had no idea what the creature was, but he would die before he let it hurt Sara.

The woman held up her hands. "Wait, hold on. We're friends. Sara, tell him that we're your friends."

"Radek, it's okay. I know them. Please calm down."

Sara's low voice spoke in his ear, but his wolf was in complete control and it refused to listen to her.

He growled, "Come near her and I'll kill you."

The man hissed again before giving him a disdainful glare. "Do you think I'm afraid of you, little boy?"

"Val! Don't antagonize him for God's sake!" The woman said. She took a step forward and Radek snapped his teeth at her. The man named Val thrust the woman behind him and made his own snarl of fury.

"I will kill you, boy, make no doubt of that."

"Call me boy again and I'll tear your guts out, creature," Radek snarled.

"I'd like to see you try." The creature grinned at him and Radek howled again and began to shift.

"Radek! Enough!"

His alpha's voice cut through his wolf's persistent howling and he snapped his head to the left. Kane was standing in the doorway of the small shack and he glared at Radek. "Get away from the woman, Radek."

Radek snarled at him and Kane growled viciously. "Do not make me embarrass you in front of her."

Radek bared his fangs as Sara touched his back.

"Radek, please look at me."

He whipped around, panting harshly as a low growl emitted from his chest. She smiled at him and touched his naked chest. "They won't hurt me. I promise you."

He stared at her for a moment longer before shifting quickly. With one last snarl at Val, he loped from the shack and disappeared into the forest.

"Radek!" Sara ran to the door and made a squeak of fear when the giant standing just inside the cabin took her by the arm.

She stared wide-eyed at him as he said, "He'll be fine, girl."

"There are creatures in the woods and -"

"Aye, he can take care of himself." The giant let go of her arm and Abby spun her around before throwing her arms around her.

"Oh, Sara. I was so worried about you! Are you all right, my love?"

She nodded. "Yes, I'm fine. Radek protected me."

"He has an odd way of protecting someone," Val said dryly.

Sara turned scarlet and Abby, pressing her mouth together to stop from laughing, tried to glare at him. "Val! Enough. You're embarrassing Sara."

He grinned at her as Sara buried her face in Abigail's throat and groaned. "I want to die."

"Hush, don't say that, my love. It's no big deal."

The younger woman groaned again as Kane gave them an impatient look. "We must go. There is another storm coming and it is a long journey home."

Abigail touched the leaves that were covering Sara's back. "What are these?"

"I was attacked in the forest by a large bird. Radek said it was a floran and after he killed it he put the leaves on my back and legs. He said they had healing properties and I wasn't to remove them."

Abigail started to peel them away and Kane shook his head. "No, leave them. Radek is right. It's best to leave them on. We will have Adina look at her wounds when we get home."

Abby nodded before suddenly frowning. "I should have brought warmer clothes for her. She's not even wearing shoes."

"Val and I will take turns carrying her," Kane said. "Come, we must go."

"I'm not leaving without Radek," Sara said in alarm. The koran rubbed against her leg and she picked it up and held it against her chest.

Abby blinked at it before turning to Val. "There are lions in this world?"

"Lions?" Val cocked his head at her. "What are lions?"

"That?" Abby pointed to the koran in Sara's arms. "I mean, it looks like a baby lion – mostly."

Kane gave it a look of disgust as Sara clutched it tighter.

"It's called a koran," he said. "They live deep in the forest. Let's go."

"Not without Radek," Sara repeated. "We have to find him and -"

"He will be fine, girl," Kane said impatiently. "He is probably on his way home as we speak. Leave the koran kitten and let's go."

She shook her head. "No. Its mother was killed and it's too little to survive on its own. It will die if I abandon it."

"The little thing you hold now will soon be three times your size, girl. It will be able to kill you easily," Kane said.

"It won't hurt me," she said stubbornly. "I will not abandon it."

"Humans," Kane muttered before picking her up abruptly. She was so little and he was so large that he carried her in the crook of his arm like she was a small child. Without speaking he ducked out of the cabin and Abigail and Val followed.

CHAPTER 9

"Ugh." Abigail stared at the dead man as Sara, her stomach churning, looked away.

"What happened to him?" Abby asked as Val rolled the man onto his stomach and pulled the bow and quiver of arrows from his back.

"Turn around, little dove."

Val strapped the bow and the arrows to her back as Abby stared curiously at him. "You know how to use a bow and arrow, Val?"

"Doesn't everyone?" He grinned at her and she returned his smile before turning to Kane.

"Can you tell what happened to him, Kane?"

Kane gave the dead man a brief, uninterested look. "Radek from the looks of it."

"He killed him?" Abigail couldn't hide her surprise.

"He was attacking me," Sara said immediately. "Radek killed him because he was trying to kill me. He had no choice, Abby."

Abby squeezed her arm reassuringly. "I believe you, my love."

She studied the dead man again. "Do you think we could peel off the top fur and use one of the ones below it for Sara? There probably isn't as much blood and –"

"No," Sara interrupted. "I will not touch anything that belongs to him."

"Sara, I -"

"No!" She said. "I will not, Abby. You cannot make me."

"The girl will be fine," Kane said. "I will keep her warm enough on the journey home."

Abby gave him a doubtful look and Sara smiled tentatively at her. "It's true, Abby. They're, uh, very warm. I would have frozen to death if not for Radek's ability to keep me warm."

"Yes, we all saw how he was keeping you warm," Val said teasingly.

"Val, enough," Abby said. She turned away from Sara to hide the smile on her face as Val winked at her.

"We need to keep moving," Kane said with a touch of impatience. He turned and strode away from the dead man.

THEY WERE WALKING FOR NEARLY TWO HOURS WHEN RADEK reappeared. Sara breathed a sigh of relief and relaxed against Val. Kane had handed her over to Val a few moments ago and she was clinging to the vampire's back. She was scanning the forest anxiously the entire time, and the sight of the large black wolf finally slowed down the nervous beat of her heart.

He shifted into his human form and growled at Val, "Give her to me."

Val stared unblinkingly at him. "The girl is fine with me."

Radek growled again as Sara said timidly, "Radek, you will be warmer in your wolf form. He won't -"

"Give her to me," Radek said slowly.

"And if I don't?" Val asked.

Abigail was holding the sleeping koran in her arms and she rolled her eyes. Val was being an ass on purpose and she whacked him discreetly on the thigh. He turned and winked at her before returning his gaze to the naked shifter.

"Will you try and take her from me?"

"I will kill you, creature. Have no doubt of that. Now give the woman to me before I lose my patience completely."

"Val, give Sara to him," Abby said quickly.

Val shrugged lazily and allowed Sara to slide from his back. Her feet had barely touched the snowy ground when Radek was hoisting her onto his back. His hands cupped her thighs familiarly and she patted one broad shoulder.

"Thank you, Radek."

He grunted in reply before striding ahead of the others.

KANE LEANED AGAINST THE TREE AND STUDIED RADEK AND the human. They had stopped for a brief rest and a bite to eat. Val and Abby were sitting together on a large flat boulder, and Kane did not think it was his imagination that Radek had carried Sara as far from them as possible. He was sitting on a fallen log with the woman on his lap, and he handed her another charka as he continued to stare at the vampire distrustfully. The girl peeled the charka and offered half of it to Radek. He shook his head and put his arms around her. He pressed her into his naked chest and growled under his breath when Val leaped gracefully from the boulder and stretched.

"Radek, let the girl visit with her friends. I wish to speak with you," Kane said.

Radek shook his head. "She stays with me."

Kane stared steadily at him and Radek flushed and bowed his head.

"Her friends, Radek. Now."

Radek stood and slowly carried Sara to her friends. His arms tightened around her and he glanced back at Kane. Kane raised his eyebrows and Radek glared at him before turning to Abby.

"She cannot sit on the stone. It is too cold for her."

Abby shrugged out of her sweater and draped it over the rock. Radek placed Sara on the sweater and snarled at Val when he stepped closer.

"Keep your distance from her, creature."

Val rolled his eyes. "Go on, doggie. Your master is calling for you."

"Val!" Abby said furiously as Radek started toward him. Sara slid off the rock and threw her arms around Radek's waist.

"Please don't, Radek!"

Already she was starting to shiver and Radek picked her up quickly and placed her back on the large rock. He brushed the snow from her feet and held them for a brief moment as Kane made an impatient growl.

"I'll be fine, Radek," Sara said.

He turned and strode to Kane with his fists clenched and his back stiff. Abby released her breath and frowned when Val started to sit next to Sara.

"Val, come sit beside me."

He grinned at her. "There is more room beside the young Sara, little dove."

"Val." She gave him a warning look. "Stop deliberately goading him. He obviously has a thing for Sara."

"He doesn't," Sara said quickly. "He hates me."

Val laughed as he sat next to Abby and put his arm around

her waist. "Hates you, does he? Makes sense. I know the first thing I do to a woman I hate is bury my face in her pussy."

Sara turned a brilliant shade of red and Abby elbowed Val in the stomach before putting her arm around the young woman. "Ignore him, Sara. He's being an ass."

She kissed Sara's head. "How are your back and leg?"

"My leg is very sore," she admitted. She was still staring at her hands and Abby squeezed her gently.

"Why do you think the shifter hates you?"

"He hates all humans," she said. "He says I disgust him."

Abby frowned. "Honey, I know this is embarrassing for you but Val is right – a man doesn't do what he was doing to you if he's disgusted by you."

Sara shrugged. "He was teaching me to kiss because he felt sorry for me. Radek said the only way I'll survive in this world is if I find a mate in his pack. Shifters don't, um, like women without experience."

Val laughed again. "That is an odd way to teach someone to kiss.

Abby grasped Sara's chin and forced her to look her in the eye. "Honey, the shifter is wrong. You don't need to find a mate to survive. I will teach you how to protect yourself and, until then, Val and I will take care of you."

"Is it true what the shifter says, Abby?" Sara asked. "Are we on another world?"

Abby nodded. "It is."

"How will we get home?"

"We cannot. I'm sorry, my love," she said.

Sara's lip trembled and she began to cry. Val, looking deeply uncomfortable, slid off the rock. "I'll be right back."

He disappeared into the trees as Abby drew Sara into her embrace. "I'm so sorry, Sara. Truly."

"WHAT IS IT?" RADEK ASKED ANGRILY.

Kane folded his arms across his massive chest. "Watch your tongue, Radek. We may be like brothers but I am still your alpha and you will treat me as such."

Radek bowed his head. "Aye, I am sorry, Kane."

He snuck a glance behind him. His body relaxed a little when he saw that the vampire was sitting beside the dark-haired woman.

"Radek!"

He turned to his alpha. "Aye, Kane?"

"I asked what is going on with you and the human. Are you mating with her?"

"Of course not. I – I hate her."

"And you were showing her how much you hate her by eating her pussy?"

Radek flushed before glaring at him. "This is all your fault."

"My fault?"

"I stumbled onto the human in the woods. She was being attacked by a floran. Before you fell in love with Reese, I would have left the human to her fate but you had to bring a human into our pack who saved my sister's life and made me feel as though I owed her."

He glanced again at Sara. "She was babbling about a bright light and I knew she was like Reese. I was only bringing her back to our pack because I thought your mate would like a friend who was like her."

"Oh, is that why?"

"Aye! I was doing your mate a favour!"

"Was spreading the female out on a table and eating her pussy a favour for my mate as well?"

Radek glared at him. "A mistake that I now regret. The human has been relentless in her attempts to seduce me."

"Aye, she does seem to be quite the temptress," Kane replied dryly.

"Did you know that the creature you travel with drinks human blood? That he keeps them like pets to feed from and to fuck? He dresses her in that ridiculous outfit and forces her to wear a collar around her neck like a dog!"

"Aye," Kane said calmly. "Abigail and Val have told me. I also know that Val does not participate in the same practices that others of his kind do. It was not him who forced the small female into slavery. Did she tell you it was?"

"No," Radek said reluctantly. "But I do not trust the creature. The way he looks at her…"

"He is in love with the female named Abigail. That is plain to see. He has no interest in your human."

"She is not my human!" Radek snapped at him. "I may have accepted that Reese is your mate and that you love her, but I will and always will, hate the humans. Do you hear me, Kane?"

"Aye," Kane said mildly. "I hear you, Radek. But you -"

He sighed as Radek stiffened before nearly running back to the small female. She was crying brokenly in Abigail's arms and Radek snatched her away from Abigail and held her against his chest.

"What did you do to her?" He snarled.

"Nothing," Abigail said mildly as Val appeared at her side. "She is upset to learn she can never return home."

Radek carried Sara back to the fallen log. He sat down and curled his hand into her hair, pushing her face into his throat as he rubbed her upper back with his other. Sara clung to him for a few moments before wiping her face and sitting up.

"I'm all right, Radek."

He didn't reply and Kane walked toward them. Despite what Radek had told him, the shifter was already treating the female like she was his mate and he was curious to see how far he could push him.

"Give the female to me, Radek. I want you to shift and go ahead of us. There are mantorians in the area and you will ensure that our way home is clear. Go a few miles and then come back and report to me."

Sara frowned at him and wrapped her arms protectively around Radek's thick neck. "It is too dangerous for him to go alone."

"Be quiet, little one," Kane said sternly. He ignored Radek's warning growl as he held out his arms. "Give her to me and do what your alpha requests, Radek."

Radek hesitated a moment longer before standing. He handed Sara reluctantly to Kane and as he settled her in the crook of his arm, took Kane's arm in a hard grip. "Do not allow the creature to touch her, Kane."

"Aye, I won't, Radek."

"How much further?" Abby asked Kane. She was staring nervously at the lightening sky as they trudged through the forest.

Radek had returned an hour ago and shifted to his human form. He had immediately held his arms out for Sara and Kane had handed her to him without speaking. She had fallen asleep, slumped against Radek's back with the koran kitten wedged between her body and Radek's.

"Another hour or so." Kane glanced at the clouds. "More if we do not beat the storm."

"Val, you should go ahead." Abby squeezed his hand. "You can move faster than the rest of us. Go to the cabin and I will see you there shortly."

He shook his head. "I'm staying with you, little dove."

She gave him a look of frustration. "Val, you're not getting caught in the sunlight because of me."

"It is a chance I am willing to take." He kissed her hand. "Or you can climb onto my back and I will take you with me."

She glanced at Sara. The woman was still sleeping soundly against Radek's back and Abby made a sudden decision. "Take Sara with you. Reese and Adina can look at her and -"

"No," Radek said. "She is not to be alone with the creature."

"Why not, little boy?" Val said cheerfully. "Are you afraid that, like you, I hate her so much I will just have to taste her pussy? Or perhaps that she will enjoy the touch of my tongue more than yours?"

"Jesus Christ, Val!" Abigail snapped as Radek's eyes turned green and he began to growl. "Give it a rest!"

Kane placed a restraining hand on Radek's arm before turning to Abby. "Both you and Val will go ahead. We will not make it home before the sun rises."

"I don't want to leave Sara again," Abby protested.

"We will not allow her to be harmed," Kane said. "Go. Tell Reese I will see her soon."

"Come, little dove." Val guided her behind him and helped her onto his back. "Hang on tight." She kissed his cheek and the two shifters watched as they disappeared in a blur.

Radek relaxed slightly and Kane gripped his arm for a moment. "Abigail is from the same world as Reese, and Val is her mate. I have promised Reese that we would treat them well. Do not harm the creature, Radek."

"If he touches the human - if he tries to force her to wear his collar - I will kill him, Kane," Radek said angrily.

"He will not. I told you, he does not keep the humans as slaves."

"How do you know that? You only just met him."

"Abby says he does not and Reese believes her. I trust in my mate's judgement," Kane said.

Radek made a harsh noise of frustration. "The girl is a virgin, Kane, and the creatures would still have fucked her without caring about her innocence or if they hurt her. They murdered her brother and stole her like she was nothing more than cattle. Just because the creature says he is not like them does not mean

"How do you know she is a virgin?" Kane interrupted.

"She told me."

"That seems like an odd thing to share with someone you just met." Kane raised his eyebrow at him and Radek flushed.

"The girl never stops talking."

Kane laughed. "Aye, I know what that's like. Although my mate did not reveal such personal details after knowing her for only a day or two."

"She offered me her virginity in exchange for my protection. She said I could have it if I kept her safe until she found other humans."

"I'm going to assume you did not take the girl up on her offer," Kane said sternly.

Radek gave him a hurt look. "Of course I did not. You know me better than that."

"Aye, I do. Although I feel we are drifting apart, as of late."

Radek shrugged. "You have a mate now, Kane, and you are the alpha of our pack. You do not have time to -"

"Bullshit," Kane said bluntly. "Do not blame my mate or my new duties as an excuse for your absence, Radek. You are distancing yourself from me and Raina and the pack. I understand your reasons, but you need to know how painful it is for Raina and for me. We miss you."

Radek sighed and stared at the sky. "Kane, I do not know what you want me to say. I am trying but I hate the humans and to see them every day is difficult."

"You do not seem to hate the young Sara."

"I feel sorry for her, nothing more," Radek snapped. "She will not last long with her fragile body and her broken spirit."

"Broken spirit?" Kane asked. "She may not have the fiery spirit of Reese or the bravery of Abigail, but her spirit seems just fine to me."

"You barely know her," Radek replied. "I have spent the last three days in her company and, believe me, the woman will not survive if she does not find a mate in our pack to protect her."

"Perhaps you?"

"Do not be ridiculous, cousin!" Radek glared at him and Kane grinned widely.

"It is not me who is ridiculous, Radek. You have not stopped touching the woman since we found you and you seem to find her attractive enough. If what we walked in on in that shack was any indication."

"I told you – the woman spent hours attempting to seduce me in order to gain my protection. She may be a virgin, but she is no innocent."

"Really?"

"Aye, really," Radek lied. "She will have no problem finding a mate in our pack."

"Then I suppose that is good for her," Kane said mildly. "I know Teagan is looking for a mate. Perhaps he will find her pleasing and -"

"Teagan is not to touch her!" Radek growled angrily. "He has no idea how to please a woman and he would hurt her badly just trying to take her."

Kane laughed. "What do you know of Teagan's love-making skills?"

"I have heard the rumours," Radek said darkly. "The human needs someone gentle, she weighs next to nothing, and Teagan will not understand that. He is used to female shifters."

"She is a tiny thing." Kane agreed as he looked Sara up and down. "But I'm sure someone in our pack will be gentle enough for her. If she rides them, she can control the pace and -"

"Watch your tongue, cousin," Radek said sharply.

Kane grinned to himself. As Radek's alpha, his cousin was speaking out of turn but for the first time in weeks Radek was speaking to him like he used to and he could not correct him for it. He missed his cousin and he could sympathize with what was happening to him. He wondered how long Radek would continue to deny his attraction for the small female. He hoped not as long as he had done with Reese. Teagan wasn't the only shifter in their pack looking for a mate and the woman would have no shortage of potential mates to choose from. Reese and Adina, and even shy Ghita, had made a good impression on his pack in the last couple of months. If Radek continued to deny his feelings but kept other shifters away from the girl it would cause tension in the pack.

Radek shifted Sara on his back and she woke with a soft

snort. She straightened, looking about blearily, before her eyes widened in alarm. "Where is Abigail?"

"They went ahead," Kane replied. "The sun was rising and she did not want her mate to be caught in the sun."

"Oh, right." Sara lifted the koran to her face and smiled when it licked her with its scratchy tongue.

"You should leave it to its fate, little one," Kane said not unkindly. "Korans are not known for their loyalty."

Sara shook her head. "I will not abandon it to die a painful death. Stop telling me to do so."

Radek squeezed her thighs. "Do not speak to our alpha in such a manner, human."

"He's not my alpha," Sara muttered defiantly.

Kane's mouth twitched as he fought to hide his grin. Radek was a fool if he truly believed the girl had a broken spirit. She might be timid but her spirit was far from broken.

"Quiet your tongue, human," Radek growled.

The koran kitten hissed and batted the back of his thick neck with its sharp claws. Radek flinched and Sara quickly gathered the kitten into one arm, giving Kane a rather smug look of triumph.

Radek glared at Sara. "Your little pet has drawn blood."

"You should be nicer to me then," she replied.

He growled again and bared his fangs at the koran when it hissed once more.

"Oh stop it. Both of you," Sara said. She tapped Radek on the back. "I can walk now. I know your arms are growing tired."

"Do you forget you wear no shoes?" He snapped at her.

"It's fine." She wiggled against him and his hands tightened around her legs. "Put me down, Radek. If my feet get too cold, I'll tell you."

"No," Radek grunted.

She scowled at him. "Put me down."

He ignored her and she sighed in frustration as Kane said, "Put the girl down, Radek."

Radek made a low growl of anger before suddenly dropping her to her feet. "Fine. I grow tired of listening to you speak anyway, human."

He shifted and bounded forward, disappearing into the trees as Sara shoved her skirt down and set the koran kitten on the ground. It scampered ahead, sniffing and peeing on different trees as Kane glanced at the human.

"You must be happy to have found your friends, little one."

She nodded. "I am. I didn't even know for certain that we were on the same world." Her breath hitched in her throat and she stared at the ground as she blinked rapidly.

"I'm sorry that you were taken from your own world," Kane said.

"Thank you." She wiped at her face. "I believe I will find a way back though. I only need to wait for the next storm and -"

"Are you certain that would work? From what my mate has told me, there is no guarantee that you will return to your own world."

"Is she from mine?" Sara asked.

Kane shook his head. "No, she is from the same world as Abby."

"But Abby is from my world, isn't she?" She frowned at him.

He shook his head. "No."

Sara took a deep breath. "I really have no idea what is happening."

She suddenly winced and grabbed at her leg.

"Are you all right?"

"Yes. My leg is a bit sore."

"We have a human female who is a healer, she will help you," Kane replied.

"Do you enjoy being alpha?" She suddenly asked.

"Why do you ask?"

She shrugged. "Radek said you had only just became alpha and that before you showed no interest in it."

"Aye, I did not. But our previous alpha was threatening my mate and I was left with no choice."

"You're married to a human, right?"

"I am."

"Do many shifters marry humans?"

He shook his head. "It is not common, although it is becoming more and more common to find shifters interacting with humans."

"So, do you like being alpha?" She persisted.

He stared thoughtfully at her. "Aye, I suppose I do."

She was silent for a moment. "Why does Radek hate humans?"

"That is for Radek to share, not me."

She sighed in frustration. "He finds me disgusting. I doubt he'll share such personal information."

"Aye, perhaps not. Although you seem to be fine with sharing with him."

"What do you mean?" She said cautiously.

He suddenly stopped and took her arm in a gentle grip. "May I give you a word of advice, human?"

"Yes."

"Do not offer your virginity to other members in my pack as a way to protect yourself. They will not be so quick to turn you down as Radek was."

She flushed a brilliant red and tugged her arm free before

staring at the ground. "Why did he tell you that?" She whispered.

Kane shrugged. "We are like brothers, little one. There are no secrets between us."

"He shouldn't have told you! It's none of your business what I – I do or offer to someone!" She said hotly.

He took her chin in a firm grasp and lifted her face to his. "Will you heed my warning, human? Do not offer this gift to another of my pack brothers."

"Why shouldn't I?" She spat at him. "I have no way of protecting myself, no way to keep from dying on this stupid world! Why shouldn't I offer the only thing I have of value?"

Kane, his eyes glowing, leaned down and she made a small squeak of fear as his warm breath washed over her face. "My pack mates are good men, little one, but they are not known for their gentleness with their mates. Do you understand what I am saying?"

She swallowed heavily and fear gleamed in her eyes. "Yes, I think so."

"They would not mean to hurt you but they are not used to someone as fragile as you."

"Radek was – was gentle," she whispered.

"I am glad to hear it but that does not mean the others in our pack will be," Kane replied. "If you decide to find a mate within my pack, you must choose wisely. And if I tell you not to choose one or another, you must listen to me and trust that I am doing what is right for you. Do you understand?"

She nodded, fascinated by the glow in his eyes and the sound of his deep voice. For the first time since she met Kane she understood why Radek, a strong and powerful shifter, bowed to his will. The shifter was an alpha through and through, and she wondered for a moment at the woman who would sleep with him. She would have to be very brave, she decided. The shifter was not unattractive but she would rather face down a floran than join him in his bed.

"Get away from her, cousin." Radek stalked out of the trees and bared his fangs at Kane.

Kane dropped his hand as Radek put his arm around Sara's waist and pulled her against his hard body. He cupped her throat possessively with his other hand as he glared at Kane.

"Do not touch her again."

Sara craned her head to frown at him. "Radek, Kane wasn't -"

"Hush, human," he said harshly.

"I was simply giving her a word of advice, cousin."

"You do not need to touch her to offer advice," Radek snarled. His face was red and a pulse throbbed steadily in his temple. "If I see you touching her again, I will –"

"Can I give you advice, cousin?" Kane interrupted.

Sara winced at the tone in his voice, her eyes automatically lowering to the ground as Radek glared at him.

"What is it?"

"If you are intending to claim this woman as your mate, then you should make your intentions known as soon as we arrive home."

Radek's mouth dropped open. "My mate? My mate? Kane, have you gone mad? I hate humans. They disgust me and this female is no exception."

Sara made a harsh sound of hurt before stomping on his foot. He flinched and released her and she stumbled away from him. Kane took her arm before she could flee into the woods and, with tears glinting in her eyes, she scowled at Radek as the koran rubbed against her legs.

"Why the hell you would ever think I would want this weak little human as my mate is beyond me, Kane," Radek snarled. "I know things have changed since you mated with a human and became alpha but do you honestly believe that I would ever feel anything more for a human than hatred? The woman is -"

"If you are not planning on asking her to be your mate," Kane said, "then stop behaving as though she belongs to you, Radek."

"I – I do not," Radek sputtered.

"Do you not? You were pleasuring her with your mouth when we found you."

Sara flushed bright red but Kane didn't seem to notice as he stared at Radek. "You refuse to stop touching her, you will not allow her to visit with her friends, and you challenge your alpha when he touches her."

"I am trying to protect her!" Radek snapped. "I do it for you and especially for your mate. Is it wrong of me to try and make my alpha's mate happy? Should I not be protecting someone as fragile as she is? Why are you -"

"She no longer needs your protection, Radek," Kane said harshly. "She has found her friends and they have vowed to keep her safe. Either ask the woman to be your mate or leave her be."

Radek's gaze dropped to Sara. She stared silently at him, her stomach churning at the strange look of need and anger and confusion that crossed his face. She swallowed and gave him a tentative smile, remembering the way he had kissed her and the sweetness with which he had touched her.

A mask dropped over his face and he curled his lip at her before nodding. "Aye, you are right, my alpha. My time with this whining, weak human is done. Let her find another in our pack to keep her safe."

He shifted and ran ahead of them. Sara, her face bright

red and struggling not to cry from a combination of anger and embarrassment, glared at Kane.

"I hate him! I hate him so much! He's the – the meanest person I've ever met in my entire life!"

Now the tears were starting to slide down her face and Kane's expression softened before he picked her up and cradled her in his arm. She buried her face in his thick neck and he patted her back soothingly before starting after Radek.

She muttered something and he sighed before squatting and scooping up the koran kitten. It batted at his chin as he tucked it into the girl's arms and she hugged it before burying her face back into his neck.

"I hate him," she said again.

"Aye, I know, little one." He tried to sound gentle. "But Radek is not intentionally cruel."

"He is!" She snapped.

"I promise you he isn't." He patted her back again. "Try and get some rest, we will be home soon."

CHAPTER 10

K ane strode across the clearing toward his cabin, ignoring the rest of his pack. They were staring in fascination at the girl in his arms, and he rolled his eyes as he entered the cabin and shut the door behind him.

"They act as though they've never seen a human before," he grumbled.

Reese glanced up from the pot of soup she was stirring over the fire. "How many humans are you planning on bringing home to me, my love?"

He grunted and carried the girl into the second bedroom. Reese followed and watched as Kane set the girl on the bed. She was sleeping and she curled into a ball, her skirt rising up over her small ass. Kane looked away as Reese pulled the covers over her and touched the girl's curly hair.

"What happened to her back and leg?"

"She was attacked by a floran," Kane replied.

"That's those giant bird things, right?"

"Aye."

"Well, she's a pretty little thing. I'm glad you found her safe and sound," Reese said.

Kane grunted with surprise when Violet flew out from Reese's hair. The little pixie twirled happily. Glittering dust floated down as she landed on the sleeping Sara. She tiptoed across her chest and pressed gentle kisses against the girl's lower lip before draping her tiny body across Sara's neck.

The girl still held the koran kitten in her arms and Reese carefully pulled it free. The koran stared at her curiously as she petted the top of its head.

"Radek stumbled onto her in the forest and kept her safe."

"Yes, Abigail mentioned that to me."

"Where is Abigail now?" Kane asked.

"She's sleeping." Reese petted the koran's throat, grinning delightedly when it began to purr.

"Did she also tell you what Radek was doing to the girl when we found them?"

Reese nodded. "She did. I was," she paused and gave him an impish grin, "a little surprised."

"Is Radek back?"

"Yes, he came back about half an hour before you did. He went straight to his cabin and has not come out since. Raina checked in on him and said that he's in a terrible mood."

"He acts as though the little human belongs to him, Reese."

"Already?" Reese frowned. "He's known her for what – three days?"

"Aye but he treats her as though she is his mate. If anyone touches her but him, he grows…agitated."

"Agitated?" Reese cocked her head at him. "If he's anything like you are, it's a little more than agitated."

"That's different. You are my mate," Kane said. "Radek barely knows the girl."

"Sometimes it doesn't take very long to fall in love," Reese said.

"It is not love," Kane said immediately. "It is his wolf who is lusting after her. Radek is a good man but he is not capable of looking past his hatred for humans."

"I don't blame him for that," Reese said.

"Aye, nor do I. But he told the girl she needed to find a mate within our pack to protect her and she believes him."

"There are a few in our pack who are looking for a mate," Reese replied. "She has no way to return to her world, I don't see the issue if she falls in love with someone from our pack."

"Aye, perhaps," Kane sighed. "But if Radek continues to act like she is his while she actively seeks out a mate, it will cause tension in the pack."

Reese studied him carefully. "Will you speak to him about it?"

"I already have," Kane replied. "He assured me that he had no interest in the human and he was happy to be rid of her company."

Reese sighed. "I suppose you had this conversation in front of her."

Kane gave her a cautious look. "Aye, we did."

"Kane, that was unkind of you," Reese scolded.

"It did make her cry," Kane admitted. "But she now hates him and he says he hates her so…"

He shrugged and suddenly smiled at her. "I guess I have solved the problem."

Reese grinned. "Are you certain of that?"

"Yes?" He gave her an adorably uncertain look and she laughed and reached upward to give him a brief kiss.

"Tell me what exactly I'm holding here." She studied the koran in her arms. Its eyes were a bright and vivid blue and it met her gaze unblinkingly. "It kind of looks like a lion cub to me."

"Aye, that is what Abby called it as well," Kane said. "It

is called a koran and the little human rescued it after its mother was killed. I should do us all a favour and end its life."

"Kane!" She scowled at him and held the baby a little closer. "It's only a baby."

"Aye, but that baby will grow larger than me in a very short time."

"How short?" She asked.

"A moon's time," he said.

Her mouth dropped open and she stared at the koran in her arms. "You're kidding me."

"I am not. They grow quickly and they are lethal and cunning hunters. They have no loyalty, and this little thing in your arms will probably try and murder us all."

"How do you know that it has no loyalty? Have you raised a koran baby before?" She asked immediately.

"Of course not," he replied.

"Then you don't know," she said. "I don't want you hurting this little one, Kane. Do you hear me?"

"Aye, but you'll feel badly when it rips my arm from my body, will you not?"

"I might," she said with a small grin. She lifted the koran's tail and studied its back end. "Well, assuming it has the same anatomy as cats on my world, he's a boy."

"Excellent," Kane said dryly. "They're larger and stronger than the females. I will probably lose a leg as well as my arm."

"Oh hush," Reese said. "We have no milk to feed it. I'm worried it's going to starve."

He shook his head. "It does not need milk. It would have started eating meat only a few days after its birth."

"Good. Will you be a dear and grab me some raw meat from the storage area?" She asked sweetly.

"I am the alpha, Reese," Kane said with a tinge of arrogance. "It is beneath me to run errands for my mate."

She laughed and poked him in his flat stomach as he gave her a wicked grin. "Of course, if there were to be some sort of compensation for the errand, I might be persuaded."

"Of course," she said innocently. "You do the errand and I will be more than happy to allow you to eat my pussy tonight."

He grinned again and slapped her on the ass before walking toward the door. "When I return, you are to be naked and in my bed."

"When you return," she said, "you're going to feed the koran while I find Adina and ask her to look at Sara's wounds."

"I prefer my suggestion."

"Later, my love. I promise it will be worth the wait," she said cheekily.

He growled happily at her before leaving the cabin.

He was crossing the clearing with a hunk of deer meat when Davin approached him. "My alpha, Teagan and I were out in the forest and scented a bear."

"Are you certain it was not a bear shifter?"

"Aye, Kane."

Kane's eyes gleamed. Most bears were in hibernation by this time of the year and to find one not yet in its sleep was excellent luck. If they were really lucky, it would be large with plenty of meat.

"My alpha? Shall we hunt?" Davin asked.

"Aye," Kane replied. "Give me a moment."

Adina was just emerging from her cabin and when Kane called her name she headed toward him.

"Good morning, Kane."

"Hello, Adina."

"Did you find Abigail's friend?"

"Aye, we did. She has been injured by a floran. Reese asks that you look at her. Will you take this to the cabin and tell Reese that we have gone hunting?"

"Aye." Adina took the chunk of raw meat and headed toward the cabin. At her soft knock, Reese opened the door and smiled at her.

"Morning, Adina."

"Hello, Reese. Kane asked me to give this to you and tell you that they have gone hunting."

Adina followed Reese into the cabin and watched curiously as Reese set the meat in front of the koran kitten. The kitten smelled it gingerly before making a low growl and pouncing on it. It tore voraciously at the meat with its tiny fangs, making growling noises of happiness, as Reese laughed.

"Why do you have a koran kitten?" Adina asked. "Do you know how big they get?"

"Yes, Kane told me. Apparently, Sara found it in the woods. Its mother was dead and she decided to save it."

"What happens when it's full grown and tries to eat all of us?" Adina asked as Reese led her toward the bedroom.

Reese grinned at her. "Kane wants to know the same thing."

She opened the door and they moved to the bed. Sara hadn't moved from her position on the bed and Adina studied her curly hair.

"I have never seen such curly hair before. Have you?"

"Yes," Reese said. "In my world, there were women with hair like hers."

Adina touched a curly lock as Violet sat up and stretched prettily. She leaned against Sara's collarbone, watching curiously as Abigail pulled down the covers and helped Adina to remove the leaves from Sara's back and legs.

"Kane said she was attacked by a floran," Reese said as Adina studied the puncture wounds on her back.

"Aye, they're vicious creatures. Cowardly though – they only go after the weak or injured." Adina said. "When I was a girl, one trotted into our village like it belonged there. It immediately went after the children that were playing in front of the school. My brother and I had to climb a tree to escape it."

"What happened to it?" Reese asked curiously as Adina lifted Sara's leg and touched the swollen flesh.

"The dogs killed it," Adina said absently. "Reese, this is not good."

"They look like they're healing," Reese said tentatively.

"The flesh is healing but there is an infection. Can you see the lines?"

Reese leaned closer and stared at Sara's leg. Thin red lines were moving upward from the deep scratches on her legs and the flesh was swollen and bruised.

"It is good that she put the liptus leaves on her wounds but it wasn't enough," Adina said.

"Radek was the one who did that," Reese replied. "He found her in the woods and kept her alive through the storm."

"Really?" Adina gave her a surprised look. "Radek kept a human alive?"

"I know, right?" Reese said. "Maybe we're starting to win him over."

Adina snorted. "I doubt that."

She prodded the flesh around the wounds and Sara moaned pitifully in her sleep and tried to pull her leg free of Adina's grip.

Adina sighed and Reese gave her a worried look. "What

medicine can we use, Adina?"

"There is no medicine."

"What?" Reese asked as Violet walked down Sara's body and sat on her hip. She stared at Adina as Adina shook her head.

"There is nothing in the forest that will stop this type of infection. I could try and coat the wound with the sap from a Bavrin tree – it has healing properties – but that will not get rid of the infection. It will slow it down, give the girl a bit more time before the infection reaches her heart and kills her but other than that…"

She trailed off and Reese gave her a sick look. "She's so young, Adina. There must be something we can do."

"There is not," Adina said.

"Shit!" Reese snapped. "Sometimes I hate this fucking world."

She studied Sara's pale face as Adina reached for the covers. "We will keep her as comfortable as possible over the next few days. We can give her tea for the pain and -"

She frowned as Violet rose in the air and hovered over Sara's leg. She began to clap her hands together rhythmically as Adina and Reese watched.

"What is she doing?" Adina whispered.

"I don't know," Reese replied.

They both gasped in surprise when the glittery dust fell from her clapping hands. Violet flew back and forth over the wounds on Sara's leg, her hands clapping so quickly they were a blur, until the entire calf was coated in the softly-glowing dust.

She flew upward to Sara's back and quickly coated each puncture wound before landing on her hip. She sat down and gave Reese and Adina a smug look as she combed her long purple hair with her fingers.

"What is that?" Adina leaned forward until her nose was nearly touching Sara's leg. She touched the dust with the tip of her finger.

"It tingles." She gave Reese a look of surprise.

"Really?" Reese asked.

"Aye," Adina waited a few moments before blowing on the dust that covered the smallest scratch. She made a small grunt of surprise before quickly blowing the rest of the pixie dust away.

"Holy shit," Reese said. "Are you seeing what I'm seeing?"

"The wounds," Adina reached out and touched Sara's smooth flesh, "are completely healed over and there is no sign of infection."

"Violet, how did you do that?" Reese asked the tiny pixie as Adina quickly brushed away the dust from Sara's back.

Violet shrugged before studying her fingernails. Reese leaned closer and touched the pixie's leg. "You just saved her life, Violet. Do you realize how amazing you are?"

A broad grin crossed the pixie's face and she jumped up before shooting upward into the air above Reese. She twirled prettily with her long hair whipping around her face, as dust fell onto Reese's upturned face.

Reese laughed as the dust tingled pleasantly for a moment before subsiding. "You're something else, Violet."

The little pixie gave her another smug look before diving into Sara's hair. She disappeared among the gold curls as Adina sat back and stared at Reese.

"I have never seen anything like it. The girl was going to die, Reese."

"And now she isn't," Reese replied happily.

"Aye, and now she isn't," Adina repeated.

She pulled the covers up over Sara as Reese said, "What

is going on between you and the blond vampire?"

"What do you mean?" Adina said nervously.

"You know what I mean. The other night I thought you were going to let him bite you right in front of us."

"I only wanted to see him up close," Adina said. "I have never seen a creature like him before."

"No one in this world has," Reese pointed out. "But you didn't see anyone else letting him lick their neck."

Adina flushed and moved into the kitchen. "I didn't let him do that. It just sort of happened."

"Adina," Reese took her hand, "you need to be careful. Faren is dangerous. Abigail says that once they bite you, it starts an obsession – one you can't control. Do you really want that?"

Adina didn't reply and Reese squeezed her hand. "I know that there's something – well – intriguing about the vampires, believe me I feel it too. But I don't think becoming Faren's food source is something you really want. Nor do you -"

"Enough, Reese!" Adina said harshly. "I am not your child nor am I a member of this pack that will be told what to do by the alpha's mate. I am a grown woman and I am entirely capable of making my own decisions."

Reese took a step back, hurt flashing across her face. "I – I'm sorry, Adina. You are right. It's none of my business."

Adina glared at her before sighing. "I'm sorry I snapped at you, Reese."

"I deserved it," Reese said with a shrug. "I was overstepping my bounds. I just – I don't want you to get hurt, Adina."

"I won't," Adina said. "The other night meant nothing – I was only curious."

"Right," Reese said unconvincingly.

"I'd better go. The man named Michael still has a fever and I want to try a different kind of tea with him."

CHAPTER 11

S ara rubbed at her eyes before staring around blearily. The room was unfamiliar and she sat up in the bed and pushed the covers back before swinging her legs over the side of the bed. A flash of purple caught her eye and she grinned happily when Violet hovered in front of her.

"Hello, Violet," she said as the pixie zoomed forward and kissed her on the nose. "I'm so happy to see you."

She stood up and stretched before yanking at the bottom of her skirt. She really needed to find some new clothes. These ones were dirty and smelly and –

Her hand reached around and traced the small of her back before she studied her leg. "My wounds – where are they?" She said stupidly.

Violet clapped her hands and spun in the air, pixie dust floating to the floor.

"I don't understand," Sara craned her head to try and look at her back. "I don't -"

The door opened and she spun around, nearly falling over in her haste. She stared wide-eyed at the tall, dark-haired woman standing in the doorway.

"Hello, Sara. My name is Reese."

"Hi." She took a nervous step back.

"Don't be frightened. I'm human like you and I won't hurt you," Reese said.

"Where am I?"

"You're in mine and Kane's cabin."

Sara's eyes widened. "You – you're Kane's mate."

"Yes."

Sara looked her up and down as Reese held her hand out. "Abigail is with Val in their cabin. As soon as it's dark, I imagine she'll come to check on you. In the meantime, why don't you come with me? I have some hot food and a hot bath waiting for you."

"A bath?" Sara's eyes lit up and Reese grinned at her.

"Yes. Come – I'll show you."

"SHE REALLY HEALED ME?" SARA STARED IN WONDERMENT AT Violet as Reese rinsed her hair with a small jug of water.

"She really did."

Sara smiled at Violet. "Thank you, Violet."

The little pixie, after watching Sara climb into the metal tub, had stripped off her dress and dove into the tub of water with her. She had washed her hair and her tiny body as Reese washed Sara's hair and now she was floating on her back at the other end of the tub, her long purple hair trailing in the water around her. She grinned happily at Sara before diving back under the water.

Sara laughed when Violet suddenly shot straight out of the water with her naked body steaming in the cool air of the cabin. She spun in the air, her wings fluttering madly. She didn't stop until her hair was a wild, wind-blown mess. Reese grinned at Sara when Violet landed on the edge of the tub, picked up her dress and wiggled into it.

"I think she's happy to be clean."

"Yes, as am I," Sara replied. "Thank you for your kindness, Reese."

"You're welcome, honey." Reese patted her bare shoulder. "Once you're ready to get out, you can have a bite to eat and we'll find some warmer clothes for you, all right?"

"All right."

Reese studied her. "You're much smaller than the female shifters so we might have some trouble finding clothes that fit you. We may have to ask Raina for some of her clothing."

"Raina – that's Radek's sister, right?" Sara asked.

"Yes."

"Does she hate humans as well?"

"No. Raina is very sweet," Reese said.

"Why does Radek hate humans?"

"That isn't for me to say," Reese replied. "Although from what Kane tells me, Radek does not seem to hate you."

Sara flushed brightly. "Does everyone know what Radek and I were doing?"

Reese patted her shoulder again. "No, honey, not everyone. But it is difficult to keep secrets within the pack."

"Radek hates me," Sara said. "He told Kane I was weak and that he was happy to be finished with me."

"Radek sometimes speaks without thinking," Reese said. "Don't take it personally, Sara. He has his reasons for hating the humans and -"

"That's what everyone keeps saying but no one will tell me why!" Sara said angrily. "It's very frustrating!"

"I'm sorry," Reese said.

Sara sat forward and clasped her arms around her raised

knees. "Don't be. I – it doesn't matter why he hates humans. I don't even like him so I don't care."

"Right," Reese said.

Sara glanced at her. "I don't like him, Reese. At least not in that way. I would be willing to be his friend but he wants nothing to do with me."

Reese ran the soap over Sara's bare back as Sara rested her forehead on her knees. "Do you like being married to Kane?"

"I do. I love him very much."

"He's uh, a very big man."

"Are you frightened of him?" Reese asked.

Sara shrugged. "No, I don't think so. Should I be?"

"No. Kane is a strict but fair alpha. If you join our pack, you will see for yourself."

"Radek says the only way I'll survive in this world is if I find a mate from your pack."

Reese shrugged. "I suppose that is one way to ensure your safety. Shifters are very protective of their mates."

"Are they all as big as Radek and Kane?"

Reese nodded. "Yes, mostly. Kane is the biggest and there are a few who are on the smaller side but for the most part, shifters are a big bunch."

Sara twisted her head to look at Reese. "Are they – I mean, is Kane…"

She trailed off and Reese smiled encouragingly at her. "Is Kane what, Sara?"

"Is he gentle? You know, in the – I mean, when you are together?" She blushed again.

"Kane is very gentle," Reese said. "But not all the shifters in the pack are aware of the fragility of a female human, especially one as little as you."

"Radek was very gentle too," Sara blurted out.

"That's good," Reese said. "Do you want to find a mate in the pack, Sara?"

"I don't know. I don't want to die," she replied moodily. "But Abigail says that she and Val will teach me to protect myself and that I don't need to find someone to keep me safe."

"Well, that's a good thing then, isn't it?" Reese smiled at her. "You can learn to fight and -"

"Reese!"

The door to the cabin flew open and Raina ran in. Sara sank lower into the water as Raina stared curiously at her for a moment.

"Hello, human."

"Um, hi."

"Raina, this is Sara," Reese said as she stood and dried her hands.

"Hi, Raina. It's nice to meet you."

Raina grinned at her. "It's nice to meet you too. You smell differently from Reese. What world are you from? My brother won't tell me a thing. He's been in a terrible mood ever since he returned. I think you drove him nearly mad."

"Raina," Reese said. "Why are you here, my love?"

"Oh!" Raina gave Reese a started look. "Right – Kavine and Verna are in a fight and they are both threatening to kill each other.

Reese sighed. "Again?"

"Aye. They won't listen to anyone – not even Anna. She told me to run and fetch you because Kane is still out hunting. She wants you to speak to them before they shift and start fighting. They'll listen to our alpha's mate if she tells them how ridiculous they are being."

"Sara, I'll be right back, okay?" Reese said as she hurried toward the door.

"That's fine," Sara said. She rested her head against the tub and closed her eyes as Reese and Raina left the cabin.

———

RADEK STOOD BEHIND TEAGAN'S CABIN, THE SHIFTER'S CABIN was right next to Kane's, and watched as Raina and Reese walked swiftly across the clearing. He could hear the faint sounds of Kavine and Verna screaming at each other from the cabin they shared, and he rolled his eyes before moving toward the door of the alpha's cabin.

I want her! Give her to me!

He snarled inwardly at his wolf's excited demand. The stupid thing was ridiculously happy at the thought of seeing the human again. It had spent most of the day whining in an embarrassingly undignified way about being separated from Sara. Unable to stand its continuous badgering a moment longer, he had made the decision to just check on her. It would quiet his wolf and perhaps he could finally get some sleep.

Bring her back to our bed, his wolf demanded. *Give me what is mine and then you can sleep.*

Enough! We will check that her wounds are healing, nothing more, and then you will quiet your ridiculous whining.

His wolf snarled in reply and he clenched his fists before opening the door to the cabin without knocking. He paused in the doorway, his heart stopping in his chest for a brief moment as he stared wide-eyed at Sara. She was standing with her back to him in a tub of water and his dick hardened as he stared at her wet, naked ass.

His wolf howled with delight as she stretched to reach the towel that was placed on a small table to the left of the tub. It was just out of reach and she made a sigh of frus-tration.

"Reese? Do you think you could hand me the towel?"

Radek continued to stare at her. Vaguely he was aware that the wounds on her back and leg were gone but he couldn't stop staring at her small, firm and decidedly perfect ass.

AS THE DOOR OPENED TO THE CABIN, SARA MADE A SIGH OF frustration when she couldn't reach the towel. Afraid of slip-ping in the tub, she said, "Reese? Do you think you could hand me the towel?"

There was no reply. She glanced behind her and shrieked with surprise when she saw Radek standing there. She lunged forward in the tub. Her feet slid out from under her and she fell back into the water, banging her head painfully against the side of the tub. She gasped and water flowed into her mouth and up her nose.

Hands reached into the water and Radek hauled her out of the tub. Naked and dripping wet, she coughed wretchedly into her hands as Radek wrapped a towel around her before pounding her on the back. She pitched forward and he cursed before catching her around the waist. He patted her on the back again, this time more gently. She coughed up a final mouthful of water before wiping her lips with a shaking hand.

"What the hell, Radek?" She choked out as he stared anxiously at her.

"I'm sorry, human. Are you all right?"

"What are you doing here?" She coughed again. Her entire body was trembling from the cool air and Radek scooped her up and carried her toward the fire. He sat down in the armchair beside it, holding her on his lap, and growled at her when she smacked at his chest.

"Stay still, human. You might be injured."

"Because of you! Why would you just walk in on a person bathing?" She snapped. "Have you heard of knocking?"

"I didn't know you were in the tub. Now stop squirming so I can examine your head."

"It's fine," she said sulkily but she stopped wiggling as he touched her wet scalp.

He parted her hair, searching for a wound, and she glared again at him as she pulled the towel more securely around her. When his fingers ran over the small bump rising on the side of her head, she flinched and tried to pull away.

"Don't move!" He growled.

"That hurts!"

He ignored her protests and examined the bump carefully. "It's not bleeding."

"Oh good," she said snidely. "I'll die from a head injury but at least I won't bleed to death first."

"Stop being so dramatic," he said.

"You're the one who walked in on me!" She said. "Why are you here?"

"I came to check on you!" He snapped. "I was trying to be nice."

"Nice? Why would you start now?" She said. "Hey! Stop that!"

He ignored her and gripped the back of her neck as he pushed her forward and tugged down the back of the towel. He studied her smooth back and she smacked his leg when he ran his fingers over the skin.

"Where are your wounds?"

"Why do you care?"

"Enough, human. Tell me why your wounds have disappeared or I'll put you over my knee and spank you."

"You wouldn't dare!" She said indignantly.

"I would. Tell me," he said.

"Violet healed them."

"Violet? Who is Violet?"

A flash of purple darted past him and he stared at the tiny creature hovering in front of Sara.

"What is that thing?"

"That *thing* is Violet," Sara said angrily. "She's a pixie and she healed me with her pixie dust."

"What? Something that little healed you? I don't believe it," he said.

The pixie frowned and Sara snorted laughter when she made a rude gesture at the shifter.

"Just because something is little doesn't mean it's useless," she said. "Let go of my neck, Radek. You're holding me too tightly."

He relaxed his grip but didn't release her completely. "How did she heal you?"

"I told you – with pixie dust."

Violet stuck out her tongue before flying across the room. The koran kitten was asleep on a pile of blankets in the corner and she dropped onto its body. She scratched its throat with her tiny hands, smiling when the kitten began to purr, before curling up under its chin and closing her eyes.

Sara clutched the towel to her naked breasts when Radek's gaze lowered to her chest. "Stop looking at me like that. You're done with me, remember?"

"Aye, I remember," he said without tearing his gaze from her breasts. "Have you found a mate within my pack to protect you?"

She gave him a look of astonishment. "I just got here,

Radek. I haven't even left this cabin. How on earth would I have found a mate already?"

"So you are looking for one?" He said as his hand tightened around the back of her neck and he shifted her on his lap.

"You told me I needed to, did you not?" She said heatedly. "You said that I would need someone to…"

She trailed off as she felt his erection against her ass. He grinned wickedly at her when her cheeks flushed. "Radek, what is that?"

"You know what it is, human," he said.

RADEK'S EYES GLOWED BRIGHT GREEN AND HE TRACED HIS fingers along Sara's damp collarbone. For the first time since he had left her in the woods with Kane, his wolf had stopped its whining and howling. He closed his eyes and took a deep breath.

"Radek, you – you don't want me," she whispered.

"Aye, that is true," he rasped as his fingers floated along the edge of the towel. "But my wolf wants you badly and I am tired of denying it."

"Y-your wolf?" She stuttered nervously and he leaned forward and licked her throat.

"I would never hurt you, human."

"But your wolf might?" She asked.

He shook his head before tugging her head toward him. "Never. I only want to help you, to show you how to please a potential mate, remember? You need a mate to keep you safe."

"I do not," she said faintly. "I – Abigail said she would teach me to protect myself."

"You are too little, sweet one," he said persuasively. "There are many dangers in this world and you need a mate - a shifter - to protect you."

His mouth hovered above hers and she licked her lips as he smiled at her. "Shall I give you another lesson in kissing, sweet Sara?"

"Yes," she whispered.

It was wrong to allow Radek to kiss her, she knew it was wrong. But sitting on his lap and hearing him say her name in that deep voice made her forget how mean he was. She pressed her ass against his erection and he made a raspy groan that lit her nerve endings on fire.

He kissed her, his lips pulling on her bottom lip, and she moaned before parting her mouth. His tongue darted into her mouth to touch the tip of hers and she licked at it eagerly as his hands slid into her wet hair.

"Your hair is so pretty, Sara," he murmured against her lips.

"Thank you," she whispered.

He bit her top lip lightly, smiling at the way she trembled in response before kissing her throat.

"Tilt your head back, my sweet," he demanded.

She lifted her head and moaned again when he licked from the hollow of her throat to her earlobe.

"You taste so good." He sucked on her earlobe before claiming her mouth again.

Sara, her head swimming and her entire body aching for release, ground her ass against his cock and made a low pleading sound.

"You crave my touch, sweet Sara. Do you not?" He asked.

She nodded and a satisfied grin crossed his face for a moment. "Of course you do."

Anger at his smug tone overrode her desire and she tried to push away from him. His arms tightened around her. "Do not leave me."

"It is very kind of you to have taught me how to kiss, Radek, but I don't believe I need further lessons. I'm sure that someone in your pack will find me pleasing enough in bed if I decide I need a mate."

His hand clamped down on her narrow hip and he glared at her. "Do not speak of being in another's bed. It is my bed and only mine that you will warm, human."

"I will warm whatever bed I choose," she said. "You have no right to tell me who I can and cannot sleep with."

He growled at her and she gave him a defiant look. "Growl all you want. I'm not afraid of you."

"You have no need for further lessons?"

"That's right," she replied.

"So you know how to touch a man then, human? How to bring him pleasure with your hands and your mouth?"

She flushed bright red and he grinned wickedly at her before taking her hand and placing it on his dick. "Go ahead then, show me."

Her eyes widened, "Radek, I don't think -"

"Go on, human. Show me how you will please your mate. Unless you are too afraid," he taunted.

She glared at him and he inhaled sharply when she rubbed his cock through his pants. "I'm not afraid, Radek. I'm not weak or useless or anything else you believe me to be."

She rubbed harder, a part of her wanting to hurt him for making her so angry and so turned on at the same time, but he groaned with pleasure and stared hungrily at her. Lust unfurled in her belly as her anger dissipated and her hand slowed.

"Am I hurting you, Radek?"

"No, human," he replied. His hand was still holding the back of her neck and he leaned forward and kissed her as she continued to rub at his cock.

She squeezed him and then moaned when his other hand cupped her breast and he teased her nipple through the rough material of the towel. He kissed her neck, licking away the moisture on her soft skin as she arched her back and moaned again.

"Radek, wait!" She gasped out.

He growled but released her immediately and leaned back in the chair. His hands gripped the arms of the chair as he stared unblinkingly at her, his frustration evident. Her hands trembling, she reached for the buttons on his pants. His look of frustration disappeared and he knocked her hands away before quickly unbuttoning his pants and freeing his cock.

Lust and anxiety warring in her belly, Sara wrapped her fingers around him and squeezed. She snatched her hand away and gave him a horrified look when he jerked in the chair and made a harsh, growling groan.

"Radek, I'm sorry, I didn't mean to hurt you," she whispered.

He guided her hand back to his cock. "You didn't hurt me, sweet one."

"Are you sure?" She asked doubtfully.

"Aye, keep going," he bit out.

Sweat was breaking out on his forehead and his eyes glowed bright green as she carefully stroked him up and down. His cock was hard, much harder than she thought one would be, but the skin was strangely smooth. She squeezed him before rubbing firmly and then lightly. He was panting, his hips rising and falling with the rhythm of her hand. She placed her other hand on his shoulder to steady herself on his lap. His cock was thick, her fingers couldn't reach her thumb when she held him, and once again she wondered how something this large could fit into her. Instead of being frightened by the thought, it sent a flood of wetness between her thighs. She ran her thumb over the wide head and he twitched so wildly she nearly fell off his lap.

"Radek?"

"Do not stop, sweet one," he rasped. He picked up her hand from where it rested on his shoulder and sucked two of her fingers into his mouth.

"Oh my God," she moaned as he sucked and licked at her fingers. It made her entire body throb with lust to watch his mouth sliding up and down her fingers and to feel his wet tongue. She shivered all over when he kissed the tips of her fingers and then linked his fingers with hers.

She stared down at her hand still wrapped around his cock. "I want to use my mouth," she whispered.

His hand tightened painfully around hers and she gave him an anxious look. "Is that – do you want that too, Radek?"

"Aye," he said hoarsely. "Very much, sweet one."

She smiled weakly at him and he pulled her forward and placed a gentle kiss on her mouth. "Only if you truly want to, Sara."

"I want to," she said.

She kissed him again and he teased her tongue with his own as his hand curled into her wet hair. She sucked on his lower lip and then pulled away, smiling nervously at him before sliding from his lap. She knelt between his legs and he smoothed her hair back from her face as she stared at his cock.

Her pussy was throbbing heavily and she squeezed her legs together for a moment before leaning forward. Radek's hands threaded through her hair and held her head. As she opened her mouth, the door to the cabin opened.

"I'm sorry that took so long, Sara, but Raina and I picked out some clothes for you to – oh!"

Sara scrambled to her feet, her face red with mortification as Reese and Abigail stared at them. Radek cursed under his breath and stuffed his cock back into his pants as Raina tried to peer over Reese's shoulder.

"What's going on? Radek? Why are you here?"

Reese turned and nearly shoved the young shifter out of the cabin. "Raina, I need you to run back to your cabin and find a sweater for Sara to borrow."

"But we have one already," Raina said. "Why do I - "

"She should have at least two," Reese said. "Go on, please. Find another."

Grumbling under her breath, Raina turned and left as Abigail stormed across the cabin. She shoved Radek hard in the chest. He gave a grunt of surprise and staggered backward as Sara made a soft cry of dismay.

"Were you forcing her, asshole?" Abigail shouted before shoving him again.

"Do not touch me again, human," Radek snarled at her.

Abigail shoved him for a third time. "Keep your dick away from her or I'll cut it off."

Radek's fangs popped out and he growled at Abigail as Reese hurried forward. "Radek, don't -"

Radek stepped toward Abby. "It matters not to me that you are friends with my alpha's mate. If you threaten me again, I will -"

"You'll what?" Abigail snapped. "I'm not afraid of you,

asshole. If you think I'm going to stand by and just let you force Sara into -"

"Radek! Stop!" Sara shouted as Radek howled angrily. She darted forward and threw her arms around Radek's waist. "Please, don't."

Nostrils flaring, he stood stiffly as Sara said, "He wasn't forcing me to do anything, Abby. I swear it."

"Sara," Abby gave her a look of confusion, "Reese told me of Radek's cruelty to you."

Sara flushed and Radek growled again. "I was not cruel to her."

"Really?" Abby said disdainfully. "Telling her she was weak and you couldn't wait to be rid of her isn't cruel?"

His cheeks went a dull red and he pushed away from Sara, his hands clenching into fists as he stared angrily at Abby.

"Radek, leave," Reese said.

He ignored her and she stepped in front of him. "Raina will be back any moment. Do you want her to see you like this? How will you explain your behaviour to her?"

His body slumped and the anger faded from his face. He stared at Sara for a moment before glancing at Reese.

"What is happening to me?" He whispered.

Sara's stomach twisted at the confusion and misery on his face and she reached for him. "Radek, don't -"

"Do not touch me!" He twisted away from her and ran from the cabin, slamming the door behind him.

Abigail cupped Sara's shoulders. "Sara, be honest with me. Did Radek make you do anything you didn't want to do?"

"No!" Sara said angrily. "I told you I wanted it. Why do you not believe me?"

"Honey, you're young and innocent and I -"

"I'm not that young," Sara interrupted. "I can make my own decisions, Abigail."

She hurried over to Reese and took the clothes from her. "Thank you, Reese." She disappeared into her bedroom as Abby began to pace back and forth.

"Abby?" Reese said tentatively. "Radek wouldn't hurt Sara. He dislikes humans but he wouldn't purposely hurt her."

"Everyone keeps saying he dislikes humans but that's twice now I've caught him and Sara half-naked," Abigail said. "If he dislikes them so much why won't he stay away from her?"

"Kane says that Radek's wolf wants her. It's why he's having so much difficulty."

"His wolf?" Abby frowned. "Do shifters really think of their wolves as separate from them?"

Reese nodded. "They do. I know it's kind of weird but they all do it."

Abby sat down at the kitchen table and rubbed at her forehead. "I'm worried about Sara. I don't want her getting hurt more than she already is. I'm grateful to Radek for saving her from that bird thing but I don't…"

She trailed off and stared at Reese for a moment. "The wounds on her leg – were they – they were gone, weren't they?"

"Yes," Reese said. She sat down next to Abby. "They were infected and Adina told me there was nothing we could do and that Sara would die within a few days. Violet was there and she – this is going to sound strange – she clapped her hands and -"

"Healed her," Abby interrupted.

"Yes!" Reese said excitedly. "This dust floated down and

when Adina blew it away the wounds were completely gone!"

Abby smiled fondly at the little pixie who was still curled up with the koran kitten. "She saved my life as well."

"Really?"

Abby nodded. "Yes. I nearly died because of a damn poisonous flower but Violet saved me."

Reese's mouth dropped open. "Holy shit. I was nearly killed by a flower!"

"You're kidding me!" Abby said.

"I am so not kidding you! I leaned down to smell this big purple flower, I was starting to get sleepy and the next thing you know Kane hit me like a freight truck and knocked me out of the way. He said it would put me in a sleep that I wouldn't wake from."

They stared silently at each other for a moment before Reese grinned at her. "Should I make us some tea and we can discuss all the other ways we've nearly died since being sucked into alternate worlds?"

Abby laughed. "Yes, I think you should."

CHAPTER 12

Sara knocked on the cabin door. Raina opened the door and smiled faintly at her.

"He is not back, human."

"I'm sorry, Raina."

The young shifter shrugged. "Why? It is not your fault he's gone. Well, maybe it is a little since he hates humans so much but then why did he save your life in the forest?"

She motioned for her to come in, the koran kitten trailed behind Sara, and flopped down dramatically in the chair in front of the fireplace. "It has only been two days. I'm sure he'll return soon."

Sara gave her a guilty look. Radek had disappeared into the forest after they were caught by Reese and Abigail and no one had heard from him since. Her stomach tightened with anxiety.

He's fine, Sara. He's a shifter and he can take care of himself.

Raina picked up a piece of string and trailed it along the floor. The koran kitten crouched down, its bum wiggling, and pounced on it. She smiled again before petting his soft fur. "He has grown already."

"Yes, he eats like a horse." Sara sat down next to her.

"Have you named him?"

"I was thinking Meeka. What do you think of that name?"

"I like it." Raina glanced at her hair and Sara smiled.

"You can touch it, Raina."

Raina hopped up and ran her fingers through Sara's hair as the koran kitten stretched out in front of the fire. She wondered how long it would take before the shifters stopped being so fascinated by her hair. Raina wasn't the only one who wanted to touch it. Every day she would feel fingers tugging on the soft curls and yesterday the female shifter named Verna had actually tried to discreetly cut off a piece of it. Reese had scolded her fiercely and the shifter had apologized but it hadn't stopped her from trying again later that day. Sara had allowed the shifter to take a small lock of it. She could feel a smile creeping across her face as she remembered the look of glee on Verna's face.

"Your hair is so funny," Raina said as she pulled on a curl until it straightened and then released it. "I have never seen hair like this before."

She continued to play with Sara's hair as she said, "Do you have any siblings, human?"

"I had a brother named Garen."

"What happened to him?"

"He died," she said.

Raina's hands stilled in her hair. "I'm sorry, human. Radek drives me crazy sometimes but I couldn't imagine what I would do if he died."

She leaned down and sniffed at Sara's hair. "You smell differently from Reese and Adina and Ghita. Is it because you are from a different world?"

"I guess," Sara said.

"You must miss your home."

"I do, very much."

"Reese says that there is no way to return to your world. I guess you are stuck with us," Raina said.

"I guess." Sara smiled at her as Raina began to braid her hair.

There was a knock at the door and at Raina's shout to come in, Verna and Kavine walked in. Verna smiled at Sara but Kavine stared sullenly at her as they joined them in front of the fire.

"He's not back, Kavine," Raina said.

Kavine sighed. "I hate it when he leaves."

She stared at Sara. "It's her fault he's gone."

"It is not!" Raina snapped.

Sara looked away guiltily. It was her fault, although not for the reasons that the other shifters believed, and she bit at her bottom lip as Kavine scowled at her.

"Kavine is in love with my brother," Raina informed Sara. "I don't know why. He's messy and bossy and he barks in his sleep."

Sara studied the dark-haired shifter. She was gorgeous with straight brown hair and dark eyes. Her body was tall and curvy in all the right places, and her stomach dropped at the thought of Radek touching her.

"So you and Radek are, uh, together?" She asked casually.

Kavine nodded. "Aye."

"You are not," Raina said. "You just want to be with him."

"Hold your tongue, Raina," Kavine said. "When I am your brother's mate, you will learn to have better manners."

Raina snorted as Kavine smiled stiffly at Sara. "I am

surprised that Radek saved your life in the forest. Do you know of his hatred for humans?"

"Yes," Sara said.

She shook her head at Verna when the shifter, a small sharp blade in her hand, crept up behind her. The shifter blushed dully and retreated.

"Was he cruel to you?" Kavine asked.

She hesitated and Kavine smiled. "He was. You deserve it after what the humans did to him."

"Kavine!" Verna said sharply. "Be nice to the human. She is not like the others."

"How do we know that?" Kavine said. "We know nothing about her. She could be as wretched as the rest of them."

She looked Sara up and down. "The rumour is that you're going to try and find a mate in our pack. You're much too skinny and none of our males will want to bed you. They'll break your fragile human bones."

"You're such a bitch, Kavine," Verna laughed. "Leave the human alone. It's not her fault she has no meat on her bones."

"She will never find a mate within our pack. She should go to the humans' village and find a mate there," Kavine sniffed.

Sara stood up abruptly and make a clicking noise with her tongue. The koran kitten climbed to its feet and followed her to the door. "I should be going now. Bye, Raina."

"Bye, Sara," Raina glared at Kavine as Sara left the cabin. "My brother doesn't like you and he never will."

"Shut up, Raina," Kavine growled.

"HELLO, VAL."

Val shifted over on the fallen log he was sitting on and smiled at Sara. "Hello, little Sara. How are you this evening?"

"Fine."

She sat down beside him and stared at the large fire. It crackled pleasantly and she held her hands out to its heat. Despite the cold weather the entire pack had gathered around the fire for their evening meal. Many of them were in their wolf form and she studied the mixture of shifters and humans.

Abigail was sitting with Maria, Neil and Sienna and even from across the fire, Sara could see her staring worriedly at Maria. The older woman had a blanket wrapped around her and was staring silently into the fire. She shook her head when Abby spoke to her.

She cleared her throat when Val hissed. The man named Michael was approaching them and he gave Val a cool look before turning to Sara. "I owe you an apology."

She frowned at him. "No, you don't."

"I do. I let go of your hand. I'm sorry."

"It was an accident. Do not trouble yourself about it," she said. "How are you feeling tonight?"

"Better, thank you."

"Good. Would you like to join us?" She patted the log beside her and Michael, after another look at Val, shook his head.

"Thank you, but no."

Val hissed again as Michael made his way to Abby and the others. He sat down beside Abby and she smiled happily at him and put her arm around him, squeezing his shoulders affectionately. Val stiffened and Sara smiled tentatively at him.

"They are only friends, Val."

He didn't reply and she cleared her throat again. "I wish to ask you for a favour."

"And what might that be, young Sara?" Val asked.

"Will you teach me how to use the bow and arrow?"

He nodded. "I can do that."

"Really?" She said with surprise. She hadn't expected the vampire to agree so quickly.

"Yes. Abigail is correct in that you must learn to protect yourself. Especially now that your shifter has disappeared into the wild."

"He's not my shifter," she said.

"Of course he is not," Val said with a small grin.

She ignored his comment. "When can we begin?"

"Why not right now?" He stood and she followed him to his cabin.

"In the dark? How will I even see if I hit the target? Perhaps we should wait until it is light and…"

She trailed off as she realized her stupidity and Val laughed. "I am afraid you will have to adapt to learning in the dark, young one."

"I'm sorry, that was dumb of me," she muttered.

He ducked into the cabin and returned with the bow and quiver of arrows. "Come, we will ask the wolves if they have some torches we can use to light your training area."

"Maria, you hardly ate anything." Abby touched Maria's shoulder.

"I am not that hungry, Abby."

Abby gave Neil and Michael an anxious look. Neil shrugged slightly and patted Maria's arm. "Maria, she's right. You need to eat."

Maria didn't reply and Abby leaned closer. "Maria, honey, I know what you're going through. It's horrible to suddenly find yourself on a different world but it gets better. I promise you. All that matters is that we're together and safe."

"Yes, I know," Maria said.

"The shifters seem nice," Sienna said. "And it is better than being kept as a slave for the leeches, is it not?"

Neil squeezed Sienna's hand and kissed her knuckles before patting Maria's shoulder again. "I know you are homesick, Maria. I am too but -"

"Enough, Neil," Maria interrupted wearily. "I'm tired and I don't want to talk about home."

"Hello, humans."

Abby watched curiously as Maria's cheeks reddened. The shifter standing in front of them was older with long, grey hair and a grey beard and she didn't think she had met him yet.

"Hello. I'm Abigail," she said.

"My name is Asher."

"It's nice to meet you. This is Michael, Neil, Sienna and Maria," Abby replied.

Ignoring the others completely, Asher crouched in front of Maria. She was staring at the snow between her feet and she jerked when Asher touched her short hair.

"Hello again, human."

"Hello, Asher." Maria didn't raise her gaze.

There was an awkward moment of silence and Abby's mouth dropped open when Asher said, "I wish to mate with you."

Neil had just taken a drink of tea and he coughed and choked at Asher's statement, spraying tea everywhere as Sienna pounded him on the back.

Maria, her eyes wide and her own mouth agape, finally looked at him. "What?"

"I wish to mate with you. Your scent is very pleasing to

me. Join me in my cabin." He straightened and held his hand out to her.

"No," Maria said.

He gave her a surprised look. "Why would you not? I will not hurt you, human. I promise."

"I – I don't even know you," Maria sputtered. "I'm not going to – to mate with you."

"Do you not find me pleasing to the eye?" He cocked his head at her as Maria flushed again.

Michael made an odd choked noise and Abby glanced at him. The man was obviously trying not to laugh and she could feel the giggles rising in her throat. She pressed her lips together and glared at Michael. "Stop it."

He bent his head, his entire body shaking with silent laughter. She clapped her hand over her mouth to hide her grin as Asher touched Maria's hair again.

"Well, human?"

"You – you look fine," Maria muttered. Her gaze lingered on his broad chest for a moment before she looked away.

A smile crossed Asher's face and he inhaled. "You want me. I can smell it. Come, I will take you to my cabin and give you pleasure."

He took her hand and tugged her to her feet. Maria, her face a bit dazed, actually took a few steps with him before she shook her head and pulled her hand free. "No, I can't."

A look of disappointment crossed Asher's face as Maria sat back down on the log and pulled the blanket around her. Her body was trembling and he tried a final time. "I will help keep you warm, human. I can see you shivering."

He took her hand and slipped it into the opening at the top of his shirt, resting it against his naked chest. "Do you feel how warm I am?"

"Yes," Maria whispered. She rubbed her fingers through

the hair on his chest before snatching her hand free and taking a deep breath. "I'm sorry. I don't want to sleep with you."

"Perhaps tomorrow night?" Asher said hopefully.

"Um, I -"

Maria gave Abigail a helpless look and Abby, her hand still clamped over her mouth, shrugged.

"I will leave you for tonight, human." Asher pointed to a cabin that was close to them. "That is my home if you change your mind about mating with me."

He nodded to the others and left. Maria smacked Neil on the arm when he burst into laughter.

"Not a word, Neil! Do you hear me?" She said fiercely.

"Shifters are very straight-forward, are they not?" Sienna said.

"Oh my God." Maria glared at Abby who was giggling. "And that is enough from you as well, Abigail."

"I'm sorry," Abby snorted. "But the look on your face when he said he wanted to mate with you was priceless."

"It's not funny," Maria said.

"No, it's awesome, Maria. You were just hit on by a random shifter!" Abby said. "You still got it, girl."

A small smile crossed Maria's face and Abby squeezed her leg. "He was pretty handsome."

"And he finds your scent pleasing," Neil said with a straight face before leaning over and sniffing Maria.

"Stop it, Neil!" Maria smacked him again and he put his arm around her and hugged her before kissing her forehead.

She returned to staring silently into the fire but Abby's worry for her lifted a little. She looked more like herself and Abby had a feeling that Asher was exactly what Maria needed.

"You seem very happy tonight, my love." Kane pulled Reese a little closer to him despite the heat from the fire.

"I am," she said.

"I am glad you have a friend from your own world," he said.

"I am too," Reese replied. "But it's more than just that."

She stared around the clearing. The entire pack with the exception of Radek was in the clearing. Raina was sitting with Mia and her family, her usual cheerful face pinched with worry. Deena and Borek had joined Asher and a few others and were eating a second round of raw meat. The younger male shifters were just beyond the clearing and wrestling in their wolf forms, while the single female shifters stood next to the fire, giggling and pretending not to watch. Abby and Val were teaching Sara, by torchlight, how to use the bow and arrow.

Well, she amended, Val was. She watched as Abby said something to Sara. Sara nodded and handed her the bow and an arrow. Val put his arms around Abby and helped her pull the bow back. He whispered in her ear and she nodded briefly. He stepped back and she aimed at the target only a few feet away. She released the arrow and it fell into the snow just a few inches from her. Val grinned at her and she rolled her eyes and handed the bow back to Sara.

Reese squeezed Kane's hand and kissed him on the cheek. "It's just nice to see shifters and humans getting along."

"Aye, it does seem to be going well," he acknowledged. "Even the creatures are fitting in."

Reese suddenly frowned. "Where is Faren?"

"I overheard him telling Val that he was going hunting," Kane replied.

"Adina is missing," she said. "Did you see her go into her cabin?"

Kane shook his head and Reese gave him an anxious look. "Do you think she is with Faren? She's been acting odd ever since she saw him."

"She might be," Kane said and stopped her from standing. "She is a grown woman, Reese."

"Kane, if he bites her – if he hurts her -"

"He will not," Kane said simply.

"You don't know that," she said.

"I do. The creatures are not stupid. They are outnumbered by us. If they hurt a member of our pack, we will not hesitate to destroy them and they know it."

"I'm worried about her," Reese said. "I think she wants him to bite her."

"Perhaps but that is her decision."

He pulled her into his lap and nuzzled her throat. "You're getting cold, my love. Perhaps I should take you back to our cabin and warm you up in front of the fire."

She smiled at him. "Sara is staying with us, remember? We can't be having sex all over the cabin anymore."

He scowled. "There must be an empty cabin she can move to."

"There isn't. Now stop pouting, you can still ravish me in our bedroom."

"What does ravish mean?" He asked.

"Uh – it means to have your dirty, wicked way with me," she said and laughed when his eyes lit up.

"I plan to ravish you many times tonight, my love," he said arrogantly.

***

SHE WATCHED THE CREATURE FEED FROM THE FALLEN DEER, feeling an odd tingle of excitement in her belly when he lifted his head and she saw his sharp fangs. He wiped the blood from his mouth and sat back on his haunches.

She exhaled slowly. She had hidden herself well in the cluster of bushes but she wondered if he could smell her. If he could smell her excitement.

Don't be barto. He's a vampire not a shifter.

True but who knew what abilities the vampires had. Nothing like them existed in this world and she didn't –

She gasped in surprise when an arm reached through her shelter of branches and a hand wrapped around her wrist. She was dragged from her hiding spot and she made a soft squeak of fear when Faren pushed her against a tree.

"What are you doing here?" He snapped.

"I – I was taking a walk, that's all," she said.

"Liar," he breathed. He buried his face in her throat and inhaled. "I can smell your blood, Adina."

She made a little moan of excitement when she felt his erection pressing against her belly. She widened her legs, her body trembling at his look of dark approval, and he moved between them. She pressed her soft thighs against his hard ones and let her head fall back.

"Drink, Faren," she whispered.

His fangs were still out and she clutched at his arms as he bent his head to her neck again. He scraped them against her skin and she cried out with disappointment when he lifted his head.

"I'm not hungry."

"Please," she said a bit desperately. "I want this."

"Yes, it would seem you do," he said before licking her mouth. "But I'm not hungry."

Disappointment flooded her face and she struggled to free herself. "Fine. Let me go."

He lifted her arms above her head and trapped her wrists

against the tree with one hand. "I am not hungry for your blood, Adina. My cock, however, wants to be buried in your warm pussy. Will you deny me?"

"No," she whispered.

He grinned, his fangs flashing in the moonlight as he lifted her and braced her against the tree. She wrapped her legs around his narrow hips as he cupped one full breast through her thick jacket and squeezed it. She had changed into a skirt before leaving the warmth of her cabin in search of the vampire. It was a foolish move considering how cold it was, but a dim part of her mind wondered if she had done so specifically for this reason.

He pushed her skirt around her waist and reached between her legs. She moaned when he traced his fingers over her panties before tearing them from her body. He touched her pussy, smiling again when he felt her warmth and her wetness.

"Ready for me so quickly, Adina," he teased, "I've barely touched you."

"Please, Faren," she whispered.

He rubbed her clit as he bent his head to her ear. "Unbutton your jacket."

Her fingers trembling, she unbuttoned her jacket and then her shirt. He inhaled sharply at the sight of her naked breasts and dipped his head to suck her nipple into his mouth. She made a sharp cry of need. Her hands threaded through his hair and clutched as he kissed his way to her other breast. He sucked until her nipple was swollen and throbbing with pleasure.

He lifted his head and kissed her deeply. She sucked at his tongue before sliding hers over the tips of his fangs. Another shudder of desire went through her and she was only vaguely aware of his hand between them unbuttoning his pants.

He lifted her a little higher and she moaned into his mouth when his cock brushed across her clit. He groaned and shifted her until he was at her tight entrance. As the head of his cock breached her warmth, she cried out and he made a strangled curse before thrusting into her fully.

"Faren!" She squeezed his waist with her thighs as he started a slow deep rhythm within her.

"So wet, so tight, Adina," he muttered into her ear. "Your pussy feels so fucking good around my cock."

"Harder," she whimpered.

His eyes glowed and he thrust rapidly in and out of her. The air around them was cold but Adina was burning up with lust and need. She clung to Faren's shoulders as he pushed her further and further toward her release.

"Yes, yes, just like that," she panted into his ear as he kneaded her breast. "Don't stop, Faren, don't…"

She trailed off, her eyes squeezing shut and her back arching as her orgasm rushed through her. He muttered a curse and plunged into her a final time before coming inside of her in a hard and satisfying rush. His fangs lengthened and she threw her head back as he pressed his mouth to her throat.

"Do it," she begged as her pussy milked his cock.

Faren snarled angrily and pulled out of her. Panting harshly, he dropped her to her feet and backed away as she shoved her skirt down and clutched her jacket closed.

"Faren?"

The vampire's body was shaking wildly and he had a look of feral hunger on his face. "Leave me."

"Did I – did I do something wrong?" She asked.

"Leave me, Adina!" He suddenly shouted.

"Why will you not take what I'm offering?" She took a step toward him. "I want you to feed from me, Faren."

He snarled again and she watched in astonishment as he turned and disappeared into the dark.

"Faren! Come back!" She shouted. There was no reply and with tears starting to drip down her face, Adina turned and hurried back in the direction of the others.

CHAPTER 13

"**G**ood morning, Kane."

Kane split the piece of wood, the axe whistling through the air, before smiling at Asher. "Good morning, Uncle."

"Do you find it tedious to cut so much firewood?"

Kane shrugged. "It is needed to keep my mate warm. I cannot use my heat to warm her all the time."

"Aye, the humans are a fragile species, are they not?"

"Not that fragile." Kane laughed. "But when it comes to the cold – aye, I suppose."

Asher was silent for a moment and Kane gave him a curious look. "Is there something I can help you with, Uncle?"

"Aye, there is. I require your advice," Asher said. "I wish to mate with the older human female."

Kane, who was just setting another piece of wood on the stump to split, jerked wildly and knocked it over. "What?"

"The older human – I wish to mate with her and I need your advice on how to convince her to mate with me," Asher said patiently. "I have asked her a few times in the last week and she refuses. Which is odd because I can clearly smell her desire for me."

Kane stared at him and Asher scowled. "What?"

"Since when have you wanted to mate with anyone, let alone a human?"

Asher's scowl deepened. "I may be old, Kane, but it does not mean I have lost all desire to mate."

"I know, Uncle, it's just strange that you suddenly wish to mate with a human."

"Not that strange. She is attractive even with her peculiar, short hair. How did you convince your human to mate with you?"

"Well," Kane split the piece of wood with a loud grunt. "first you must learn to call her by her name, instead of human. Do you even know her name?"

"Aye. Maria."

"So call her Maria instead of human."

"I can do that," Asher said. "What else?"

Kane set the axe down again. "You must sweet talk her, Uncle."

"Sweet talk? What is that?" Asher asked.

"It means to use your words to convince her to mate with you."

"I am. I have asked her numerous times to mate with me," Asher replied.

Kane laughed. "No, Uncle. You must be sweet to her. Tell her she is pretty, compliment her eyes or her hair, and…"

He trailed off and frowned at the ground for a moment. "Wait, that is not right. I mean, it is right, but you cannot make it all about her looks. Reese says human women also like to hear that they are smart."

"I do not know if she is smart, Kane. I've barely spoken with her," Asher said.

"You need to make the effort to get to know her before you mate with her, Uncle. Human females like that."

Asher sighed. "Human females are much more work than female shifters. Your aunt knew I wanted to mate with her and was more than willing to do so without me telling her she was pretty or smart."

Kane grinned at him, "Human females are not like our females, Uncle."

"Aye, I am beginning to realize that."

"You can also give her little gifts. Reese says that in her world, men will often present their females with items they think they will like."

"Like what?"

"Flowers and small, shiny rocks."

"Rocks?" Asher said in confusion and Kane shrugged.

"That's what Reese said."

Asher shoved his hands into his pockets and stared at the cloudy sky as Kane split another piece of wood.

"Is it worth it, Kane?" He finally asked.

"Aye, Uncle. It is," Kane said.

"SHUT UP, MIA! HE IS COMING BACK! AND HE PROBABLY left not because of the humans but because you and Kavine are always mooning over him!"

Sara strapped her bow across her back and hurried in the direction of Raina's and Radek's cabin. She was practicing for most of the morning and her arm and hand were throbbing and burning. She flexed her hand gingerly as more shouting was heard from the cabin. She knocked and then opened the door just in time to see Mia throwing a chair at Raina.

"You take that back right now, Raina! Radek did not leave because of me!" Mia screamed angrily.

Raina growled at her, the simple shirt and pants she was wearing beginning to split at the seams as her body swelled. "You're always chasing after him! Always annoying him with your constant chattering! No wonder he keeps leaving! Between you and Kavine he has no time to himself!"

"Girls!" Sara clapped her hands together sharply and the two shifters turned and growled at her. She took a step back as fear trickled through her veins, before taking a deep breath and scowling at them.

"Both of you stop! Right now!" She said.

"Are you going to make us, human?" Mia snarled at her.

"No, but I will find your alpha and he will punish you for fighting," Sara said.

Mia's face paled and she glanced uneasily at Raina before stepping back. Sara marveled at the power that Kane had over his pack. She was fairly certain that Kane's punishment would be nothing more than a verbal warning – she had been with the pack for over a week now and she had never even seen the alpha raise his voice in anger with any member of his pack – but the young shifters obviously respected and feared him.

She stared sternly at both of them. "Why are you fighting? You're best friends."

"Mia says that Radek is never coming home again and that he has left our pack for good," Raina said heatedly. "It's her fault he keeps leaving in the first place."

"It is not!" Mia snapped. "He hates the humans and he's left because of them."

She turned and glared at Sara. "Because of you!"

"Shut up, Mia!" Raina shouted again. Her face was bright red and Sara could see tears in her eyes. "Radek will be back and he will tell you himself that he keeps leaving because of you and stupid Kavine!"

"I am not stupid!" Mia shouted back.

"I didn't say you were stupid! I said Kavine was stupid!"

"Enough!" Sara said again. "Mia, I think you should go home. You and Raina can talk this out later when you're both calm."

"I'm never speaking to her again!" Mia shouted before storming past Sara and out into the cold.

Raina stalked to the door and shouted, "Fine with me, Mia! I don't want to ever speak to you again either!"

She slammed the door shut and punched the wall before stomping to the kitchen and collapsing dramatically on one of the chairs. She buried her head in her arms and her body shook as she sobbed.

"Oh, Raina. Honey, don't cry." Sara hurried over and pulled a chair up next to her before sitting down and rubbing her back. "It'll be okay, don't cry."

Raina threw herself into Sara's arms. "Why does he keep leaving me?"

"Oh, honey," Sara held her and rubbed her back again. "He's just – he's confused right now and needs some time."

Raina stared up at her. "He keeps leaving me all alone and doesn't even care that I'm by myself. I hate him!"

"You don't, honey," Sara said. "I know you're angry with him but you don't hate him."

Raina sobbed quietly for a few minutes before wiping at her face with her hand. "Aye, I don't. But I'm so mad at him."

"I know and you have every right to be. It isn't fair to you that he keeps leaving you," Sara replied.

Raina continued to lean on Sara. She didn't mind. There was no fire in the fireplace and it was cold in the cabin. Raina's warmth was the only thing keeping her from shivering. She stroked the young shifter's hair. "I'm sorry, honey."

"It's not your fault. Well, maybe it is," Raina said. "Although I wasn't lying when I told Mia that Radek is tired of her and Kavine mooning over him."

She was quiet for a few moments before sighing again. "I'm so lonely. What if Mia is right? What if Radek really has left for good?"

Sara shook her head. "He hasn't. He loves you, Raina and wouldn't leave you like that." She hesitated before saying, "Do you want me to stay with you?"

Raina popped up and stared at her. "Would you, human?"

Sara nodded. She was staying with Reese and Kane and although the alpha was perfectly friendly to her, she had a feeling that he would prefer to be alone in the cabin with Reese.

"Yes. If there's room in your cabin," she said.

"There is!" Raina said. "We have three bedrooms. You can sleep in mama and papa's room."

"Then it's settled. I'll stay with you until Radek returns." Sara smiled when Raina kissed her cheek.

"Thank you, human!"

"You're welcome. But we'll need to have a fire going. I will freeze to death if we don't." Sara grinned at Raina before standing and holding out her hand. "Why don't you come with me to Reese's cabin while I tell her?"

"All right." Raina took her hand and squeezed it. "We are going to have so much fun together, Sara!"

———

"WHAT DOES IT FEEL LIKE WHEN THEY BITE YOU?"

Abigail stared at the blonde woman before her gaze flickered to Maria. Maria was staying in Adina's cabin and Abby had stopped by to visit with her. She didn't know Adina very well, the woman kept to herself and Maria had told her that Adina didn't talk much even when it was just the two of them.

"Does it hurt?" Adina asked when Abby didn't reply.

"Yes," she said honestly. "A little."

Adina stared into her mug, giving Maria a distracted smile of thanks when the older woman filled it with tea.

"Adina?" Abby leaned forward and touched the woman's hand hesitantly. "Are you – do you want Faren to bite you?"

"Of course not. Why would you think that?" Adina said quickly. "I am just curious."

"Adina," Maria sat down across from her, "when you are bitten by a vampire it starts an obsession that cannot be controlled. You will go mad if they do not keep biting you."

Adina frowned. "I find that hard to believe, Maria."

"Aye, I know it seems strange but believe me – it is true. If Faren bites you and then does not continue to feed from you, the only way to stop the madness is by not seeing him again. Eventually, if the vampire is not near you the obsession will fade but it takes a long time and is very painful. Especially if they have been feeding from you for a while."

"It's true," Abby said.

A shiver went down her back. When she was stolen from Val, the withdrawal was worse than anything she had ever experienced before. She shuddered again, remembering the pain and the need. She had spent more than two weeks in bed, her entire body wracked with pain and her mind screaming at her to find Val, while Michael and Wesley and the others had waited to see if she lived or died.

When Adina gave her a questioning look, she smiled

faintly at her. "I was separated from Val after he had bitten me. The pain and the withdrawal were...intense."

"Yet you allowed him to bite you again," Adina pointed out.

"Yes, but that's because I love him and I was saving his life," Abby said. "If I didn't love him, I would not have allowed him to bite me again. It isn't just the obsession with being bitten. Vampires are a, well, very sexual race. Most of them enjoy having sex with a human before they bite them. It's not just the feeding you obsess for but the sex too."

Adina's face went a brilliant shade of red and she quickly bowed her head. Abigail frowned in confusion but Maria touched Adina's shoulder. "Adina? Have you had sex with Faren?"

Adina rubbed her forehead with one shaking hand. "Aye, last week."

"What? How?" Abby asked.

She smacked herself in the head as a small grin slid across Maria's face. "Wait, never mind. That's a stupid question."

Adina sighed heavily. "He would not bite me."

Both Abby and Maria gaped at her and Adina's flush deepened.

"You're kidding me," Maria said faintly. She stared at Abby. "Have you ever heard of a vampire having sex with someone without biting them?"

Abigail's own cheeks reddened. "Well, yeah. Val slept with me without biting me when we were reunited. But Faren – I find it hard to believe that he didn't bite you, Adina. He has no problem feeding from humans."

"Well, he didn't!" Adina suddenly snapped. "I have practically begged him twice now to feed from me and he will not."

"I know that I don't know you very well but I'm hoping

you'll take my advice. Faren is dangerous. He wouldn't deliberately hurt you, at least I don't think he would, but he does not have the affection for humans that a vampire like Val does. Most vampires don't. Val is, well, he's different," Abby said.

"He is," Maria agreed. "Letting Faren feed from you would not be wise."

"It doesn't matter. I told you – he won't feed from me," Adina said.

"That's a good thing," Maria said.

Adina didn't reply but Abby could see the disagreement on her face. "Adina? Why do you want Faren to bite you?"

Adina paused before finally meeting her gaze. "All my life I have been the – the good girl. I did what my parents told me to, I became a healer like my mother because that's what she wanted me to do. When my brother sold me to the slavers to save his own hide, I wasn't even that angry with him. I told myself I understood why he did it and that good girls like me needed to just accept what happened to them."

She stood up and paced restlessly back and forth in the small kitchen. "Do you know that the previous alpha nearly picked me for his mate? His name was Dagon and he was cruel. He had killed all four of his previous mates but I told myself and Reese that it didn't matter. That I had to accept I would be his mate and do as he asked and hope to bear him children so he wouldn't kill me as well. Because that's what good girls do."

"Oh, Adina," Maria said.

Adina whirled around to face her. "I do not ask for your pity, Maria! I am tired of always doing the right thing, of always being careful and safe, and just once I want to know what it feels like to do something – something stupid and reckless!"

She folded her arms across her torso and stared at the floor. "And I am attracted to Faren. Not that it matters. He is not attracted to me."

Abby frowned. "If he had sex with you, Adina, then he's attracted to you."

"Then why will he not feed from me?"

"That is weird," Abby admitted. "I don't know why he won't."

Maria shrugged. "Perhaps for the first time in his life he feels something more than blood lust for a human."

"I don't think that's possible for Faren," Abby said.

There was a knock at the door and Maria crossed the room to open it. Abigail grinned when she saw Asher standing in the cold.

"Hey, Asher," she called.

"Hello, human," he replied without looking at her. He stared intently at Maria who blushed furiously before clearing her throat.

"What do you want, Asher?"

"Hello, hum –" he paused and cleared his own throat. "Hello, Maria."

She gave him a startled look as Abigail and Adina joined them at the door.

"Come in out of the cold, Asher," Abby said brightly as Maria glared at her.

The shifter nodded and stepped into the cabin, kicking the door shut with his foot. He had both hands behind his back and he smiled at Maria.

"Your hair is very pretty today, Maria."

Maria touched her hair self-consciously as Asher's gaze lowered to her chest and then her pelvis.

"Um, thank you."

"You're welcome, Maria. Do you know how to read, Maria?" He asked.

"Yes." Maria gave Abby a confused look as the younger woman grinned like a lunatic. Even Adina was smiling faintly and Abby nudged her playfully as Asher continued to stare at Maria.

"You're very smart, Maria," Asher said.

"Thank you?" Maria said hesitantly.

There was an awkward silence and Abby, still grinning widely, said, "Do you know how to read, Asher?"

"I do not. I am not as smart as Maria," he said gravely.

"Nonsense. I bet Maria would teach you how to read," Abby said.

"Abby!" Maria elbowed her discreetly before smiling nervously at Asher.

"Would you, hum – Maria?" Asher asked. "I would like to learn to read."

"I don't have anything to teach you with," Maria said.

"I can bring books, Maria," Asher replied. "Anna teaches our young ones how to read and write and has what you need."

"Why not get Anna to teach you then?" Maria asked.

Asher hesitated, clearly not sure of what excuse to give, and Abby jumped in. "I'm sure Anna doesn't have enough time to teach the young ones and you. Isn't that right, Asher?"

"Aye, that is right." Asher gave her a grateful look and Abby winked at him.

"Well, Maria? Will you teach me to read, Maria?" Asher asked.

Maria hesitated before nodding and Asher gave her a broad grin. "Thank you, Maria."

He turned to leave and Maria, Adina and Abby stared at the weeds he held in his right hand behind his back.

"Asher? What are those?" Abby said as Maria booted her in the shin. She winced and rubbed her leg as Violet stuck her head out from Abby's hair, clasped her tiny hands under her chin and made an exaggerated kissy face at Asher and Maria.

"I almost forgot, Maria. These are for you, Maria," Asher held out the limp bouquet of weeds.

"Thank you, Asher," Maria took the weeds. They were soaking wet and Asher smiled hesitantly.

"I had to dig them out from under the snow, Maria."

"They're beautiful," Maria said.

"I have another gift for you, Maria," Asher held his tightly-clenched left fist out. "Open your hand, Maria."

"What's with all the 'Maria's'?" Abby whispered into Adina's ear. The blonde woman shrugged and Abigail bit back her laughter when Asher dropped five small stones into Maria's hand.

The stones were polished until they gleamed in the dim light and Maria stared blankly at them as Asher gave her an eager look. "Do you like them, Maria?"

"They're very…shiny," Maria replied.

"Aye, they are. I spent many hours polishing them, Maria," Asher replied. He gave her a nervous look. "Small, shiny rocks. My alpha's mate says that is what human females like. Is she wrong?"

Abigail made a choked noise of laughter and turned away as Maria studied the rocks in her hand before smiling at the shifter. "No, she isn't. They're lovely and I like them very much. Thank you, Asher."

"You're welcome, Maria. I will come by tomorrow so you can teach me to read, Maria," Asher said.

He left the cabin and Abigail and Adina burst into soft laughter as Maria slipped the rocks into her pocket.

Adina grinned at Abigail. "What kind of world are you and Reese from that men give you small stones as presents?"

Abigail giggled. "Oh my God. If you could just – f I – oh shit, this is the funniest thing ever."

She wiped at the tears in her eyes before shaking her head. "In my world, we have jewels - precious jewels - that are dug from the earth. There are a bunch of different ones and the most coveted one is the diamond. They're worth a lot of money and men give them to women when they get married or even just as presents. Diamonds are often referred to as 'rocks' and they are small and shiny. That's what Reese meant."

She laughed again as Maria, her cheeks still flushed, shrugged. "It's not Asher's fault he didn't understand."

"Nope, it isn't," Abby looped her arm around Maria's shoulders and kissed her cheek. "I like him a lot, Maria. You should sleep with him."

"Abby!" Maria slapped her gently on the hip. "Go on, now. I don't want to hear anything more about sex with Asher. He gave me those gifts because I agreed to teach him to read."

"Oh, of course, that's why." Abby rolled her eyes and walked away.

CHAPTER 14

"You are doing very well, young Sara," Val said.

"Do you really think so, Val?"

"I do. Much better than the little dove," he said.

"Hey!" Abigail gave him a mock look of anger as he grinned at her.

"It is true, Abigail."

"I know. God, I miss my sword." She studied the target in the glow from the torches. She had fired five arrows and only one had even hit the target. Sara had also fired five and all of them were embedded deep within the middle of the target.

"You have a knack for it," Val said to Sara as she collected the arrows.

"I've been practicing a lot," Sara said.

"I heard. Abby told me you've been practicing for hours every day for the last month," Val said as Abby kissed him on the cheek before joining Michael beside the fire. A dark look crossed his face and a soft hiss escaped before he could stop it.

"She's in love with you, Val," Sara said.

"I know. But I am the jealous type." He winked at her and

she grinned before following him toward the shifters and humans gathered around the fire.

As Val joined Abigail and Michael, she sat beside Raina and the young shifter leaned against her affectionately as Deena sat beside her.

"Hello, Deena," Sara said politely.

Deena touched her hair and smiled. "Pretty hair."

"Thank you," Sara said. "I like your hair too. Where is Borek?"

"Hunting," Deena replied before touching her hair again.

They sat in silence for a few minutes before Sara looked at Raina. "You're quiet tonight, Raina."

"I'm fine," the young shifter said moodily.

"Are you sure?"

"Aye," she said shortly.

Sara bit her lip. She had been living with Raina for the last month and had gotten to know the girl very well. She was fairly certain she knew what was wrong. She squeezed Raina's hand. "He will return soon."

"It has been an entire moon. He has never been gone this long before," she said. Tears were starting to drip down her face and she wiped at them angrily. "He could be dead for all I know."

Panic stabbed Sara directly in the heart. The young girl had finally vocalized what she was worried about for weeks and she tried to smile reassuringly at her. "I'm sure he isn't. He can take care of himself."

"I know he is dead," the teenager whispered. "I can feel it."

"He is not dead, Raina." Kane's deep voice came from behind them and the three of them turned to stare at him.

"You don't know that, Kane," Raina whispered.

"I do, my love," he said kindly. "I saw him in the forest not two days ago."

"What?" Raina jumped up and grabbed Kane's hands. "You spoke with him!"

"No. He was in his wolf form and would not let me get close to him. But he is not dead."

"Why won't he come home?" She whispered forlornly.

"I do not know," Kane said as his gaze slid to Sara.

Guilt flooded through her and she stared at the snowy ground, only barely aware of Deena's hand stroking her hair.

"Raina? Come sit with mama and me." Mia had appeared. The two girls had made up only a few days after their fight. Raina nodded and followed Mia to where her mother sat. The woman put her arms around Raina and Mia and hugged them.

Her spot was immediately filled by a young shifter with black hair and light blue eyes. He grinned happily at Sara.

"Hello, human. I mean – Sara."

"Hello, Davin." Sara returned his smile. "How are you this evening?"

"Very well, and you?"

"I'm good, thank you."

A gust of cold wind blew and she shivered. Davin draped his arm across her shoulders and tugged her against him. "I will keep you warm, Sara."

She shifted away from him. "Oh, that's fine, I -"

"I don't mind," he interrupted. "Do you have enough firewood for your cabin?"

"We do. Thank you again for chopping the wood for us. It's very kind of you."

He squeezed her shoulder and she tried not to wince as he said, "It is my pleasure. I know that humans are fragile."

"Aye, they are, Davin. You're hurting the young Sara."

Kane was still standing behind them and Sara gave him a grateful look as Davin loosened his grip.

"I'm sorry, human," he said with a guilty look at Kane.

"That's all right," she replied.

"Join your friends, Davin. I wish to speak to Sara," Kane said.

"I am keeping her warm, my alpha," the young shifter protested.

Kane stared sternly at him. "Deena will keep her warm. Go on, Davin."

He hesitated a moment longer. His cheeks flushed a dull red when Kane growled under his breath, and he stood reluctantly. "I will speak with you later, Sara."

"Sure." She smiled cheerfully at him and he grinned back delightedly before trudging past the fire to sit with the other young shifters.

Kane sat down with a soft grunt as Deena put her arm around Sara and stroked her curls. She leaned against the female shifter, grateful for her heat, as Deena said, "You are precious to him."

Sara didn't reply and Kane glanced at her. "Deena is right. Davin has a crush on you."

"I know," Sara said.

Reese joined them and sat on Kane's lap. "What are you guys talking about?"

"Hello, flower," Deena said.

Reese smiled at Deena, "Hello, Deena."

"We are discussing Davin's crush on Sara," Kane said bluntly.

Sara blushed and Reese tapped Kane on the back. "Did you ask Sara if she wanted to talk about it?"

"No," Kane said. "Should I have?"

"Yes, my love."

Kane stared at Sara. "Do you wish to speak with me about this, Sara?"

"Oh, um, sure I guess," Sara said. She didn't actually want to talk about it but it seemed rude to say so.

"He would be a good mate for you," Kane said. "He is your age and I do not believe he has mated yet. It would be easy enough for you to teach him gentleness when mating."

Sara's blush deepened and Reese whacked Kane on the back. "What Kane is trying to say, honey, is that Davin is a very sweet boy and would treat you well."

"He's been very nice to me," Sara said.

"Do you wish to mate with him?" Kane asked.

"Kane!" Reese whacked him again before smiling at Sara. "Are you interested in dating Davin?"

"He won't be interested when he finds out that I am, un, inexperienced." Sara was blushing so hard she could feel sweat breaking out on her forehead.

"Why do you say that?" Reese asked curiously.

"Well, because shifters like their mates to have experience in the, you know, bedroom," Sara said.

"What?" Reese gave her an odd look.

"Is it different because he hasn't mated before?" Sara asked.

Both Kane and Reese were looking at her like she had lost her mind and she squirmed uncomfortably against Deena. "Why are you looking at me like that?"

"Why do you think shifters want mates with experience?" Reese asked. "Shifters don't care about that sort of thing." She glanced at Kane. "Do they?"

He shrugged. "Perhaps some do but I know of no shifter in our pack who cares whether their mate is experienced in sex."

"No, that's not true," Sara protested. "Radek told me that

shifters only want to sleep with women who have experience. It's why he would not take my virginity in exchange for his protection. It is why you found us the, uh, way you did – he was teaching me what to do so I could find a mate in your pack."

Reese snorted. "I know Radek is your cousin, Kane, but the minute he gets back I'm ripping him a new one for lying to Sara."

"It isn't true?" Sara whispered.

"No, young Sara, it is not," Kane said.

"Why would he lie to me?"

Kane sighed. "Probably because his wolf wishes to mate with you and his human side does not know how to handle it."

Sara squeezed her hands together in her lap and stared into the flames as Deena stroked her hair again.

Kane sighed again. "When Radek returns I will speak to him about lying to you, Sara."

"No, don't. It doesn't matter," she said quickly. "I don't care whether he lies to me or not."

"Then the matter is finished." Kane smiled at Reese who rolled her eyes.

"Are you interested in mating with Davin then?" Kane asked.

"Kane." Reese gave him an exasperated look and the shifter stared at her in bewilderment.

"It's fine, Reese," Sara said. "I do not know if I am interested in him or not. He's very kind and handsome but…"

She trailed off and Kane frowned. "But what?"

"No spark," Reese said.

Sara nodded as Kane shrugged. "Sometimes it takes a little longer for an attraction to grow. Give Davin a chance, young Sara."

Sara didn't reply and Reese touched her shoulder. "Radek isn't the right choice for you, honey."

"I know that," she said quickly.

"It is only his wolf who desires you," Kane said.

"I *know*," she said a bit crossly before scowling at the shifter. "He left because of me."

"Aye, he did," Kane said.

Sara flinched and Reese frowned at Kane before touching her shoulder again. "Don't feel bad, Sara. Radek is a grown man and if he chooses to run away rather than deal with his issues, that's not your fault."

"Raina misses him terrible," Sara said guiltily. "I – I think I should leave."

"No," Reese said immediately. "You can't go out on your own."

"I could go to the human village," Sara said. "As long as I'm here, Radek won't return and Raina is without her brother. It isn't safe for Radek out in the forest, and I couldn't live with myself if Radek died and Raina lost him the way I lost my brother."

"Kane will find Radek tomorrow and speak to him," Reese said. "He will convince him to return to Raina and to the pack. Don't worry, honey. We'll fix this. Right, Kane?"

Kane remained silent and she pinched him discreetly on the back. "*Right*, Kane?"

"Aye, my love," he said with a remarkable lack of conviction.

HE TROTTED INTO THE CLEARING AS THE COLD LIGHT OF DAWN peeked over the trees. He sniffed at the ring of stones in the middle, the fire had died long ago, as the wind ruffled his fur.

He loped to his cabin and stopped to stare briefly at his alpha's cabin before shifting to his human form. The wind bit at his flesh and he stepped inside his home, closing the door behind him. The cabin was oddly warm. Flames still flickered in the fireplace and he frowned at the wood stacked neatly beside the hearth.

Why would Raina have a fire going, he wondered as he crouched naked in front of it. It was cold but normally they just slept in their wolf forms. It was especially odd that she would keep a fire going all night.

The door to his parents' bedroom opened and his eyes widened when Sara stepped out into the main room. She yawned and stretched and his eyes dropped to the hem of her shirt as it rose up. She was wearing one of his shirts, he realized, and his wolf made a soft growl of happiness at the sight of her slender, pale thighs.

She ran a hand through her hair. The curls were a mass of bedhead craziness and she yawned again before heading toward the kitchen. Although the kitchen and living space were one open room, she hadn't seen him. He stayed where he was as she filled a pot with water from the bucket on the counter, humming to herself as she did.

SARA ADDED A BIT MORE WATER TO THE POT. SHE HAD WOKEN early this morning and couldn't fall back asleep. Like usual, her mind had turned to Radek and she had tossed and turned for nearly an hour while her mind worried incessantly about him.

Stop worrying, Sara. Kane will find him today and bring him back. He's fine.

Yes, he probably was, but it hadn't helped her to sleep and

she had finally decided to just get up and make tea. She turned toward the fireplace and at the sight of Radek standing naked by the fire, dropped the pot. It fell to the floor with a loud clatter and water splashed her feet and legs. It dripped down her calves as she stared wide-eyed at the naked shifter.

"Radek?" She whispered.

Without speaking, he stalked into his bedroom and slammed the door behind him. She stared at the water and pot on the floor, wondering for a moment if she was simply dreaming. The idea was shattered when Radek's door whipped open and he reappeared wearing a pair of pants.

He stood in front of her and she studied his face as he watched her silently. Confusion and anger flickered across it and for just a moment, a flicker of lust. He took a step back. "What are you doing in my home?"

"Radek, you're back," she whispered.

"What are you doing in my home, Sara?" He repeated.

"I – Radek, where have you been? Do you know how worried I've been about you?" She asked.

He leaned forward and inhaled, his eyes dropping to her breasts. She flushed, feeling that familiar tingle of lust, and he stiffened before stepping toward her.

"Tell me why you're here and why you were sleeping in my parents' room," he said in a soft voice.

"She's here because you left me alone."

Raina had emerged from her bedroom. Radek's face lit up and he turned toward his sister. "Raina!"

He started toward her and she held her hands up and scowled at him. "Don't, Radek."

"Raina? What's wrong?" He asked.

"What's wrong? What's wrong?" She shouted. "You left me for a moon, Radek! An entire moon! I was all alone and you didn't even care!"

187

"Raina, I do care." Radek said in confusion. "I didn't mean -"

"No you don't!" Raina shouted. "If you cared about me you wouldn't have left me all alone."

"You weren't alone," Radek protested. "You had Kane and Uncle and the entire pack."

"It isn't the same! I would have spent every evening alone in this stupid cabin if it had not been for the human," Raina snapped. "Don't you dare be angry with her for staying in mama and papa's room! At least she has been here for me unlike my own brother!"

"Raina, I'm sorry," Radek said.

"It's too late for being sorry!" She shouted. "You keep leaving me over and over, Radek, and it isn't fair! I hate you!"

"Raina, don't say that." Radek gave her an anguished look and reached for her. She shoved him in the chest, burst into tears, and ran to her room. She slammed the door and Radek ran his hands through his hair before turning and staring at Sara.

"Radek, I'm sorry," she said. "Raina didn't mean that. She loves you very much, she's just upset."

"Aye," he muttered.

The look on his face was breaking Sara's heart and she took a hesitant step toward him. He flinched and backed away, disappearing into his bedroom and shutting the door behind him.

"ABBY, WAIT UP!"

Reese jogged from her cabin toward Abby. "Why are you up so early?"

Abby grinned at her. "I haven't actually gone to bed yet. Val just went into his daysleep. I'm going to join him shortly, I just wanted to get a bit of sunshine."

"It must be difficult to spend most of your time in the darkness," Reese said.

Abby shrugged. "It's not as bad as you think. When I was eighteen my foster parents kicked me out, and I ended up working the night shift at this creepy factory that made plastic containers for nearly a year. So, I have some experience being up all night."

"I'm not sure that I could do it," Reese said.

"You get used to it," Abby said. "Why are you up so early?"

"I woke up early and thought I'd check on Asher. He's been going to his cabin early every evening for the last few nights and that's not like him. He's usually so social with the pack. I'm a bit worried about him. I know he's an early riser so I thought I'd have breakfast with him and see if there was anything bothering him."

"That's nice of you," Abby said. She followed Reese toward Asher's cabin. "Asher is Kane's uncle, right?"

"Yes." Reese knocked on Asher's door before opening it. "Asher? Are you awake? I thought we could have – oh my God!"

Abby's mouth dropped open and Reese turned bright red. She slammed the door shut and stared at Abby. "Did you – ?"

"Yes," Abby said solemnly.

"Was Maria…"

Reese trailed off and stared blankly at Abigail.

"Riding him like a pony?" Abby suggested.

"Yeah."

"Yep, she was."

"Oh my God," Reese repeated. "I guess I know why he's been retiring early."

The two women stared at each other before bursting into simultaneous giggles.

"Shh!" Reese said frantically. "They'll hear us! Come on."

They hurried away from the cabin, both of them still giggling, as Kane came out of their cabin.

"What's so funny, humans?" He asked.

"Uh, nothing," Reese said.

"Did you check on Uncle? I thought you were having breakfast with him."

"He's busy right now," Reese replied.

"Busy doing what?"

Reese hesitated and Abby, a wicked grin on her face, said, "Maria."

"Maria? What do you…" He trailed off and a small smile crossed his face. "My advice about the rocks worked."

"You gave your uncle dating advice?" Reese laughed.

"Aye, and it was good advice," Kane said smugly.

"Yes, Maria loved the small, shiny rocks," Abby snickered.

"Shiny rocks?" Reese gave her a puzzled look and Abby burst into laughter again.

"I forgot to tell you! A few weeks ago, Asher came to see Maria and gave her some rocks because -"

The door to Radek and Raina's cabin opened and Sara slipped out into the cold. Her face was pale and Abby frowned as she walked slowly toward them.

"Sara? What's wrong, honey?"

"Radek is back," she said. "Raina was very angry with him and said that she hated him. The look on his face, Abby, it was so awful. Now Raina won't come out of her room – I could hear her crying."

Abby hugged her as Reese glanced at Kane. "You need to speak with him, Kane, and I'll speak with Raina."

"Aye," Kane sighed.

"He's in his room. I knocked on his door but he wouldn't come out," Sara said. "I think you should give him a bit of space."

Kane studied her carefully before nodding. "Perhaps you are right, little one."

CHAPTER 15

"Thinking of leaving again, cousin?"

Kane joined Radek at the edge of the forest. The younger shifter was leaning against a tree staring moodily into the woods and he glanced at Kane before shaking his head.

"No."

"Good." Kane clapped him on the back. "You've been missed, Radek."

He laughed bitterly. "Have I? Raina hates me and will not speak to me."

"Aye, I know. Reese is speaking to her now in our cabin. She will help to smooth things over with your sister."

"I'm not so sure about that. I have never seen Raina so angry before."

"Can you blame her? You left her for a moon."

"I should not have done that. I know that now. But I needed time by myself to think, to clear my head, and figure out what to do in regard to the humans living in our pack."

"And have you?" Kane asked.

"Aye," Radek replied. "I realize now that not all humans

are like the ones who tortured me as a pup. Your mate and the others do not deserve to be treated the way I have done. I will do better from now on, my alpha. I promise you."

"And the young Sara?"

"What about her?" Radek asked.

"Will you take her as your mate?"

"Of course not. My time alone brought me clarity in many ways and my desire to mate with her has passed."

"Has it?" Kane said.

"Aye, it has," Radek said. "In fact, it does not bother me that she lives in my home. She can continue to stay there for as long as she likes."

"That's generous of you, Radek, but not necessary," Kane said.

"What do you mean?"

"I mean that the young Sara has already been offered a new place to stay."

"With who?" Radek asked.

"Young Davin has opened his home to her."

Kane watched as anger flickered across Radek's face. "His cabin only has one bed."

"Aye, that's true," Kane said briefly.

Radek scowled at Kane. "Is she fucking him?"

"That is none of my business, nor is it any of yours. Besides, you are over your attraction to the human, remember? What do you care who she fucks?"

"I don't," Radek said. "Has she accepted his offer?"

Kane shrugged. "I do not know."

Radek started toward the cabins and Kane grabbed his arm. "Where are you going?"

"Back to my cabin."

"Sara isn't there, Radek."

Radek hesitated before saying casually, "Do you know where she is?"

"I believe she told Reese she was going hunting this morning."

Radek stiffened and stared into the woods. "Hunting? You let the human go into the woods alone? Have you gone mad, Kane?"

"The young Sara is not the same, Radek. She has become quite good at -"

Radek yanked his arm free of Kane's grip and snarled at him before running into the woods. Kane sighed. He was happy his cousin had returned but the longer he continued to deny his feelings for the human, the more discord it would bring to the pack. Perhaps the young human was right – it would be better if she left and joined the humans.

SARA, NEARLY HIDDEN IN THE THICK UNDERBRUSH, RELEASED her breath as she fired the arrow. She made a soft squeal of delight and stepped out from the bushes. She stared at the fallen floren. Her arrow had pierced it through the head, killing it immediately, and she smiled in satisfaction before crouching beside the dead beast. She ran her hand over its feathered body. The floren was a big one and there would be more than enough feathers to fill the pillows and quilt that Ghita was helping her to make. Theran's mate was an accomplished seamstress and she had happily agreed to teach Sara.

She stiffened when she heard the low growling. She yanked the arrow from the floren's head and stood, loading her bow quickly as she turned around. She aimed the arrow into the trees and waited. When the wolf appeared with his fur gleaming in the sun, she scowled at him and lowered her weapon.

"Radek, you nearly got yourself shot with an arrow. Do not sneak up on me like that again."

The wolf ignored her and stalked forward on stiff legs. His head was lowered and he growled continuously as he stared into the bushes to her left.

"What? What is -"

The animal slipped out of the bushes and stared at the human and the wolf. Its yellow eyes glowed and it made its own growl when the wolf darted forward and positioned himself protectively in front of the human.

***

THE KORAN WAS MASSIVE, THE BIGGEST OF ITS KIND THAT Radek had ever seen, and it growled again in warning. Its golden mane rippled in the wind and its paws were three times the size of his own. Radek crouched down and snarled at the koran. He would die before he let the beast anywhere near Sara. He would –

"Radek! Stop it!"

To his astonishment, Sara positioned herself in front of the koran and aimed her arrow at Radek. "Leave him alone, Radek!"

He barked a warning, his heart nearly stopping in his chest when the koran ran forward. Instead of tearing Sara to pieces, it bumped its massive head into the top of her back and began to purr.

Sara smiled and set down her bow and arrow before turning and hugging the koran. It was much taller than her, and it hung its head over her shoulder and stared unblinkingly at Radek. Sara ran her hands through his thick mane and scratched at his throat.

"Who's my good boy, Meeka? Hmm? Who's my sweet baby?" She crooned to the beast.

Its jaw opened, revealing large razor-sharp fangs. Sara giggled and sputtered when he licked her entire face with his scratchy tongue.

"Meeka, no. That hurts." She took a step back and the koran butted his head against her chest. It knocked her off her feet and she staggered upward before giggling again and patting him on one meaty shoulder. "You need to go on a diet. You're starting to get a bit chubby."

The koran purred again before stepping around her and sniffing at the dead floren. Radek shifted to his human form and stared at Sara.

"What?" She said defensively. "I told you the koran kitten would never hurt me."

"That is the koran kitten?" He said faintly.

"Yes. His name is Meeka."

"Sara, he is dangerous. You should not -"

"He isn't dangerous," she said immediately. "He's my baby and I love him."

"Sara -"

"Enough, Radek. You don't get to lecture me about Meeka. You know nothing about him and – Meeka, no!"

Radek's jaw dropped when Sara hurried over to the large beast and slapped him on the rump. "Get away from that, Meeka!"

The koran, who had begun to tear at the floren's belly, immediately moved away and dropped to his stomach. He stared at the ground. Radek could swear he saw shame in its eyes as Sara scolded him fiercely.

"You know you're not allowed to eat what I kill. Don't

pretend you don't, Meeka. You're big enough to catch your own meals now."

Meeka made a low grumbling noise and Sara frowned at him. "Don't talk back to your mama."

The koran whined and rested its head on its massive paws before staring pitifully at Sara. Her expression softened and she crouched beside Meeka and rubbed the side of his face. "It's all right, baby. If you help me bring the floren back to the cabins, I'll give you some of its intestines as a special treat. Deal?"

He rumbled noisily in response and Sara kissed him on his nose. "That's my good boy. Stay."

The koran continued to lie on the ground as Sara picked up the head of the floren. She tugged at it, grunting with the effort, but the dead bird didn't move despite the slippery snow. She turned to Radek. "Are you just going to stand there or are you going to help me?"

Radek, his face a mask of confusion, picked up the dead floren and rested it across the koran's massive back. The koran climbed to its feet as Sara picked up her bow and slung it over her back. She started toward home with the koran following docilely. Radek hurried after her.

"Sara, how did you learn to use that?" He pointed to the bow on her back.

"Val taught me. He says I have a knack for it." There was a tinge of pride in her voice. She glanced at him, studiously ignoring his naked lower half. "What are you doing out here?"

"Kane told me you were hunting and I was worried about you."

"You don't need to worry about me, Radek. I'm not the same person I was before," she said. "I can take care of myself."

He frowned at her. "The woods are too dangerous for someone as little as you, human. Even with your arrows and your," he glanced behind them at the koran, "pet."

She shrugged carelessly. "I'm not as weak as you think I am."

They walked in silence for a few moments before Radek said, "Are you moving in with Davin?"

"He has offered to let me stay with him now that you're back," she said.

"Aye, I know," he said moodily. "That was very kind of him."

"He's a kind man," she said briefly.

"Are you going to move in with him?" He asked again.

"I suppose I probably will. I can't stay with you and Raina and I feel like a third wheel at Kane's and Reese's so…"

"You do not have to leave my home," he said.

She laughed. "Of course I don't."

"I mean it," he persisted. "You can stay for as long as you'd like."

"No thanks," she said. "I'd rather not stay with someone who hates my guts."

"I don't hate you, human."

"Do you not?" She asked. "You left your pack for a month because of me."

"I was – I was confused and needed time to think."

"And now?"

"I'm fine," he said.

"Are you? If you leave again, Raina will never forgive you and I already feel guilty enough."

"You have nothing to feel guilty about," he said.

"Sure I don't," she said.

He gave her a slightly desperate look. "Please stay with

us, Sara. Raina is still angry with me but I know she won't want you to leave. Especially if she continues to refuse to speak to me."

"She won't stay angry with you for long, Radek. She missed you terribly."

"I missed her too," he said. "Will you stay with us? It makes more sense than staying with Davin. He has only one bed and we have an extra for you."

She bit at her bottom lip. "Can I think about it?"

He gave her a frustrated look. "What is there to think about, human? What I am saying makes perfect sense and you know it."

"There are a lot of things to consider." She glared at him.

"Like what?"

"Like the fact that you hate me but your wolf wants to mate with me. Do you want to live with that weird tension night after night?"

"My wolf no longer wants to mate with you," he said abruptly.

A look of hurt flashed across her face. "Oh."

She quickened her pace and Radek hurried after her. "Are you mating with Davin, human?"

"That is none of your business, Radek."

He grabbed her arm and pulled her to a stop, ignoring the koran's low growl behind them. "Tell me, human."

"I won't," she said. "I told you – it's none of your business."

"Human, you will -" he paused and sniffed the air, his face drawing down in a scowl as Davin appeared in front of them.

"Hello, Sara. Hello, Radek."

"Hi, Davin," Sara said as Radek grunted in reply.

Davin fell in beside Sara and put his arm around her shoulders. "I see you caught a floren."

"I did."

"He's a good size," Davin said admiringly before grinning cheerfully at Radek. "You must be glad to be home."

"Aye," Radek said shortly. His wolf was growling at him to knock the younger shifter's arm from Sara's shoulders and he was finding it hard to ignore.

"What are you doing out here?" He asked abruptly.

Davin shrugged. "I came to find Sara and see if she wanted help to move her things to my cabin."

A growl slipped out before he could stop it and Davin stared at him curiously as Sara said, "Davin, it's very kind of you to offer to let me stay with you but -"

"Your lips are blue," Davin interrupted before pulling her closer to him. "When you stay with me I will make sure you are warm enough."

Radek snarled under his breath. They had reached the cabins. Hanif was just leaving his and joined them.

"You caught a floren!" Hanif said. "Well done, little human."

"Thank you, Hanif," Sara said.

"She is becoming quite the hunter," Davin said proudly before kissing Sara on the cheek.

She ducked out of his grip as Radek growled again before shifting to his wolf form. He loped toward his cabin and Sara bit worriedly at her bottom lip as Davin put his arm around her again.

"Shall I help you move your things now, Sara?"

"Davin, it's very kind of you to offer but I think I'm going to stay with Raina and Radek for now."

"Why would you do that?" Davin asked. "Radek hates humans and he will not want you to stay with him."

"He already said that I could. Raina and I have grown close and I would miss her terribly if I moved out."

"But I would like to get to know you better, human," Davin said. He pulled Sara to a stop and glanced at Hanif. The older shifter grinned at him before walking away.

"Sara, I like you," Davin said plainly. "Do you not like me?"

"I do, but only as a friend. I'm sorry," Sara said.

A look of disappointment crossed the shifter's face. "Are you certain? I would make a good mate, Sara. I will keep you warm and protect you."

"I know, but I just don't feel that way about you," Sara said. She patted his arm. "I really am sorry."

"Aye, I am too," Davin said. "Are you certain?" He asked again.

"I am," Sara replied.

He nodded and she watched him walk away. She leaned against Meeka and scratched at his throat. "I'm an idiot, Meeka. I still want Radek but he doesn't want me."

The koran rumbled and peered at the floren on his back. Sara laughed and patted one fur-covered shoulder. "Always thinking with your stomach, Meeka. Come on."

"RAINA?" RADEK KNOCKED ON HER BEDROOM DOOR BEFORE opening it. The girl was sitting on her bed and she stared at the floor as he sat down beside her.

"I'm very sorry, Raina. Please forgive me."

"Aye, I know you are, Radek. I'm sorry I said I hated you – it isn't true."

He put his arm around her and she leaned against him as

he kissed the top of her head. "It was wrong of me to leave you for so long."

"It was. You can't keep leaving me like that, Radek."

"I know."

She finally looked at him and he wiped away the tears that were starting to drip down her cheeks. "I was so lonely and afraid that you were dead. If it had not been for Sara, I would have gone mad. I know it."

"I'm sorry," he said again.

"And now you're going to make Sara move out and I like her, Radek. She isn't an awful human. She's sweet and kind."

"I'm not making her leave," Radek said.

Raina gave him a look of surprise. "You aren't?"

"No. She is welcome to stay here for as long as she wants," he said.

"But you hate humans." She stiffened against him. "Are you leaving again? Is that it?"

"No," he said immediately. "I will never leave you again, Raina."

"Do you promise?"

"Aye, I promise," he hugged her and she kissed his cheek before smiling at him.

"You will like the human, Radek, I swear it. Just give her a chance, please?"

"Aye, I will," he said.

Raina smiled happily and leaned against him as he stared blankly at the bedroom wall. *The problem wasn't in learning to like the human*, he thought dismally, *but keeping his hands off of her.*

Raina squeezed him before standing. "Come, let's join the others. It is almost dinner."

"RADEK!"

Kavine's loud squeal of happiness echoed across the clearing and Sara watched as the shifter threw herself at him. She wrapped her legs around his waist as he staggered back, and kissed him hard on the mouth.

Jealousy surged through Sara and she stared into the fire as Raina made a loud snort of annoyance. The young shifter sat down beside Sara and linked her arm around Sara's arm. "Guess what, Sara?"

"What's that, Raina?"

"Radek said you can continue to stay with us! Isn't that wonderful?"

"It is." She concentrated on the shifter and not the way Kavine was continuing to cling to Radek.

"Ugh," Raina snorted again. "Kavine is already all over my brother. It's disgusting to watch."

"He doesn't seem to mind," Sara replied.

Raina rolled her eyes. "He hates it."

"Then why is he letting her sit on his lap?"

Raina peered across the fire. Kavine was indeed sitting on Radek's lap and his sister snickered when Radek gently but firmly pushed her from his lap and onto the log beside him. Kavine pouted but wrapped her arm around Radek's and leaned against him.

"Not anymore. He really does hate it when she clings to him like that," Raina said.

Sara didn't reply but she felt a tingle of satisfaction when Radek stood and joined Borek, Deena and Asher. He sat between Asher and Borek, leaving no space for Kavine, and nodded to his uncle when he spoke into his ear.

"See, told you," Raina said. "Are you cold?"

"A little." Sara pulled her sweater closer to her body. Raina had given her a few changes of clothing but her sweaters were thin and didn't do much to block the cold wind. She really needed to find some warmer clothing before she froze to death. She didn't want to spend the entire winter stuck indoors next to the fire. Besides, although Raina didn't seem to mind how warm the cabin was, Radek would probably not allow her to keep the fire going so much. The male shifters were much warmer than their females.

Raina snuggled closer. "It must be awful to be unable to keep yourself warm. Your lips are always blue."

Before Sara could reply, Michael stood and cleared his throat. "Kane, how far is the human village from here?"

"A few days, if the weather holds," Kane replied. "Why?"

Michael glanced at Abby. "There are supplies I would like to purchase."

"With what?" Val said. "You have no money."

"Reese said the village relies mostly on trading." Abby said.

"Aye, that is true," Kane acknowledged. "They are fond of the furs and pelts we bring them."

"Planning on skinning a deer?" Val said mockingly to Michael.

"Enough, Val," Abby muttered. "He is not the only one who wants to go to the village."

"You cannot be serious," Val said.

"I need a sword, Val," Abby said, "We need warmer clothing – Sara in particular."

"There are pelts and fire to keep her warm," Val said. "It is not worth the risk."

"It is," Abby insisted.

"It will be a dangerous journey, even if the weather holds," Kane said.

"We know," Michael said. "Would you tell us the way and loan us a few furs for trading?"

"Aye, I could give you some of our furs, we have plenty," Kane said. "But to make the journey on your own is not wise."

"I'll go with them," Hanif spoke up. "It has been a while since I've been to the village."

"Or went on an adventure." Theran grinned at him and clapped him on the back.

"Thank you, Hanif," Abby said.

"I will accompany you as well," Kane said. "One shifter will not be enough protection against the dangers in the forest."

"I'm going too," Reese said.

"No," Kane replied immediately. "It is too dangerous, Reese."

"I can take care of myself," she said.

"Aye, my love, I know. But you are still not going."

He held his hand up when she opened her mouth. "There will be no arguing with me about this. You will stay with the pack."

She frowned at him and he kissed her on the forehead before staring at the rest of the shifters. "Is there any other who wishes to make the journey?"

"I want to go," Sara said.

"No, little one," Kane said.

She glared at him. "You are not my alpha, Kane, and I am more than capable of protecting myself. I'm going."

The shifters stared uneasily at their leader. Kane, a small smile crossing his face, nodded. "Very well, young one. You are welcome to join us."

"NO!"

Radek had stood and he glared at Kane. "She is not going, my alpha."

"She is, Radek," Kane said calmly.

"I forbid it," Radek said.

Before Kane could reply, Sara scowled at him. "You forbid it? It is not your place to forbid me from doing anything. I'm going, Radek, and you cannot stop me."

"No, you are not," Radek growled.

"Yes, I am," Sara snapped.

"Human, you will listen to what I say and -"

"Like hell I will!" Sara shouted. "I'm not -"

"Enough!" Kane's deep voice cut through her protests and the shifters made an uneasy whine.

"If Sara wants to go, she can," Kane said to Radek.

"She will freeze to death, Kane," Radek said. "She can barely stand the cold here in our home where there are fire and pelts. She will not -"

"I will go with them and keep her warm," Davin interrupted.

Radek snarled at him. "You will do no such thing, Davin."

"Why do you care whether she lives or dies, Radek?" Davin asked. "You hate humans, remember?"

"You are not to touch Sara. Do you understand? Not for warmth or for any other reason," Radek said.

"Who are you to give such orders?" Davin asked. "Do you think I will obey you because you are the cousin of our alpha?"

"If I see you touching her, I will -"

"You'll what?" Davin stood, his hands clenching into fists. "What will you do, Radek?"

Radek's fangs popped out and he snarled again at Davin. A thick beard began to grow on Davin's smooth cheeks and he made his own growl before stalking toward Radek.

"Stop it!" Sara's voice rang out over the clearing. The two shifters turned toward her and she glared at them both. "I am going to the village with Abby and the others. I appreciate the offer, Davin, but I do not need you to keep me warm. I'll be fine."

She sat back down, trying hard not to shiver, and squeezed Raina's knee gratefully when the shifter put her arm around her.

Kane stared at the clear night sky. "We will leave the morning after tomorrow. If the weather holds and we move quickly, it will take us two days to get to the village."

"You forget that I cannot travel during the daylight hours," Val said.

"I have not forgotten," Kane replied. "It is impossible for you to go with us. Travelling at night is unwise."

"I'm going," Val said. "Either I go or Abigail does not."

"Val," Abby stroked his long hair, "you know you can't go. I'm sorry, I wish you could, but Kane is right. It's safer to travel during the day."

"You are not going without me, little dove," Val said.

She stared solemnly at him and he cursed before standing and stalking to their cabin. Abigail sighed before following him.

"Radek, you will be in charge of the pack while I'm gone," Kane said. "If there is -"

"I'm going with you," Radek said.

"For what reason?" Davin asked. "You have never shown any interest in the village before. Why would you be so eager to be around the humans? I have already offered to accompany our alpha and the humans and there is no need for another shifter. Is that not right, my alpha?"

Radek stared desperately at Reese. He had no hope that Kane would understand his silent request but Reese might. His hands clenched into fists and his stomach was a tight knot of anxiety as Reese studied him silently. She curved her hand around Kane's thick neck and tugged his head down. She spoke into his ear and he glanced at Radek before frowning at Reese. She smiled at him and spoke rapidly into his ear again and the alpha sighed before standing.

"Radek will join us. Davin, you will be needed here to assist Theran. He will be alpha in my absence and he will require your help."

Davin's mouth dropped open before his back straightened and he gave Kane a look of pride. "Aye, my alpha. I will be happy to do that."

"Good." Kane took Reese's hand before standing. "It is getting late. Return to your cabins, my pack."

Raina held her hand out to Sara. "Come, Sara. I'm so happy that you are still staying with us."

"I am too, Raina," Sara said.

She followed the young girl to their cabin as Radek trailed silently behind them.

CHAPTER 16

"Radek, we have to keep the cabin warmer," Raina lectured as she added a few logs to the fire.

"Aye, I know," he said.

"Well, I do not want to hear you complaining about how hot it is. Poor Sara is always cold. It will be good for her to find warmer clothing in the human village," Raina said.

She pulled Sara a little closer to the fire. "Perhaps you will find a human mate at the village, Sara."

"We will not be there long enough," Radek said. "A day or two is not long enough to find a mate."

"I suppose not," Raina said. "But there is no harm in looking."

She squeezed Sara's arm. "If you do find a human mate, I will miss you, Sara."

"I will not be finding a mate. Your brother is right – a day is not long enough."

"Mama and papa only knew each other for a month before papa bit her," Raina said. "Mama said she knew he was the one only a few days after she met him."

"It's different for shifters," Radek said. "You know that, Raina. Humans cannot smell a mate's desire for them."

"Aye, I suppose not," Raina said before sitting on the rug in front of the fire. "Sit with me, Sara. I would hear you sing again."

Sara leaned down and kissed the top of Raina's head. "I'm very tired, Raina. I think I will go to bed."

She nodded to Radek and disappeared into her bedroom. Raina frowned at Radek. "You make her nervous, Radek."

"I am being kind," he protested.

"Aye, I know." His sister stood and sniffed in his direction. "Perhaps it is a good thing that humans cannot scent another's desire."

Radek flushed bright red. "I do not desire the human, Raina."

"Whatever, Radek." Raina rolled her eyes before disappearing into her room.

Sara leaned against her bedroom door and listened as Radek walked past her room and into his bedroom. His room was next to hers and she crossed the room and placed her hand on their connecting wall before pressing her ear against the wood. She couldn't hear anything and she ran her fingertips over the rough wood before slipping into Radek's shirt. She had stolen it from his room and couldn't bring herself to return it to him. She climbed into bed and burrowed under the bear pelt. The bedroom was cold and she was already beginning to shiver. On more than one occasion she had taken the pelt and crept to the main room to lie in front of the fire when the cold had woken her from her sleep. She couldn't ask Raina and Radek to heat the cabin more than they already were – they were probably much too warm as it was – and she really needed to remember to ask Reese for another pelt.

She closed her eyes and tried to relax as she shook lightly.

She had a bad feeling that she would never fall asleep. Not with Radek in the next room.

He's naked, you know. And warm. He could definitely help heat your bed.

She sighed irritably. Thinking thoughts like that were not going to help her sleep. She buried her cold nose in the crock of her arm and pushed thoughts of the naked Radek out of her head.

———

SHE WAS WOKEN BY HIS WHINING ONLY A FEW HOURS LATER. She lay in her bed, shivering and staring grimly at the ceiling as he barked and whined and moaned in his sleep.

Do not go to him, she told herself fiercely. *He neither wants nor needs your comfort.*

She clenched her fists, listening as his cries grew louder and her heart breaking at the fear in his voice. She was just throwing back the covers to go and wake him when Raina pounded on the wall between her bedroom and her brother's.

"Radek! Wake up! You are barking in your sleep again!"

His tortured whining ended abruptly. Her pulse beating rapidly and feeling sick to her stomach, she lay in the darkness and tried not to imagine how afraid and disoriented he was feeling.

Go to him. At least make sure he's okay.

She couldn't. He didn't want her anymore and it would only upset him if she showed up in his bedroom in the middle of the night. He would think she was using it as an excuse to throw herself at him and, truthfully, he would be right. She would not act like Kavine and constantly attempt to win the heart of a man who didn't want her. She had some pride and she –

The door to her bedroom opened and she sat up, her heart stopping for a moment when she saw Radek standing naked in the doorway. She couldn't see his face in the darkness but his entire body was shaking wildly and she silently pulled back the covers to her bed.

He shut the door and nearly ran across the room, climbing into her bed and putting his arms around her like a frightened child. She urged him to lie down beside her and she stroked his back and pressed gentle kisses into his light hair as she murmured soft words of comfort.

When his trembling stopped, she whispered, "Better?"

"Aye, thank you, Sara."

"You're welcome." She started to ease away from him and he tightened his arms around her.

"Do not leave me."

"I won't," she whispered. She relaxed as he buried his face into her throat and she stroked his back. Radek was warm as an oven and for the first time in days she didn't feel cold. His body heat made her sleepy and she was just dozing off when he said, "Have you mated with Davin?"

"Radek," she said, "that isn't any of your -"

He lifted his head. "Tell me. Please, Sara."

"Why do you think he wants to have sex with me? I have no experience, remember? Shifters want their mates to be experienced."

She waited to see if he would tell her the truth. He stared at her for a moment before looking away. "Perhaps you are allowing Davin to teach you what you need to know."

She knew she should have been angry with him for continuing to lie but instead a small thrill of excitement went through her. Radek was jealous and God help her, she wanted to use his jealousy and his lies to get what she wanted.

"I have had no more lessons since the day you left," she said.

His hand which had wandered down to her hip, squeezed compulsively.

She sighed sadly. "I am afraid I will remain a virgin forever unless I find a human in the village who does not have the same…requirements as shifters."

"A human will not be able to protect you the way a shifter can," he said.

Tell him you don't need any protection, her inner voice said indignantly. *Tell him that you are more than capable of protecting yourself.*

She really should, but the feel of his hard body had her libido in overdrive and it promptly ignored her inner voice as she said, "That may be true but there is nothing to be done about it."

"There is," he whispered.

"What do you mean?" She asked innocently.

He cleared his throat. "I am still willing to teach you, human."

"No, thanks," she said. "I'm not so pathetic that I would ask someone who doesn't even want me to show me how to please a man."

"I lied," he said in a low voice.

She hid her smile of triumph. "What was that, Radek? I did not hear you."

"I lied," he repeated. "I do still want you, Sara. Very much."

"How am I to know that is the truth?" She asked. "You could be -"

He pressed his mouth against hers and she moaned before opening her mouth. He thrust his tongue between her lips and she kissed him back feverishly as flames of lust licked at her belly.

He cupped her small breast through her shirt and she arched her back. He teased her nipple through the soft fabric and she groaned in frustration before reaching for the hem of her shirt. He helped her to strip it off and inhaled sharply when her naked body was revealed.

"You're so beautiful, Sara," he growled before dipping his head and placing light kisses across her upper chest.

She pushed on his head and he nipped at her collarbone before licking a slow path to her nipple. She arched her back again, her hands threading through his hair. She muttered a soft curse when he licked the underside of her breast before tracing his tongue around her nipple. It had hardened into a stiff peak and she whimpered when he brushed his stubble across the tip of it.

"Radek, please," she moaned.

He sucked hard on her nipple, his cock hardening at her soft cry of pleasure, and teased it with his lips and tongue until she was moaning. He switched to her other nipple and teased it into a hard point.

"I love how sensitive your nipples are, Sara." He pressed a light kiss between her breasts before claiming her mouth again.

They kissed repeatedly, tasting and licking and sucking at each other's tongues until they were both panting harshly. Sara traced Radek's broad back with her fingers. She smiled at the way it made his eyes lighten before nibbling on his thick neck. "I want you so badly, Radek."

"I want you too, Sara," he whispered.

She parted her legs eagerly when he trailed his fingers across her flat stomach. He stopped to caress the blonde curls and she pushed impatiently at his hand. A grin crossed his face and he kissed her again as his fingers slipped across the wet lips of her pussy.

"Ohhh," she sighed and didn't object when he used his leg to widen her thighs. His rough fingers found her swollen clit and he rubbed at the pink bud as she moaned and thrust her hips at him. He slid his finger into her tight opening, kissing her soothingly when she tensed, and rubbed her clit with his thumb.

"Radek," she whispered, "will you go slowly?"

"Aye, sweet one, I will," he promised. "And I will stop if you ask me to."

RADEK HOPED THAT HE COULD STOP IF SHE ASKED. HIS COCK was throbbing almost painfully and his wolf was howling at him to take the soft female. He rubbed her clit more firmly, watching her face as she moaned and panted. He smiled again when her pelvis thrust helplessly against him. He dipped his head and sucked on her swollen nipple. She cried out with pleasure and he growled happily when her pussy tightened around his finger and she came with another harsh cry. He slid a second finger into her, stretching her tight opening, as she collapsed against the bed. Her entire body was shuddering with the aftershocks of her orgasm and he gave her a moment before kissing her.

She smiled tentatively at him. "Do you want me on my hands and knees, Radek?"

Lust flared within him at the thought of Sara on her hands and knees, but he shook his head. "No, sweet one. Not this time."

Despite his assurances there was a part of him that was worried he would hurt her. He needed to see her face as he entered her. If it was too painful for her, he would stop. The thought of hurting her made him feel sick.

"Radek? What's wrong?" She cupped his face and gave him a worried look.

"Nothing," he whispered.

"Are you certain?"

"Aye. Are you certain you want to do this? It will hurt, Sara."

"I know," she said before kissing him again. "Please don't stop now."

He stroked her tongue with his before cupping her breast again. She moaned and dug her fingers into his back as he teased her nipple before moving between her thighs. She widened them and gave him a sweet and trusting smile that brought a weird surge of heat to his stomach.

"Do it, Radek. Please."

He reached between them and guided his cock to her entrance. She was soaking wet and the head of his cock slipped into her easily. She let her breath out in a soft moan and he slid a little further in before forcing himself to with-draw. His wolf growled angrily and he snarled at it in his head as Sara touched his face with her fingers.

"It feels good, Radek."

"I'm glad, sweet one," he whispered.

He hooked one hand around her slender thigh and lifted her leg slightly before pushing into her again. He went farther this time, watching her face for signs of pain and stopped immediately when she winced. He pulled out of her and she frowned at him.

"Sara, perhaps we shouldn't do this. You're very small and -"

"No!" She pounded on his chest with her tiny fist and

gave him a look of frustration. "I do not wish to stop. It will be better if you do it quickly, Radek."

"That isn't a good idea. I think -"

She yanked his head down and bit the lobe of his ear. He grunted in surprise and she tightened her grip around his neck. "Take me, Radek. Make me yours."

Desire flared within him and his eyes glowed brightly. "Mine."

"Yours," she whispered and then gave a harsh cry of pain when he thrust fully into her. He stopped, his entire body shaking with the need to move and stared anxiously at her.

"I am sorry, sweet one."

She took a few deep breaths. "Do not be. The pain is starting to fade."

He continued to wait. Sara's walls clung wetly to him. He had never been in a pussy as tight as hers and he suppressed the urge to thrust wildly within her.

Sara stroked his hair, running her fingers through the thick strands before lifting her head and kissing his throat. "I'm ready."

"Are you?"

She nodded. "Go slowly, all right?"

"Aye," he replied. He withdrew and slid into her in a slow, smooth motion that made his balls tighten.

Sara's body tensed beneath him despite her reassurances, and he bent his head and captured her nipple in his mouth. He sucked at it as he thrust slowly in and out of her and she moaned as she clung to his narrow waist.

"Does it feel good for you, Radek?" She asked timidly.

He groaned and kissed her hard nipple before lifting his head. "Aye, Sara. So good."

He kissed her, tangling his tongue with hers as he moved

a little faster. She sucked on his upper lip before whispering, "I feel so full, Radek. I like this very much."

A small smile crossed his face. "I like it too, sweet one."

SARA STARED UP AT RADEK AND RAN HER FINGERS UP AND down his ribs. He was starting to pant and his eyes were glowing so brightly that she could see his face clearly in the darkness. He moved faster, thrusting in and out of her in a quick rhythm and she thrust her hips experimentally. He groaned and warmth rushed through her. She did it again, trying to match her timing to his. After a few awkward and completely off-pace thrusts that made her blush with embarrassment, she found the rhythm.

"Good, my sweet one," he praised her as she widened her thighs and met each of his downward strokes.

She bit her bottom lip and continued to stare at his face. Warmth was spreading through her pelvis and it was pleasant enough but she felt none of the pleasure like before. She didn't mind. She wanted to witness Radek's pleasure, to watch as her body brought him to the edge, and she urged him on with soft whimpers.

She gasped when his hand slipped between their bodies and his fingers found her clit. The warmth instantly turned into a fiery burn of desire and she began to lose her natural rhythm as her hips thrust against his hand.

"Oh God," she whimpered. "Radek, I think I'm going to…"

Her words turned into a low moan of pleasure as her body tensed and her orgasm raced through her. Her pussy clenched around him and he thrust in and out of her wildly before his own body stiffened and he came inside of her with a faint howl.

He rested his forehead against hers, his breath warm on her lips, before easing out of her. She lay trembling with her legs shaking with the force of her orgasm as he rubbed her flat belly with his large hand.

"Sara? Are you all right?" He asked anxiously.

She gave him a sleepy little smile before caressing his face. "Aye, Radek. I feel so good."

He returned her smile with relief before kissing her mouth. "Stay here for a moment."

She lay contently as he left the bedroom. He returned nearly five minutes later and she jerked in surprise when she felt the warm, wet cloth between her legs.

"Radek?"

He kissed her hip and finished cleaning her before dropping the cloth into a basin. He dried her with a second piece of fabric as she blushed furiously.

"Do not be embarrassed, sweet one," he said. "The blood is natural."

"I know," she replied. "Thank you for that."

He kissed her tenderly. "Aye, you are welcome, Sara." He handed her a wooden cup. "Drink this."

She drank half the water before handing it back to him. He finished it and set it on the floor before climbing in to the bed and pulling her into his embrace.

"Will you stay the night with me?" She whispered.

"Aye, if you wish."

"I do." She curled into him and rested her head on his broad chest before closing her eyes.

"Thank you, Radek," she whispered sleepily. "It was a very enjoyable lesson."

He rumbled soft laughter before kissing the top of her head. "Aye, sweet one, it was."

HE SLIPPED NAKED INTO HER BED, SMELLING OF PINE TREES and the snow. She shivered delicately when he cupped her naked breast with one cold hand.

"Why are you not waiting for me in my cabin?"

"I have waited in your cabin every night for the last moon, Faren. I was worried you would grow tired of me."

He grunted his disapproval. "Your door was unlocked."

"I left it unlocked for you," she whispered as she arched into his touch.

He turned her onto her back and cupped her face. "A foolish idea and one you are not to do again, Adina."

"Do you believe you have the right to tell me what to do?" She asked.

"I do not need your door to be unlocked in order to join you in your bed," he said sharply. "Promise me you will lock it at night."

A look of amusement crossed her face. "Does a vampire possess the ability to walk through locked doors?"

He slipped his hand between her thighs and rubbed at her clit. "Promise me, Adina."

She moaned and spread her legs wide before stroking his erect cock. "You are cold, Faren."

"It is a cold night." His pelvis arched against her and she squeezed him before raising her head and baring her throat to him.

"You would rather hunt in the cold and drink the blood of animals then feed from me?"

"I will not bite you, Adina. Do not ask me again." He

stroked her clit, smiling with satisfaction when moisture coated his long fingers.

She pushed him onto his back and straddled him, pinning his hands above his head and rubbing herself against his erection. He lifted his head and sucked at one hard nipple as she moaned.

"You make me barto, Faren," she moaned.

"Barto?" He scraped the tips of his fangs across her nipple and she cried out with pleasure before reaching down and sliding his cock into her.

She rode him slowly, panting and moaning as he cupped her breasts and kneaded them.

"Crazy," she whimpered. "You make me crazy."

He shook loose of her grip and sat up abruptly. He cupped the back of her head and kissed her. She sucked on his tongue as he thrust back and forth within her, and he squeezed her ass before sucking on her neck.

"You make me barto as well, Adina," he murmured against her soft skin.

She squeezed her pussy around him in response and he groaned before burying his face in her neck and losing himself in her soft warmth.

CHAPTER 17

"You look tired, Abby," Reese said as she set a cup of tea in front of her.

"I spent most of the night arguing with Val," Abby replied. "And I didn't sleep well after we went to bed."

"Are you still going to the village with us?" Sara asked.

"Yes," Abby said. "Val's unhappy about it but I need a sword. I can't defend myself without one."

She studied Sara closely. "Are you sure you want to go, Sara? I can bring you back some clothing."

"No, I want to go," Sara said.

"You're not planning on staying in the village, are you?" Abby asked hesitantly.

"Why would I?"

Abby glanced at Reese who shrugged. "To find a human mate."

Sara shook her head. "I have no desire to find a mate."

She shifted in her chair, trying not to wince. Her thighs were sore and there was a lingering ache in her pelvis despite her hot bath this morning. Radek was gone when she woke this morning and she had not seen him all day. She was trying not to take it personally but she had spent most of the day feeling sorry for herself.

Stop it, Sara. Radek offered to teach you how to please a man in bed and he has done so. His wolf wanted you and it got what it wanted. You can't honestly be surprised that he doesn't want more.

"Sara, what's wrong?" Reese asked kindly.

"Nothing. I am just a little tired, as well. And cold. I will be very happy to buy some warmer clothing," Sara replied.

The door opened and Kane entered the cabin in a swirl of cold wind. He was completely naked and Abby and Sara hastily averted their eyes as Reese grinned at him. "My love, we have company."

He shifted to his wolf form and trotted into the bedroom as Reese smiled at Sara and Abby. "Sorry. They were out hunting and he doesn't bring a change of clothes with him. The shifters have a remarkable lack of modesty when it comes to nudity."

Abby laughed. "I thought vampires were exhibitionists but shifters put them to shame."

She gave Reese a saucy grin. "There's no polite way to say this but Kane has the biggest dick I've ever seen. I don't know whether to say congratulations or give you my sympathy."

Reese laughed. "The first time I saw it my jaw dropped to the ground, I swear to God."

"Are all shifters that well-endowed?"

Reese nodded. "Not that I go around studying them in-depth but yeah, I think so. Kane's particularly big but I think they're all blessed in that department. I'm seriously happy I wasn't a virgin when I met Kane. It hurt enough with a normal-sized penis, I couldn't imagine how it would have felt with a shifter."

"It isn't that bad," Sara said distractedly as she swirled the tea in her cup. "It was painful but it didn't…"

She trailed off, her eyes widening and her cheeks going red as she realized what she said. She stared nervously at Abby and Reese as the two women glanced at each other.

"Sara, did you sleep with Davin?" Abby asked.

Sara bit at her bottom lip, "Uh…"

"Radek." Reese said.

"Oh, Sara, you didn't," Abby said. She reached out and took Sara's hand. "Honey, having sex with Radek is a terrible idea. I know you're attracted to him but -"

The bedroom door opened and Kane emerged wearing a loose cotton pair of pants. He headed toward them, leaning down and kissing Reese before smiling at her. "Our hunt went very well."

"Good," Reese replied.

"Aye, it was -"

Kane stopped and inhaled before turning to stare at Sara. Her flush deepened at the look on his face and he sighed wearily. "You have mated with Radek."

"Kane," Reese said, "you can't just blurt that out. It's something private between Sara and Radek."

Kane shrugged. "She is covered in Radek's scent. It is impossible to keep it private."

"Perhaps, but bringing it up in mixed company isn't polite," Reese replied.

"Humans are so strange," Kane said before leaning against the short counter. "Was he gentle, young one?"

Sara's face was so red, Abby thought she was going to have a stroke. She squeezed her hand as Reese poked Kane in the stomach. "That's none of your business, Kane."

Sara shook free of Abby's grip and stood up. "I should

go. It's almost dinner and I told Anna I would cook the meat for her. The smell of it makes her sick."

She hurried from the cabin as Reese frowned at Kane. "My love, you really shouldn't embarrass Sara like that."

"I did not mean to," Kane said. "If Radek was not gentle with her, it is my duty as alpha to speak with him about it."

"He's lucky I don't have my sword," Abby said. "Sara is sweet and innocent and he shouldn't be playing with her like this. If what you say is true, that it is only his wolf who wants her, then he's going to break her heart. She likes him – I don't care what she says – it's obvious."

"I think Radek likes her too," Reese said. "I don't believe he'll intentionally hurt her, Abby. He's been acting so strange since he met her and I think she's starting to change his perception about humans."

"Perhaps," Kane said. "But it may be better if the young one finds a human male in the village."

"She says she doesn't want one," Reese said. "We can't force her to find a husband."

"I should allow young Davin to join us instead of Radek. He would be a better mate for Sara."

"Would he?" Reese asked skeptically. "I am not so sure of that. Besides, you know Radek will just disobey you if you tell him he cannot go. He may not love Sara yet but he is adamant about protecting her."

"Aye, you are right," Kane replied.

"As always," Reese winked at him and he rolled his eyes before heading back to the bedroom.

Abby stared worriedly at Reese. Reese took her hand and squeezed it. "He won't hurt her, Abby. I promise you."

"I hope you're right, Reese. I really do," Abby replied.

Radek trotted toward his cabin. He shifted to his human form and stepped into the warmth. He had spent most of the day roaming the woods. He had heard Kane howling for him to join the hunt but he had ignored it. If he went near his alpha, Kane would smell Sara on him and he wasn't up to explaining why he had mated with her.

He rubbed at his forehead. He had slipped out of the bed early this morning, ignoring his wolf's demands to take Sara again. He had thought his wolf would be sated but its need was even more voracious and he had spent most of the day trying to drown out its clamouring to find Sara and bed her.

"Hello, Radek."

His head jerked up and he stared at Kavine. She was standing naked by the fire and she gave him a slow smile as she walked toward him.

"It's so warm in your cabin, Radek. How do you stand it?" She asked as she cupped one breast.

"What are you doing here, Kavine?"

"What do you think?" She said teasingly. "I am tired of being denied, Radek. I know you want me and I -"

She suddenly inhaled as shock crossed her face. She growled, baring her fangs at him. "I can smell her all over you."

"Leave, Kavine," he said. "For the last time – I have no desire to mate with you."

"I can't believe you mated with that skinny human," Kavine said as hurt crossed her face. "Why would you do that? You know I love you."

"I don't love you," he said. "Why can you not accept that?"

"Because you are mine!" She shouted. "I will kill the human for marking you with her filthy scent!"

He grabbed her arm. "Go anywhere near Sara and you will regret it. Do you hear me, Kavine?"

"You're hurting me," she snapped.

He squeezed her arm before relaxing his grip. "Stay away from Sara. I will do far worse to you if you harm her."

Her face paled and she swallowed compulsively. "You would not hurt a member of your pack, Radek."

"Would I not? Go near Sara and find out, Kavine."

She made a low whine of submission. "I – I did not mean that, Radek. I am just angry and upset."

He released her and took a step back as tears welled up in her eyes. "Will you take her as your mate? Is that it, Radek? You would mate with a human after what they did to you?"

"Get out, Kavine," he said. "Get out of my sight and stay away from Sara."

She wiped the tears from her face angrily. "Fine, Radek. I no longer want you anyway, now that you have mated with the filthy human."

He stared impassively at her and she growled again before flinging open the door to his cabin. She shifted to her wolf form and loped away and he sighed and shut the door against the cold.

Find our mate, his wolf snarled. *I need her.*

He ignored its demand and added more wood to the fire before heading to his bedroom to dress.

"Did my brother bite you?"

Sara gave Raina a startled look before glancing at the others sitting around them.

"Hush, Raina."

"Why? Everyone here knows you mated with him," the teenager said cheerfully. "Shifters can smell it, you know."

"Yes, I know," Sara said under her breath. "But I prefer to keep my private life private."

Raina shrugged but lowered her voice. "Did he bite you?"

"Of course not," Sara said. "Why would you ask that?"

"He likes you."

"Not that much."

"Enough to mate with you despite what the humans did to him," Raina said.

She stared silently at the fire before putting her arm around Sara. "I am glad you and Radek are getting along, Sara. I hope he does claim you as his mate. I would like to have you as a sister."

"Thank you, Raina, but I don't think that's going to happen," Sara said.

"Why not?" Raina glanced at her brother. He was sitting with Asher and Maria and had ignored both Raina and Sara the entire night.

"I think it was, uh, a one-time thing between your brother and me," Sara said. She wasn't about to get into the details of her "lesson" with Radek but she didn't want the girl getting her hopes up.

"Oh," Raina said. "I guess I am not surprised. It would be very odd for Radek to want to claim a human as his mate. I imagine he just wanted to know what it was like to mate with a human and will find a shifter to claim."

"Yes, probably," Sara said as jealousy filled her slender body.

She studied Kavine. The female shifter hadn't gone near Radek once since they had gathered for their evening meal and had sent a few venomous glares her way. Radek had told her that female shifters marked their mates with their scent and she was fairly certain Kavine could smell her on Radek. The thought filled her with a ridiculously smug sense of pride and she cursed herself for her foolishness. Even if she had marked Radek, her scent would fade soon enough and Raina was right – he would find a female shifter to claim. She just hoped it wouldn't be Kavine.

Kane, sitting with Reese and Abby and Val, stood and the shifters quieted down.

"It is time to retire, my brothers and sisters. The wind is a cold one and there are a few of us who have an early morning. Remember, Theran is in charge while I am gone. Be safe and watch out for each other."

Sara stood and took Raina's hand. They walked toward the cabin as Radek joined them. "Promise me you will be careful, Radek," Raina said before grasping his hand.

"Aye, I will, Raina. I will bring you back something from the human village." Radek squeezed her hand before opening the door.

"I would like that," Raina said. "Come, the two of you must sit with me for a while. I will miss you both terribly when you're gone."

She sat in front of the fire and without looking at Sara, Radek joined her. Sara glanced at her bedroom before sitting down next to Raina. She wanted to go to bed and get away from Radek before she did or said something foolish to him. But Raina was holding her hand and giving her a pleased smile and she couldn't bring herself to disappoint the teenager.

"RAINA," RADEK SAID NEARLY HALF AN HOUR LATER. "IT'S time for bed."

Raina laughed. "I am not a child, Radek."

"Aye, I know, but we are getting up early tomorrow and Sara will need as much rest as possible. It is a long and cold journey."

"You are right," Raina said. "I did not think of that. Forgive me, Sara."

"It's fine, honey." Sara tried to smile at her. She wondered if she was the only one feeling the tension in the room. She had spent the last half-hour trying not to remember how it had felt to have Radek between her thighs and failing miserably. She wanted him badly and she didn't know how much longer she could sit in the same room without throwing herself at him.

Don't be so foolish, Sara. He is finished with you – have some self-respect.

Raina bounced to her feet and kissed Radek's cheek before hugging Sara. "You will wake me before you leave, will you not, Radek?"

"Aye, Raina."

"Promise?" She said anxiously. "I want to say goodbye."

"I promise," Radek replied as Sara stood and followed Raina toward the bedrooms.

Raina disappeared into her bedroom and Sara hesitated in front of the door to her room.

Say goodnight and go inside. Don't make a fool of your-self by begging Radek for another night.

"Goodnight, Radek." She made a low cry of surprise when he spoke directly behind her.

"Goodnight, Sara."

She whirled around and pressed her back against the door as Radek stepped forward until he was nearly touching her. "How are you feeling?"

"F-fine," she stuttered.

"Not sore?" His gaze drifted down to her pelvis and heat blossomed between her legs.

"No," she whispered. "I had a hot bath this morning."

"That is good to hear."

He took another step toward her and she moaned when his chest brushed against her breasts.

"You should go to sleep," he said hoarsely. "We will be leaving very early in the morning."

"I – I'm not tired," she said.

"Are you not?"

"No." She wet her lips and he made a harsh growl of need.

"I have thought of nothing but you all day, sweet one," he said. "I would very much like to join you in your bed again tonight."

"I want that too," she said.

He smiled. His fangs were already out and she ran a trembling hand down his hard arm.

"Will you give me a – another lesson, Radek?"

"Aye, sweet one. It would be my pleasure," he muttered before capturing her mouth in a soft kiss.

She fumbled behind her for the door handle as Radek pressed light kisses against her throat. His hand covered hers and he opened the door before lifting her. She wrapped her legs around his waist and kissed him as he shut the door and carried her to the bed. He sat down and she straddled him, pressing herself against his erection before helping him pull off his shirt. She kissed his broad chest, licking and tasting his rough skin as he cupped the back of her head and growled. She sucked on one flat nipple before nipping it experimentally. He groaned and she glanced timidly at him.

"Did that hurt?"

He smiled and stroked her hair back from her face. "No, sweet one."

He tugged her sweater and her shirt over her head before cupping one small breast. He rubbed her nipple as she licked his collarbone before reaching between them and rubbing his cock.

"Will you teach me how to please a man with my mouth, Radek?" She whispered into his ear.

He stiffened and an odd look of anger crossed his face.

"Radek? What's wrong?"

He cupped the back of her neck. "I will teach you how to please me with your mouth, Sara, but only me. It is only my cock you are to touch and taste – no other. Do you understand?"

"Radek…"

"Do you understand?" He repeated with a scowl.

"Yes," she whispered.

"Good." He pushed her gently to her knees on the floor between his thighs before unbuttoning his pants and sliding them down his legs. She stared at his cock, moisture pooling between her legs, before grasping the base of it and squeezing.

"Sara," he gave her a strange look, "if you do not want to do this, you don't have to. Do you understand?"

She nodded. "I want to."

She leaned forward and pressed a kiss against the shaft. He jerked and she frowned at him. "Hold still, Radek."

"Aye, hold still," he muttered. His hand curled into her hair and he tugged her toward the head of his cock.

She slid her mouth down around his cock, making a muffled noise of surprise when he jerked again, and sucked experimentally on the head. His hands tightened in her hair and she took more of him into her mouth. The skin was velvety soft and she liked the slightly salty taste of him.

"Look at me, Sara," he rasped.

She stared up at him as she stroked the base of him with her hand and traced her tongue around the head. He groaned and petted her hair before smiling at her.

"Suck harder, my sweet one." He was almost pleading and she moaned around his cock when he reached down and cupped her breast.

"You're doing so well," he said before pinching her nipple.

She gasped and then sucked on his shaft, sliding her mouth up and down before licking him again.

His hips were rising up to meet each downward stroke of her mouth and he pressed on the back of her head. "More, sweet one. Take more of me into your mouth."

She took as much of him into her mouth as she could, her lips stretching around his thick length until he hit the back of her throat. She choked, her eyes starting to water and pulled away.

"I'm sorry," she whispered.

He shook his head. "There is no need to be sorry. Take only as much as you can."

She nodded and took a deep breath before sucking on his cock again. She varied the pressure of her hand and mouth. Her pussy throbbed with every soft groan of pleasure he made and she repeatedly tested how far she could take him.

Her jaw was starting to ache and his cock was swelling in her mouth. She felt a moment of panic – how could his cock grow even larger – and then Radek's hands were curling around her arms and he was lifting her to her feet.

"Did I do something wrong?" She asked.

He stared at her red and swollen mouth. "No I was growing too close to coming and I want to fuck you."

He leaned forward and kissed her flat abdomen. "Get on your hands and knees on the bed, sweet one."

She climbed onto the bed, feeling a moment of self-consciousness that disappeared when Radek rubbed her ass. She parted her legs and moaned in disappointment when he didn't touch her pussy.

"Radek, please fuck me," she whispered.

"Aye, sweet one, I will."

She waited with breathless anticipation for his cock. A dim part of her worried about the pain but she shoved it out of her head. It would not hurt as bad this time, she was sure of it.

She could barely contain her shriek of pleasure when instead of Radek's cock, his hot, wet tongue slid across her slit. She clutched the bedsheets in her hands and arched her back like a cat, moaning when he stiffened his tongue and slid it into her wet entrance. His fingers parted the lips of her pussy and she moaned again when he licked her clit delicately.

"Oh, please!" She cried breathlessly. "Please!"

He licked her clit repeatedly as he pushed his finger into her pussy. Her muscles clamped around him and he sucked her clit into his mouth as her orgasm roared through her in a glorious rush of pleasure that made her head spin. She twisted and writhed against his mouth before collapsing against the bed. His hands circled her waist and he hauled her back to her hands and knees. She trembled violently as he pushed the head of his cock into her pussy.

"Relax, sweet one," he murmured before rubbing her lower back with his warm hands.

She took a deep breath and forced herself to relax as he pushed further into her. There was a slight twinge of pain that turned into a mild feeling of discomfort. He withdrew and slid into her again, waiting patiently as she stretched around him. When he was sheathed fully within her, he held her hips and stroked back and forth.

Sara moaned. His cock was rubbing against the front wall of her pussy and it was sending an odd but extremely enjoyable sensation through her body.

"That feels so good, Radek," she panted.

"Good," he muttered before pressing on her lower back. She lowered her upper half obediently to the bed and he rubbed her raised ass again before thrusting back and forth in a quick, hard rhythm that stole her breath. She was making unintelligible noises of pleasure, her hands clenching and unclenching with each rhythmic push.

"Oh God," she moaned. Her legs were beginning to shake. Every stroke of Radek's cock was making her squirm in delight, and her pussy squeezed helplessly around his thick shaft when her second orgasm rushed through her.

Radek cursed under his breath and plunged in and out of her, his hands clamping down on her hips as he thrust back and forth. He arched his back, his muscles straining as he found his own release and came deep inside of her wet pussy. She made another soft cry and breathing harshly, he pulled out of her. She fell onto her side and he curled up behind her. He kissed the back of her shoulder and cupped one firm breast as she shuddered and made soft moans of pleasure.

"So good, Radek," she sighed.

"Aye, sweet one. It was." He moved her under the covers and slid in behind her. She turned and wrapped her slender body around his, resting her head on his chest as he stroked her back with the tips of his fingers.

"Will you stay the night with me?" She whispered.

"Aye, I will."

CHAPTER 18

"Promise me you'll be careful."

"I promise, Val." Abby wrapped her arms around his waist and kissed his throat. "I love you."

"I love you, little dove," Val said gravely. "Stick close to the shifter. Without a sword, you're vulnerable."

"I know." She could see small rays of sunlight through the cracks in the boards across the window and she kissed him again. "Go to your daysleep. I'll be back soon."

He pulled her back into his embrace and kissed her fiercely. "I wish you would stay."

She sighed and rested her forehead against his. "I can't, Val. I need a sword."

"Michael can bring you back one."

"I need to pick out my own sword, feel the weight of it in my hand," she said. "I'll be fine. I was on my own for over a year and managed not to die, remember?"

"I remember," he said.

Abby smiled when Violet flew out from Val's long hair. She kissed Abby on the nose and Abby shook her head when the pixie tried to disappear into her hair.

"No, Violet. It will be too cold for you in the forest. Stay with Val."

The pixie pouted and Abby stroked her tiny back. "I'll be back soon, I promise."

She touched Val's face and kissed him a final time. "I love you, I'll see you soon."

When she stepped outside, Michael and Sara and the shifters had already gathered at the edge of the forest. Raina had her arms wrapped around Radek's waist and he kissed her on the forehead before she released him and hugged Sara. Reese was standing with Kane and the alpha was whispering into her ear. She nodded. Abby could see tears in her eyes and Kane kissed her tenderly before squeezing her hip.

"Please be careful, Kane," Reese said as Abby joined them.

"Aye, I will be. You have nothing to fear." Kane smiled reassuringly at her before glancing at the others.

"Are you ready?"

They nodded and he turned back to Reese. "Do not go into the forest alone, my love. If you need anything, ask Borek. All right?"

"Yes. I'll be fine, just worry about yourself," Reese said.

He squeezed her hand and Reese kissed him again before hugging Abby. "Be careful, Abby. Stay close to Kane."

"I will. See you soon, Reese," Abby replied.

She glanced at Sara. The girl was standing with Radek and she gave the shifter a cool look before holding out her hand. "Sara, walk beside me."

"The girl stays with me." Radek took Sara's hand.

"I think the girl can make up her own mind," Abby said.

"It's fine, Abby. I want to walk with Radek," Sara said. She glanced up at the shifter and Abby frowned at her look of adoration as Kane led them into the woods.

"It will feel good to have a sword again." Michael fell into place beside her and she smiled at him.

"Yes, it will."

Hanif, dragging a wooden sleigh full of pelts, hurried to catch up to them. "What will you do if the human village has no swords?"

Michael shrugged. "Go further until I find a village that does, I suppose."

"Kane will not allow it," Hanif said. "It is risky enough travelling to this village during the cold months. We will be lucky if we do not freeze to death in a blizzard."

"Then why did you offer to come with us?" Michael.

Hanif grinned. "I never could resist an adventure. The bigger the possibility of death, the more anxious I am to join in."

Abby laughed and poked Michael in the side. "Sounds like someone else I know."

Michael rolled his eyes. "I do not have a death wish, Abby."

"Nor do I," Hanif said. "But I have no desire to sit warm by the fire when there is an entire world to explore."

Michael grinned at him. "I couldn't agree more, Hanif."

There was a rustling in the bushes to the left of them and shifter and human alike froze. Kane inhaled before relaxing and staring at Sara. "It seems your pet has joined us."

"Meeka, come here, baby," Sara called.

The massive koran emerged from the bushes and rubbed against her. She staggered back and Radek grabbed her arm to keep her from falling. Sara scratched the koran's throat and he licked her face before purring.

"You're a good baby, Meeka," she said.

The koran licked her face again before walking docilely

next to her. Kane shook his head and snorted, "A koran as a pet. I would never have thought it possible."

Abby grinned at him. "You've got to open your mind to different possibilities, big guy. Not everything is what it seems, right?"

"Aye," Kane replied before glancing at the sky. "Come, we must move more quickly."

"ADINA? ARE YOU HERE?" SIENNA KNOCKED AGAIN BEFORE trying the door. It opened and she stuck her head into the cabin. "Adina?"

Adina came hurrying out of the bedroom. The room was dark despite the bright afternoon sunshine - a blanket covered the window - and Adina smiled nervously at her before closing the bedroom door.

"Hello, Sienna. Come in."

Sienna closed the door behind her and followed Adina to the small kitchen. "Were you sleeping, Adina?"

"Um, I was just taking a nap."

"Were you?"

"Aye. What can I help you with?" Adina replied.

"Neil cut his hand this morning and Reese said you had some salve that would help heal it."

"Do you need me to look at it?" Adina asked as she pulled a jar from the open shelving in the kitchen.

"I don't think so. It's stopped bleeding."

Adina handed her the jar. "Apply this twice daily for a week. It should help."

"Thank you." Sienna hesitated before glancing at the closed bedroom door. "Are you allowing Faren to bite you?"

"That's none of your business," Adina said sharply.

"I suppose it is not," Sienna said. "But I have been bitten many times by vampires, Faren included, and know something of the obsession it creates."

"You told Neil you didn't want Faren. I heard you say it," Adina said.

Sienna sat down at the table and after a moment, Adina joined her.

"What I told Neil was not the truth. For the week after we arrived, I did feel a yearning for Faren. He was the last vampire to feed from me."

"You seemed to control it well enough," Adina replied.

Sienna sighed. "That is because Faren had not been feeding from me for long, Adina. Where I was before – the vampires took turns feeding from me. Each night it would be a different one and because of that, the need was not as strong. Do you understand?"

"Aye."

"Faren had fed from me two nights in a row and even with that short amount of time, I still wanted him when he stopped. Even though I am in love with Neil."

"Why did you lie to Neil about it?"

Sienna gave her a dry look. "Do you think the man who loves me would want to hear of how I ached for another man? Neil's wife killed herself after being bitten by a vampire. She couldn't bear the obsession."

Adina gave her a horrified look. "That's terrible."

"Aye, it is. Neil considers Val a friend but he does not trust other vampires. I do not blame him for that," Sienna said. "I suffered through my need for Faren without Neil knowing and I'm trusting you to not reveal my secret."

"I will keep it to myself. Do you still want Faren?"

"No," Sienna said. "The obsession has passed and it is only Neil I want and love."

She paused and touched Adina's hand. "I tell you this because I want to help you understand that what you feel for Faren is because he feeds from you. Your feelings for him are false and -"

"He hasn't fed from me," Adina interrupted.

"What?" Sienna said in surprise.

"He will not feed from me. I have asked him to and he refuses. He joins me every night in my bed but only after he has hunted and fed from the animals in the forest."

"I do not know what to say." Sienna sat back in her chair. "I do not know Faren but it is strange to me that he will not feed from a human who is willing."

"Perhaps there is something wrong with me," Adina whispered. "Perhaps he does not find me desirable enough to feed from."

Sienna frowned at her. "If he's fucking you every night, he finds you desirable enough."

Adina sighed and stared at the table. "Do you not wonder why I want him to feed from me, Sienna?"

Sienna shrugged. "That is your business, Adina. Who am I to judge the actions of others?"

She stared thoughtfully at the closed bedroom door. "Perhaps Faren will not feed from you because he cares for you."

"He does not," Adina said flatly. "He uses me for sex and nothing else."

"I would not be so certain of that, Adina. He spends his daysleep in your bed."

"So?"

"Vampires are most vulnerable during their daysleep. They can be woken from it but they are weak and disoriented. Vampires do not usually daysleep in a human's bed. It would be easy enough for you to stab him in the heart or take his head while he slept."

Adina gave her a horrified look and Sienna shrugged. "It is true. For him to sleep in your cabin means he trusts you."

They sat in silence for a moment before Sienna stood. "Thank you for the salve, Adina. I will return it to you in a week."

"You're welcome," Adina replied.

Sienna left and she stared at her bedroom door before rubbing at her burning eyes. She was tired and her thighs and pelvis ached. Faren had kept her up all night, fucking her repeatedly. She was still ashamed at the way she had begged and pleaded for him to bite her.

He had refused like always, and she wondered for a moment if Sienna was right. Perhaps Faren did care for her.

He doesn't. He wants sex and you give it to him. There is nothing more.

Wasn't there? A few hours before dawn when her body was worn out from the numerous orgasms Faren had coaxed out of her, he had asked about her life. He refused to share details of his own but he had listened quietly as she had spoken of her mother and her brother, and how she had learned to be a healer. Anger had flashed across his face when she had shared the way her brother had sold her to the slavers, and he had pulled her into his arms and held her until he had gone to his daysleep.

She rubbed again at her eyes before putting water to boil over the fire. Her obsession to be bitten by him had turned into something more in the last month. She cared for Faren more than she should and it would break her heart when he finally tired of her and moved on to another.

"You're seriously not building a fire."

"No, human. It is too dangerous," Hanif said.

"We're going to freeze to death." Abby scowled.

Darkness had fallen and Kane had agreed to stop for the night. Abby glanced at Sara. Her lips were blue and she was shivering violently despite Radek's embrace.

Hanif laughed. "She sounds like your mate, Kane."

"You will not freeze to death," Kane said. "Radek will keep young Sara warm, I will keep you warm, and Hanif will keep Michael warm."

"No," Michael said. "I'm not sleeping with Hanif."

Hanif grinned at him. "I will be in my wolf form, human."

"It's still too awkward," Michael replied.

"You really will freeze to death if you don't," Hanif said cheerfully.

"I'll take my chances."

"You can sleep with Meeka," Sara said. She called for the koran and it appeared out of the darkness with a soft rumbling purr.

"Meeka, you need to help keep Michael warm tonight. Do you understand?" She cupped the koran's giant face and stared into its golden eyes. "Lie down and let Michael sleep against you."

The koran hissed and glanced at Michael before returning his gaze to Sara. Sara scratched his throat and kissed his nose. "Please, Meeka. Be a good baby and help keep Michael warm."

The koran made a grumbling noise of displeasure but lay down obediently before staring at Michael.

"Go on, Michael. Meeka won't hurt you," Sara said encouragingly.

Michael glanced at Abby. She shrugged and he sighed before lying down gingerly against the koran. The koran curled around him and Michael stiffened when the beast sniffed at his hair before licking his forehead.

"He's just saying goodnight, Michael," Sara said.

"Or doing a taste test." Abby grinned.

Michael scowled at her as Kane stripped out of his clothing and shifted. He growled at Abby and she lay on the ground as Kane curled around her.

"Good God, it's like having a furry, breathing electric blanket," Abby said as Kane draped his large tail over her thighs.

Radek shifted and wrapped his large body around Sara's tiny one before licking her face. She was completely hidden by him and she said a muffled goodnight as Hanif shifted and stretched out in the snow.

KANE HELD HIS HAND UP AND THE OTHERS STOPPED BEHIND him. "We are close to the village."

"Thank God," Abby said. They had risen early and after walking steadily for the entire day she was ready for a hot meal and warm bed.

Kane turned to Sara. "Your pet cannot come into the village with us. The humans will be alarmed if a korar walks among them."

Sara nodded and buried her hands in Meeka's large mane. She scratched him roughly and he purred happily. "You have to stay hidden, Meeka. Stay in the forest and do not let yourself be seen by the humans. We will be back in a day or two. All right?"

He rumbled in reply and licked her hand before turning and disappearing into the dark. The shifters and humans walked for another ten minutes before the trees began to thin.

Abby could see the glow of lights flickering in the darkness and it wasn't long before they were at the edge of the forest.

"This is pretty big," she said in surprise as she gazed at the wooden buildings. Most of them were stores but there were a few houses scattered among them.

"Aye, it has grown since the last time we were here." Kane studied the buildings in the glow of the torches that lined the streets. "We will find lodging for the night and purchase our items in the morning. Follow me, humans."

They followed him for nearly ten minutes down a narrow street until he stopped in front of one of the larger buildings. He opened the door and Abby moaned happily at the blast of warm air. The room was small and the fire crackled loudly in the fireplace. Michael hurried over to it, holding his hands out as Kane approached the man sitting at the small wooden desk.

He was absorbed in a book and didn't look up when Kane cleared his throat. "We require lodging for the evening. Do you have any rooms?"

"Aye, we have quite a few as of late," the man replied without looking up. "How many do you require?"

"Three should be enough," Abby tugged on Kane's sleeve. "Sara and I can share a room, you and Radek can share, and Michael and Hanif can take the third one."

"Sara stays with me," Radek said immediately.

Abby rolled her eyes as Kane said, "We require four rooms."

"Thirty gold coins," the man said before finally raising his gaze. "You'll need to pay up front and…"

He trailed off, swallowing thickly at the sight of Kane's large body.

"We have pelts and furs to trade. I assume this will be agreeable." Kane leaned down and rested his hands on the desk as the man shrank back.

"Of course," he said hurriedly. "Four furs, one for each room, should cover it."

"Excellent. Hanif, show the man the furs we have brought." Kane smiled and the man made a soft moan of fear.

"Do you have a blacksmith here?" Michael asked as the man stumbled toward the door where Hanif was waiting.

"Aye. Two streets down from here," the man said before following Hanif into the cold.

"We will find our swords there," Michael said happily to Abby.

She squeezed his arm as Kane said, "Radek and Sara will share a room, Hanif and I will share the other and Abigail and Michael can have their own rooms. I think it's best if we retire for the night. We will meet here in the morning."

———

"IT IS A NICE ROOM," SARA SAID AS RADEK LOCKED THE door and closed the curtains.

"Aye," he replied before stripping off his shirt.

She sat down on the bed, bouncing a little, before removing her jacket and boots. "It will be good to find warmer clothing tomorrow."

Radek sat down beside her and curved his arm around her waist. "I will keep you warm, sweet one."

She smiled at him. "Am I to cling to your back like a monkey for the entire winter?"

"I would enjoy that," he winked at her and she leaned against him.

"Are you tired, sweet one?"

"A little. Mostly cold."

"Perhaps I should warm you up?" Radek nuzzled her throat and she smiled happily.

"I would enjoy another lesson." She stroked his firm thigh through his pants.

He tensed and she gave him a hesitant look. "Radek? What is wrong?"

"Nothing," he said tersely.

"Are you certain?"

"Aye."

She touched his naked chest timidly. "I can go to Abby's room if you'd like."

He scowled at her. "No. You sleep in my bed tonight. You are not to leave my sight while we are here. Do you understand, Sara?"

"I can take care of myself." She glanced at her bow and arrows leaning against the wall.

He didn't reply and she gave him her own scowl. "I can."

"I know but I will feel better if you stay close to me. Will you do as I ask?"

She nodded and he stroked her hair before reaching for the hem of her shirt. "Are you ready for your lesson, sweet one?"

She pressed her mouth against his. "Aye, Radek. I am."

CHAPTER 19

"For how big this place is, there doesn't seem to be many people," Abby said thoughtfully.

It was early the next morning. Kane and Hanif had taken them to what appeared to be a restaurant. After haggling with the owner, they had traded in a few furs for breakfast.

Kane grunted, "Aye, there are fewer people than I remember."

"Three of the stores we passed this morning were boarded up," Michael said.

The restaurant was on the larger side but there were only a few people sitting at the tables and Abby studied them curiously. "Do they know you're shifters, do you think?"

Hanif shrugged. "Most likely. We are bigger than humans and trading for furs is a dead give-away. It's why they're so nervous."

"Is it?" Radek wondered. "Both you and Kane have been here before - they know we are not here to cause trouble."

"Perhaps they are -"

Hanif stopped as the door to the restaurant opened. "Kane," he muttered. "Do you see that?"

Abby stared at the man standing in the doorway. Man was probably a bit too generous, she decided. The creature stood over ten feet tall and his entire body was covered in a layer of hair.

"What is that?" She whispered.

"A tagen," Hanif replied.

She could hear the fear in his voice and she glanced at Kane as Hanif said, "Why is there a tagen in a human village, Kane?"

"I do not know," Kane said. "Stay calm, Hanif."

"Aye, calm," Hanif muttered.

The tagen inhaled, his gaze landing on Kane and the others. A shiver went down Abby's back when his black eyes stared at her. A look came over his face, she wouldn't let herself believe it was lust, before he grinned at her and moved to the far side of the restaurant. He sat down at an empty table and pounded his fist on the wooden surface. It cracked beneath his hand and he chuckled to himself as the waitress approached him timidly.

"Bring me meat. Rare," he rumbled.

She nodded and cringed when he slapped her ass. The slap sent her to her knees and Hanif growled under his breath as she scrambled to her feet.

"Calm, Hanif," Kane said again. "Finish your meals quickly."

The others nodded and they ate rapidly as Kane studied the tagen silently. The tagen ignored him completely. His gaze remained on Abigail and Hanif leaned toward Kane.

"I do not like the way he stares at the human," he muttered under his breath.

"Nor do I," Kane replied.

Abby gasped when Kane hauled her from her chair and

sat her on his lap. He placed one large hand possessively on her thigh and gripped the back of her neck with his other.

"Hey, Kane?" Abby said as Sara and Michael stared at Kane in surprise. "Whatcha' doin', big guy?"

"He is showing the tagen you belong to him," Hanif said in a low voice. "He studies you too closely."

"Great," Abby muttered as Kane stared unblinkingly at the tagen.

The tagen bared his teeth at the shifter as the waitress placed a large chunk of meat in front of him. He tore into it, chewing loudly as he continued to study Abby.

"We leave – now," Kane said.

He stood and keeping his hand on Abigail's neck, steered her toward the front door. The tagen made no move to stop them and only when they were standing outside in the cold sunlight, did Kane drop his grip.

"We stick together at all times," Kane said as the others followed them down the street. "We will purchase the human's swords first and then find warmer clothing for Sara and the herbs that Adina requested. We're leaving the human's village as soon as we have our supplies. Is that understood?"

They nodded and Kane strode faster. "Hurry, it is not safe for us in the -"

"It is strange to see shifters in a human village." The voice was thick and deep and the hair on the back of Abby's neck tried to stand up. The tagen had appeared around the corner and Kane stopped immediately.

"No stranger than a tagen in a human village," he replied.

"Perhaps. Why are you here, dog?"

Hanif growled at the insult and Kane gave him a warning look. "We are not looking for trouble. We require supplies.

Once we have purchased them from the humans, we will leave."

The tagen tapped his chin thoughtfully as he stared down at them. "The thing is, this village now belongs to my brothers and me. And we don't care for dogs in our home."

"We are not looking for trouble," Kane repeated. "Step aside, let us purchase our supplies, and we will leave."

"That isn't how it works here anymore. You must pay a price to even enter our home," the tagen said.

"You are welcome to take a few of our pelts," Kane said.

The tagen laughed before belching. "We have more than enough pelts. Humans, however, are becoming increasingly rare. For some reason, they do not enjoy our rule and keep stealing away in the night."

"Perhaps it is because you rape their women," Hanif snarled.

The tagen shrugged. "Perhaps. My brothers and I do enjoy the softness of human females. Our female kind are terrible to fuck."

His gaze fell on Abby. "If you wish to stay in the village, I will allow it."

"Thank you," Kane said.

"For a price, dog," the tagen said.

"I have told you – you're welcome to a few of our pelts," Kane replied.

"And I have told you – we have no need for pelts. The woman," the tagen pointed at Abby, "will be more than enough payment."

Kane put his arm around Abby's waist and drew her back against him. "The woman is my mate and belongs to me."

"Do not worry, dog, I will make sure your woman forgets all about your puny cock when she is in my bed," the tagen replied.

Kane snarled and Abby could feel his body swelling against her back. "Touch her and I will kill you."

"Do you honestly think you can defeat me, shifter?" The tagen gave him a look of surprise.

"There are three of us and only one of you. Walk away now and we will let you live," Kane said.

"You are big for your kind, but I will kill you and your dog brothers easily enough. Give me the woman and you can walk away. I give you my word," the tagen said.

Kane glanced at Hanif and Radek. The two shifters nodded and moved forward as Kane pushed Abby behind him. "You had your chance, tagen."

"Aye, as did you," the tagen said. He charged forward, he was surprisingly nimble for his size, as the three shifters changed to their wolf forms. Their clothes shredded around them and they leaped at the tagen in unison.

The tagen bellowed angrily and swung one arm. It caught Hanif in the chest and he yelped before flying backward into the deep snow. He was on his feet and rushing forward in an instant as Kane and Radek landed on the tagen with heavy thuds. Their weight drove him to his knees and he punched Radek in the side before grabbing Kane around the throat. He squeezed tightly and then screamed miserably when Hanif tore off a chunk of his face with a loud growl. He dropped Kane and swung blindly at him as blood poured from his face. Kane ducked and the tagen screamed again when Radek bit him in the side. His teeth sank through the heavy pelt and he growled ferociously as the tagen beat at him with his fists

Kane, snarling viciously, knocked the tagen onto his back and latched onto his exposed throat. He tore through the skin, blood spraying in a wide arc, and the tagen made a low gurgling noise as his feet drummed on the ground.

The shifters backed away, blood dripping from their large

fangs, and watched as the tagen clapped his hand to his throat. Blood continued to spray from his jugular vein for nearly a minute before it trickled to a stop and the tagen slumped against the hard ground.

Kane shifted to his human form and wiped the blood from his mouth.

"Are you all right, Kane?" Abby asked.

"Aye." Kane glanced around. At the far end of the street, a small group of humans had gathered and they were staring at the shifters in shock and fear.

Kane dug through the bag that was tucked among the furs on the wooden sleigh and pulled out clothes as Radek and Hanif shifted. "We need to leave."

"We need swords," Michael said. "I'm not leaving without one."

Kane growled and Abby shook her head. "He's right, Kane. This whole trip was pointless if we don't get swords and warmer clothing for Sara."

"We move quickly," Kane muttered as he tossed clothing to Hanif and Radek. "Stay together and keep your eyes open for the other tagens."

***

"RADEK, ARE YOU SURE YOU'RE ALL RIGHT?" SARA examined the bruising that was developing on his side and Radek nodded reassuringly.

"I am fine, sweet one. Nothing is broken."

They were standing outside of the blacksmith's and Kane glanced impatiently at the door before studying the crowd of humans who were following them.

"I do not like this, Kane," Hanif said uneasily. "Where are

the other tagens and why would they take over a human village in the first place?"

"For their women, most likely," Kane said.

"Why didn't the humans band against them?" Hanif wondered. "They have weapons."

Kane glanced at Radek. He knew what Kane was thinking – there had to be a few tagens if they had taken over an entire village – and he pulled Sara closer to him.

Kane was reaching for the door when it opened and Abby and Michael emerged. They were both carrying swords, Abby had two, and she placed one of them on the sleigh with the furs. Kane took her hand. "Let's go."

They hurried down the street, the crowd of people parting silently to let them pass. A shiver ran down Sara's spine. The crowd of people had grown and it was eerie to walk through them without a sound being made. A small girl with a dirty face and matted blonde hair stared shyly at her from behind her mother's leg. Sara smiled at her and the child hid her face in her mother's leg as Radek gripped her hand and pulled her along.

"Faster, Sara," he murmured.

They were almost to the main street of the village and the edge of the forest loomed to their right. Kane said, "There is a general store just a bit further. They will have clothes for Sara and the herbs Adina needs. We will -"

"Oh shit," Abby said.

Three tagens, all of them bigger than the one they had killed, emerged from the side streets. They surrounded the small group as Kane snarled.

"You killed our brother, dog," the biggest one said. He had thick black hair and dark brown eyes, and Abby guessed his height to be around twelve feet. His arms were as thick as her thighs and he shrugged out of his pelt before pulling a wooden club from the leather strap around his waist.

"We told him to walk away," Kane said. "He chose not to."

The tagen studied Abby and Sara before smiling at Kane. "We will kill you and take your women. They will suffer greatly for what you have done."

Radek howled and then shifted with an abrupt pop. He snarled at the tagens, saliva dripping from his fangs as he stood protectively in front of Sara. She pulled her bow from her back and quickly notched an arrow into it as the second tagen leered at her.

"You're a pretty little thing. I will enjoy having you in my bed."

She raised her bow and aimed it at him and the tagen laughed delightedly. "What spirit you have. Do you think an arrow will stop me? Do you even have the strength to draw the bow back?"

"Come closer and you'll find out," she spat.

"Enough," the leader of the tagens said wearily. "Let us kill them and be done with it."

Kane and Hanif shifted and Hanif raced toward the second tagen. It raised the club it carried and swung at him. Hanif ducked and the tagen made a soft grunt of surprise when he felt the arrow lodge in his ribs. He pulled it out and gave Sara a look of astonishment. "You will pay for that, you little bitch."

Hanif barked and the tagen lunged at him as Radek and Kane surrounded the largest tagen. He swung his club in a gentle arc before smiling at them. "Come on then, you mangy dogs."

They leaped at him as Abigail glanced at Michael. He

grinned at her, his eyes lit with a fierce light, and gripped his sword. "Are you ready, Abigail?"

"Yes." She returned his grin. "Stay here, Sara." They ran toward the third tagen and Sara watched wide-eyed as they moved nimbly around him, their swords jabbing and flashing in the sunlight.

In only a matter of minutes they had driven the tagen to his knees and with a harsh grin, Michael sliced the tagen's head from his body. The head tumbled into the snow and blood sprayed from his headless stump before his body pitched forward.

"Fuck, that felt good!" Abby shouted.

There was a harsh howl of pain. The second tagen had Hanif by his front leg and Hanif howled again when he broke the shifter's leg with a loud snap.

Abby and Michael sprinted toward the tagen as he wrapped his large hands around Hanif's neck. There was a soft whoosh of air. The tagen dropped Hanif and slowly reached up to touch the arrow that was sticking out of the middle of his forehead.

"No," he whispered as blood trickled from his mouth and he fell onto his back with a thud.

"Nice fucking shot, Sara!" Abigail shouted as Sara lowered her bow and released her breath in a harsh rush.

There was a scream of pain and the largest tagen knocked Kane from his body and stumbled back. He screamed in anger over the dead bodies of his brothers and turned to flee. Radek howled and leaped onto his back, knocking him face-first into the ground. The tagen beat at him with his fists as Radek sank his teeth into the back of his neck and ripped away the flesh.

The tagen screamed miserably and flipped onto his back,

holding his hands out in a desperate plea. "No, please, I am sorry. Let me live and I will leave. I swear it."

The two shifters glanced at each other, identical grins crossing their faces, before they fell on the tagen.

Sara winced and looked away as the tagen's dying screams shattered the cold air. Hanif had shifted to his human form and he was holding his left arm grimly as Abigail and Michael helped him to his feet.

"Are you all right, Hanif?" Michael asked.

"Aye, it is only broken. It will heal in a day or two," Hanif's face was pale but he smiled grimly at Michael.

Radek backed away from the dead tagen and howled. Kane joined him and the humans in the street clapped their hands over their ears. Radek shifted and turned to Sara. His eyes widened and he gave a hoarse shout of warning as the tagen slipped out from the side street and grabbed Sara around her throat. He ripped the bow from her hand and tossed it to the ground before backing away from the shifters.

Radek, panic coursing through his veins, ran toward them and the tagen squeezed Sara's throat. "Come any closer, dog, and I'll snap her neck."

Radek froze and stared helplessly at Sara as the tagen yanked her back against him. She barely came up to his waist and she gave Radek a look of terror as the tagen petted her curly hair.

"Give me my mate," he snarled at the tagen.

"Your mate is dead if you come any closer," the tagen snapped.

"Your brothers are dead." Kane had joined Radek and he showed the tagen his blood-smeared hands. "If you kill the girl we will make you suffer in ways you cannot imagine."

The tagen lifted Sara around the waist and backed toward the forest behind him. "The girl is coming with me. If you try and follow us, I will tear her guts out with my bare hands. Is that what you want, shifter? To see your mate's guts in the snow?"

Radek howled, his body swelling and his jaw cracking as his fangs protruded from his mouth. "Give me back my mate and I will end your miserable life quickly."

The tagen was in the forest now and he shook his head as Radek and Kane stalked toward him. "You are killing her."

"Radek," Sara whispered.

"It is all right, my sweet one," Radek said. "You will be safe soon."

The tagen laughed before pulling Sara's head back by her hair. "Your mate lies to you, girl. You will be dead soon. But not before I make you pay for what your mate has done to my brothers. You will beg for death before I am done."

His eyes widened at the soft growling behind him. He turned, his entire body stiffening, and stared in horror at the giant koran crouched behind him. The koran roared and the tagen whimpered in fear before dropping Sara to the ground. He backed away, holding his club protectively in front of him as the koran stalked forward. It nuzzled Sara's hair affectionately and licked her forehead before crouching again.

"No," the tagen whispered. He glanced behind him Radek and Kane were moving toward him with their fangs bared and their bodies swelling, and he turned and darted into the forest. The koran roared again and the tagen screamed miserably when the beast landed on his back. He fell to the ground, scrabbling uselessly at the snow as the koran swiped at him with his sharp claws. They cut through his thick pelt and into his flesh and he moaned pitifully when Meeka bit into the flesh of his back. His back arched, his fists pounding against the ground as the koran tore his spine from his flesh with a wet, ripping sound. Meeka roared a third time in triumph as the tagen made a final, gasping moan and died.

"Sara!" Radek dropped to his knees beside her and gathered her into his arms. "Are you hurt, my sweet one?"

He lifted her chin and studied her throat anxiously as she threw her arms around his waist.

"I'm fine, Radek."

He kissed her, his hands threading into her hair to hold her head.

"Are you okay?" She asked when he finally released her mouth.

"Aye, I am perfectly fine."

"Gross," Abigail muttered.

Sara followed her gaze. Meeka was throwing the tagen's spine into the air, catching it in his mouth and tossing it again as blood and bits of meat splattered the snow. He rumbled happily and tossed the spine into the deep snow before pouncing on it and shaking his head wildly.

"Ugh!" Abigail backed away as drops of blood landed on her face.

Sara laughed a bit hysterically. "Meeka has a new toy."

Radek rubbed her back before hugging her as Kane squeezed Hanif's shoulder. "How is your arm, Hanif?"

"Broken," Hanif grunted. "Thank you for saving my life, little human."

"You're welcome, Hanif," Sara replied.

Kane studied the humans who had gathered behind them. "Are there any more?"

A man stepped forward. He was tall and thin with hunched shoulders and thinning hair. "No. You have destroyed all of them."

"How long have they been at the village?"

"Nearly six months." The man glanced at the other humans. "They killed most of us."

He cleared his throat and gave Kane a nervous look. "Thank you, shifter. We are in your debt."

Kane nodded. "We need more supplies and food for our journey home."

"You are welcome to whatever you need," the man replied. He turned to the humans standing behind him. "This is a day of celebration. The shifters have ended the tagens' cruel reign and we will offer them the best of what we have."

CHAPTER 20

Sara stared out the window at the street below her. The humans were still partying and the sound of their singing drifted through the glass. She and the others had picked out supplies before, at the villagers urging, joining the humans for a feast. She had enjoyed the party. The humars were nearly giddy with relief at being freed from the tagens and they were falling over themselves to thank them.

Only Radek had not joined in the festivities. He had not stopped her from mingling with the humans but he had spent the entire evening sitting at an empty table with his back to the wall as he watched the humans.

She drew the curtains closed. Despite the villagers' protests, all of them had retired for the night. They were leaving early in the morning and Kane wanted them well-rested for the journey home.

"Sara? Is there something wrong?"

The genuine concern in Radek's voice made her heart swell. She loved him, she knew that now, and she thought he might love her. He had called her his mate, and the fear on his face when the tagen had taken her was very real.

He hates humans, Sara. Even tonight he could not bring himself to enjoy their company. Do you honestly believe that he loves you? He called you his mate for the same reason that Kane did with Abby – to try and protect you from the tagen.

Bullshit. He loves you.

"Sara?" Radek's arms circled her waist and she leaned against him.

"Tell me what the humans did to you, Radek."

He tensed and started to pull away. She clung to his arms and stared pleadingly at him. "Tell me, Radek."

He studied her face for a moment before staring at the wall. "When I was a boy I went into the forest alone. I was not supposed to but I was stubborn and disobeyed my parents. I was stolen by humans. They took me to their home and tortured me for the amusement of themselves and their children."

He was beginning to tremble and she put her arm around his waist and hugged him.

"They burned me and stabbed me just to see how long it would take before I would heal. They collared me and chained me to a wall in their barn. More than once they took me to the lake and held me under the water until I nearly drowned."

"Oh, Radek," Sara whispered. She was starting to cry and she wiped at the tears as he continued to stare at the wall.

"I was so afraid, Sara. After a few days, I – I begged them not to hurt me, promised them I would do whatever it was they wanted if they would just stop hurting me. They laughed at me. They called me a worthless dog and told me I was going to die."

"How did you escape?" Sara asked.

"I didn't. My father and Kane's father searched for my scent in the forest. It took them a few days to find it – my mother said it was nearly gone by the time they found it. They and our alpha, Maven, followed it to the farm where I was being held captive. They killed the humans who had taken me and returned me to our pack."

"I'm so sorry, Radek," Sara whispered.

He stared blankly at her for a moment before frowning. "Why are you crying, sweet one?"

"Because it breaks my heart to hear the way you were abused," she said. "You were only a child and what happened to you is horrifying. I – no wonder you hate us."

"I don't hate you, Sara," he said quickly.

She rested her forehead on his sternum and he stroked her curly hair before burying his face in it.

"I don't hate you," he repeated. "Do you believe me?"

WHEN SARA NODDED, RADEK PICKED HER UP AND CARRIED her to the bed. He needed her badly. When the tagen had taken her, the fear had nearly paralyzed him. The thought of losing his mate had sent his wolf into a frenzy of terror and anger and his human side was equally terrified. He'd realized in that moment of terror that he loved her and wanted to be with her for the rest of his life.

He set her down next to the bed and smiled distractedly at her. He loved Sara and he had no idea how to tell her. Would she even believe it, he wondered. He had spent weeks telling her he hated her kind, that it was only his wolf who would ever want her, and he didn't have a clue how to convince her that he had been a fool.

Bite her, his wolf said persuasively. *Bite her and show her and everyone else that she is ours.*

He realized with a start that Sara had already undressed and her tiny hands were unbuttoning his shirt.

"Sara," he covered her hands with his own, "are you sure this is what you want?"

She frowned at him. "Why wouldn't it be? Do you no longer want me, Radek?"

He shook his head immediately before shrugging out of his shirt. "I want you so badly, sweet one."

"Good." She unbuttoned his pants and he kicked them off impatiently as she stretched out on the bed. He studied her naked flesh, drinking in the lovely sight of her pale, soft skin as she held her hand out to him.

"Radek, do not make me wait."

He lay down beside her, smiling a little when she climbed onto him and straddled his waist. "I want to be on top. Can I, Radek? We have never tried this position before."

"Whatever you want, sweet one."

He cupped her small breasts, pulling on her nipples until they hardened as she closed her eyes and arched her back. He played with her breasts until she was rubbing her pussy against his abdomen and moaning. God, he loved the sounds she made, loved the look on her face when he touched her soft skin, and he felt a wave of love for her that was nearly painful in its intensity.

She was stroking his chest, her fingers tracing small circles through the hair and he reached between her legs and stroked her warmth. She was wet and he growled happily before rubbing at her swollen clit. She lifted her body and he slipped two fingers deep into her tight core. She groaned and rocked her hips against his hand, her fingers digging into his warm skin.

"Does that feel good, sweet one?" He asked.

She nodded before whispering, "Aye, but your cock would feel so much better, Radek."

She blushed furiously at her boldness and he grinned at her. "Then take what you want."

He moved his hand away and watched as she grasped the base of his cock and guided it into her. She moaned and when he was fully sheathed within her, smiled at him. "There is no pain at all now, Radek."

"I am glad, sweet one," he said. He pumped his hips experimentally and she bit her bottom lip before groaning harshly.

"You're going to make me come," she whispered.

He flexed his hips again and she slapped him on the chest. "Don't move."

"Impossible," he groaned. "Your tight pussy drives me crazy."

She coloured at his words before leaning over him and resting her hands on either side of his head. He cupped her breasts and licked the tip of one nipple and she squirmed with pleasure.

"Radek, wait!"

He muttered a curse but stopped and she traced his jawline with her fingers. "Why did you tell the tagen I was your mate?"

His pulse pounded in his ears and he stared blankly at her. "Sara, I -"

"Tell me," she insisted when he trailed off. "Did you say it because you truly want me to be your mate?"

He swallowed thickly. "I – do you want to be my mate, Sara?"

"I asked you first," she said before bouncing up and down.

He groaned, his hands clamping onto her hips. "I – I would keep you safe if you became my mate. I promise."

"I can take care of myself, remember?" A brief look of concentration crossed her face and he nearly came inside of her when her inner walls squeezed around his dick.

"God! Do not do that, sweet one," he begged.

"Why not? Do you not like it, Radek?" She squeezed him again and he jerked against her.

"Aye, but it is bringing me too close."

"I'm sorry," she said sweetly before squeezing him for a third time.

He growled, his eyes flashing and she kissed the tip of his nose. "You don't frighten me."

"Good. I don't want my mate to be afraid of me," he replied.

"I didn't say I would be your mate."

He growled again and clamped his arm around her waist before sitting up. She moaned at the change in position and he curled one hand into her mass of hair and held her as she hooked her slender thighs around his waist.

"You are my mate, Sara. Say it," he demanded.

"It is kind of you to offer to be my mate to protect me, Radek, but I told you – I no longer need your protection. I can take care of myself," she said.

"You are my mate because I love you, not because I wish only to protect you," he said angrily. "And you may be adept with the bow but you are still very little and will need…"

He trailed off, his stomach churning as he realized what he had said. She would not believe him and she would refuse to be his mate. He would spend the rest of his life pining for her and would go mad if he had to watch her with another. He had ruined his chance with her and –

"I love you too, Radek."

He jerked again and stared wide-eyed at her. "Truly?"

She nodded. "Aye, truly."

"It is not just my wolf who loves you, Sara," he said hurriedly.

"I know," she said. "Although I am fairly certain your wolf has been in love with me since the day you met me. It's just taken a while for your human side to figure it out."

She grinned cheekily at him and he growled before capturing her mouth in a fiercely possessive kiss. "I was a fool to deny it for so long."

She cupped his face and rested her forehead against his. "I love you."

"I love you," he whispered.

"Good. Now fuck me, Radek."

"It would be my pleasure, sweet one," he murmured.

He thrust back and forth, his entire body shivering with delight at the feel of her warm, slick tightness. She wrapped her arm around his shoulders and held on as he plunged in and out of her. She gave him a shy look before reaching between them and rubbing at her clit with her fingers.

He growled his approval and watched her fingers rub at her swollen clit. He thrust harder, his balls tightening as his orgasm drew close and muttered a curse when she began to make small breathless cries of need.

"I'm so close, Radek," she moaned as her fingers circled her clit.

Bite her!

His wolf was howling at him to claim his mate and he couldn't stop his fangs from descending. He stared at her thin shoulder, his cock twitching inside of her as he thought about how it would feel to sink his fangs into her soft skin, to mark her as his forever.

"Bite me, Radek," she suddenly whispered. "Make me

yours."

She was staring at his fangs, her fingers still rubbing at her clit, and she lifted her gaze to his.

"Do it," she said.

He howled and pulled her forward, twisting her slightly so the back of her shoulder was exposed to him, and sunk his fangs into her flesh. She cried out, her pussy clamping around him as her back arched and she came all over his cock.

He growled again, his hips thrusting furiously as he came deep inside of her. He pulled his mouth away and licking her blood from his lips. She collapsed against him, panting harshly as her body trembled and he licked the wound until it stopped bleeding.

"Are you all right, sweet one?"

She nodded weakly before smiling at him. "I'm yours now. Yours forever."

"Aye, forever," he whispered before kissing her smooth cheek. "I love you, Sara."

"I love you, Radek."

"RAINA, MY LOVE, COME INSIDE. IT'S FREEZING OUT." REESE held her hand out to the shifter. Raina paced back and forth next to the dying fire as the other shifters returned to their cabins.

"They are supposed to be home tonight," Raina fretted. "It is so late, why are they not home?" She glanced up at the moon as Reese sighed.

"They're fine, my love. The snow is deep and it's probably taking them longer to walk through it then they thought."

"What if they're not fine?" Raina's lower lip was trembling. "What if they've been hurt or killed or -"

"You can't think that way." Adina had joined them and she patted the young shifter's back. "They are probably nearly home as we speak."

"I should have went hunting with Theran and the others," Raina said. "They might find them in the woods."

Reese didn't reply. Val had left his cabin and was heading toward the edge of the forest and she called his name.

He hesitated before turning around and joining them. "What is it, Reese?"

"Where are you going?"

He shrugged. "It is a nice night for a walk."

She gave him a doubtful look and he winked at her as Raina tapped him on the shoulder. "You are going to look for your human, are you not?"

He didn't reply and she gave him a pleading look. "Please take me with you."

Reese shook her head. "No, Raina."

"That's not fair!" Raina shouted. "I want to go with the creature."

"It's too dangerous, honey," Reese said.

Raina growled at her. "I can take care of myself. Besides, the creature is with me and he knows how to fight. Do you not?"

"I do," Val said, "but Reese is right. I do not need your assistance."

Raina snarled, baring her teeth at Val, and he grinned. "You have spirit, young one, but I -"

He stopped as Theran, Davin and Borek came bursting out of the trees. They were in their wolf forms and Raina gave them a curious look as they skidded to a stop in front of them.

"What's wrong?"

Theran shifted to his human form and glanced over his

shoulder at the trees. "Mantorians, a large group of them."

Raina's eyes widened and a whine of fear slipped from her throat before she clung to Reese's waist.

"How many?" Reese's heart was pounding in her chest and she rubbed at her leg as Val gave her a curious look.

"At least twenty-five. I have never seen so many together before," Theran said as Davin and Borek shifted.

"Borek, alert the others that there are mantorians and tell them to be ready to fight," Theran said. "If we are lucky they will pass by without noticing us."

"And if we're not?" Val raised his eyebrow at him.

"Then we fight," Theran said grimly.

"What exactly are mantorians?" Val asked.

Reese shuddered. "They – they're these giant, awful white creatures with wings and razor-sharp teeth, and they make this horrid buzzing sound that is just…"

She trailed off and pulled Raina closer. "They're very dangerous."

"How big?" Val asked. "Surely shifters can defeat them."

"Aye, against one or two. But with twenty-five of them," Theran swallowed thickly, "they're quick and extremely strong and they can rip a shifter to shreds with those teeth."

He watched as Borek ran to each cabin, knocking on the doors. "Davin, is everyone accounted for?"

"Aye. I did a headcount before we left to hunt and everyone was here," Davin replied.

"Did anyone leave after we went hunting?" Theran asked Reese.

"I don't think so. It seemed like everyone was here for the evening meal," Reese said.

"Good," Theran breathed a sigh of relief. "Everyone back to their cabins. Stay quiet, and -"

Adina, her face bloodless, suddenly gripped his arm.

"Faren. Faren is out hunting in the forest."

"The creature will be fine," Theran said. "He moves more quickly than the mantorians. I have seen it."

"But if he isn't? If they take him by surprise," Adina said frantically, "they will kill him."

She turned to Val. "You have to help him. He is your friend."

Val studied her silently before nodding. "I know."

Adina turned back to Theran. "Theran, please. He can't go alone."

"Adina, you would have me risk the lives of our pack members for that creature? He is not one of us."

"I am not either!" Adina snapped. "But would you leave me to fend for myself?"

"It is not the same," Theran said, "and you know that. You may be human but you're a member of our pack."

"So is Faren!"

"No, he is not," Theran said.

"Reese," Adina gave her a desperate look, "please."

Reese hesitated before turning to Theran. He groaned at the look on her face. "She is right, Theran. We can't leave him out there. I know he is different but Adina cares for him and she's a pack member."

Theran muttered a curse under his breath before turning to Davin. "We'll need more shifters. Go."

Davin nodded and ran toward the nearest cabin as Adina gave Theran a look of relief. "Thank you, Theran."

"Aye," he said grimly.

"I'm going with you," Adina said.

"No, you're not," Reese scowled at her. "You're staying here."

"I am not," Adina said. "They may need my help."

"With what?" Val said. "You're not exactly the fighting

type."

"If someone gets injured, they'll need my help," Adina said.

"Adina, no!" Reese said. "You're not going."

Adina glared at her. "If it was Kane out there, would you stay safe in your cabin while the others searched for him?"

"Adina, I -"

Reese stopped and Adina nodded in hard satisfaction. "That is what I thought. I'm going."

"Asher, please be careful," Maria said worriedly.

"Aye, I will be, Maria."

"Do you promise?" She said.

"I do. Do not worry," Asher replied. He pushed down the blanket she had wrapped around her until her shoulder was bared and licked his claiming mark. "I will return to you shortly. Lock the door behind me and stay in our cabin."

She kissed him hard and he hugged her before leaving. He joined the others as the edge of the forest and frowned at Theran. "Is this it?"

"Aye," Theran said grimly. Only Teagan, Borek, and Davin were standing with him. "The others chose not to risk their lives to save the creature and I will not force them to accompany us."

Teagan cracked his knuckles before grinning at Asher. "Five shifters are more than enough to destroy the mantorians."

He glanced at Neil and Val. "Plus, we have the creature and the human. They can act as distractions while we kill them."

Val rolled his eyes and nudged Neil who was holding a

large axe. "It has been a long time since we have battled together, my friend."

Neil nodded before swinging the axe in a gentle arc. "If I die because of your stupid vampire friend, I'll haunt your ass, Val."

"Let's go," Theran said. He glanced at Adina. "You should stay, Adina. We will be moving quickly and -"

"I can keep up," she said stubbornly. "Do not worry about me, Theran."

He nodded and she followed the others into the dark forest.

FAREN, HIDDEN IN THE SHADOWS OF THE LARGE TREE, watched as the deer stepped delicately into the moonlight. He watched silently as the deer chewed at the branch of a tree before stiffening. It stared into the distance and Faren waited patiently.

Go to Adina. Why are you feeding from animals when she has offered you her blood?

He ignored his inner voice and took a deep breath before moving forward in a blur and jumping on the deer. He grabbed its antlers and lowered its struggling body to the ground. He knelt on its upper body as it kicked and struggled, and bared his fangs. Before he could plunge them into the large vein of its neck, a weird buzzing sound emerged from the trees. It set his teeth on edge and he released the deer and hissed before standing and twisting around.

Five creatures stood behind him and he made a soft grunt of surprise. They were over eight feet tall and their bodies were covered in white feathers. Large wings sprouted from their backs and they had feelers on the tops of their heads.

The feelers rubbed against each other, producing that hideous buzzing noise, and he had to stop himself from clapping his hands over his ears.

He hissed at them as their large red eyes glowed in the darkness. "You would be wise to leave, creatures, before I lose my patience and kill you all."

They cocked their heads. The buzzing grew louder before the one closest to him opened his mouth and hissed. Its mouth was lined with large and razor-sharp teeth and he felt a trickle of fear.

"On second thought, I believe I will say good evening." He grinned humorlessly at them. Before he could flee, the sounds of wings flapping filled the cold night air and more of the creatures landed on the ground around him.

"Fuck," he muttered as they surrounded him. There were more than twenty of the creatures and the buzzing was so loud he thought he would go mad from it. The buzzing intensified as the creatures closed in on him and he hissed a final time before darting forward. He landed on the closest creature, climbing its feathered body nimbly and sinking his fangs into its neck. He tore its neck open, spitting out feathers and the bitter taste of its black blood as it screamed shrilly.

Faren, snarling and snapping his teeth, screamed hoarsely when another of the creatures tore him from the dying white bug. Its black claws dug into his back and he screamed again when it tore his flesh wide open. It threw him to the ground and it and four others fell on him, their teeth slashing into his body, as he screamed repeatedly.

———

VAL TURNED AND STRODE BACK TO WHERE ADINA WAS floundering through the deep snow. She was struggling to keep up with the rapidly-moving shifters and he turned his back to her.

"Get on," he said impatiently.

She climbed onto his back and he grunted in reply when she whispered her thanks. He moved forward quickly. The human was on the larger side but he barely felt her weight as he darted through the trees after the shifters. He could hear Neil panting heavily behind him and he called mockingly, "Out of shape are we, human?"

"Fuck you, Val," Neil panted. "You know you're jealous of my body."

Val snorted soft laughter as Theran barked at them.

"The idiot vampire is probably back at the camp, wondering where his bed warmer is," Neil puffed as he caught up to Adina and Val.

"Probably," Val agreed, "but we don't know for certain that he -"

He was cut off by a hoarse shout of pain that echoed through the night air.

"Faren!" Adina cried. "That was Faren, I know it."

Adina made a harsh cry of surprise when Val dropped her in the snow and disappeared in a blur of speed. The shifters chased after him, bounding gracefully through the deep snow as Adina struggled to her feet.

"Neil!"

He took her hand and they ran after the shifters as more screams pierced the air.

THE MANTORIAN WATCHED AS ITS BROTHERS TORE INTO THE strange-smelling creature. Its cries were growing weaker and it buzzed its satisfaction as the blood stained the snow. It touched its feeler to the mantorian standing next to it and it buzzed in reply. They would finish destroying the creature and then hunt down the scent of the shifters. It was many weeks since they had fed and the shifters would be more than enough to satisfy the hunger. It buzzed again, excitement coursing through its veins as its wings fluttered in the cold air.

If they were lucky, there would be many shifters and they could –

A breath of air passed by it and warmth flooded its chest. It glanced downward, its eyes glowing in surprise at the black blood that coated the feathers of its chest. It touched the blood with one black-tipped claw and studied it in the moonlight. It was growing oddly weak and it sank to its knees as more blood poured from its slit throat. It watched with numb disinterest as a second creature, hissing loudly, attacked its brothers who were feeding from the fallen one. It buzzed quietly and fell face-forward into the snow as howling filled the night air.

The five shifters bounded forward and snarling and barking, they attacked the mantorians feasting on Faren's body. They drove them back as Adina and Neil joined them. They formed a protective circle around Faren and Adina fell to her knees beside him.

"Faren!" She screamed his name, staring horrified at the gaping wounds in his chest and torso. He was drenched in blood and Val shook him roughly.

"Faren, open your eyes!"

His eyelids fluttered open and he stared hazily at Val before his eyes rolled to Adina.

"Hello, Adina," he rasped.

Blood bubbled from his mouth and Adina shrugged out of her jacket before struggling to sit him up. Val yanked Faren into a sitting position. The vampire screamed hoarsely as blood gushed from his chest and stomach and Adina made her own cry of pain.

"You must feed from me, Faren," she said urgently as tears flowed down her cheeks.

"No," he shook his head weakly. "I will not. Do not ask me to -"

He broke off, coughing weakly as blood flew from his mouth.

"Fuck, Faren! You are dying, feed from the human!" Val snarled at him.

"I cannot," Faren whispered. "I want her love not her obsession."

"I do love you!" Adina cried. "Do you hear me? I love you! Now drink, you fool!"

She pressed her throat against his mouth. "Drink!"

Her back arched and she cried out when Faren sunk his fangs into her throat. He drank greedily as Val stood and turned to face the other mantorians.

"Fuck - that buzzing!" Neil shouted. "What the fuck are these things?"

Val shook his head grimly as the mantorians drew closer. He glanced at Theran and the shifter bared his teeth at him. He could smell the shifters' fear but he couldn't fault them for it. He was afraid too. They were outnumbered and the mantorians were buzzing and hissing with excitement as they crept forward. Two of them flew into the air and dropped with deadly speed onto their group.

Neil swung his axe and the mantorian's head fell to the ground. Its body hovered in the air for a moment, black blood jetting from the stump of its neck and the wings flapping slowly before they stopped completely and its body joined its head in the snow.

The other mantorian screamed in pain as Theran bit through its arm. He ripped the arm free and spit it out as Borek and Teagan fell on the mantorian and tore it to pieces.

The other mantorians didn't seem to be bothered by the grisly end of two of their kind and hissing and buzzing, they flew forward. The shifters launched themselves at the mantorians as Val and Neil surrounded Faren and Adina.

Asher gave a sharp howl of pain as the mantorian he was fighting raked its claws across his chest. Blood soaked his grey fur and he was thrown backward into the snow. He struggled to his feet as the mantorian flew toward him. Before it could land on him there was a loud growling behind him and a giant, grey wolf slammed into it mid-air. It knocked the mantorian to the ground and ripped its throat out before howling. Kane returned to Asher, sniffing at the blood coating his chest before nudging him against the shoulder. Asher whined and Kane grinned fiercely at him before stalking toward the mantorians.

Val hissed as the mantorian reached for him. He dodged its claws and hissed again as a familiar scent drifted to him. Abby appeared beside him and she grinned at him before skewering the mantorian with the sword she held in her right hand. She wrenched her sword free as Michael sliced its head from its body.

"Hey, honey. Miss me?" She winked at Val and he yanked her into his embrace and kissed her hard.

"I brought you something," she said and handed him the second sword she was carrying. He swung it through the air as she studied the mantorians. "What the fuck are these things?"

"Mantorians," he replied.

"Well, let's have some fun," she said as she raised her sword and grinned again at him.

Davin backed away, snarling and growling at the two mantorians who were advancing on him. He snarled again, saliva dripping from his fangs as one of the mantorians flew forward. There was a soft whistling noise and the mantorian dropped to the ground. An arrow was embedded in one red eye and it made a final buzzing noise before dying.

He turned to see Sara lowering her bow and she nodded to him as Radek stepped in front of her and growled viciously at the mantorian approaching her. He crouched and barked in surprise when the koran leaped out of the darkness and batted the mantorian from the air with one giant paw. It spun crazily and crashed into a tree and Meeka roared happily before pouncing on it.

Theran barked at Hanif and the two shifters surrounded a lone mantorian. It flew upwards in a desperate attempt to escape, and Hanif jumped and snagged its foot. He tore it free from its leg with a wet rip and the mantorian screamed in pain, blood pouring from its foot before it disappeared into the night sky.

Faren, Adina's blood rushing through his veins, pulled his mouth from her throat. She rested weakly against him as he cupped her face. "Adina, look at me!"

She blinked blearily before touching his chest with her hand. "Faren, are you healed?"

He nodded and stroked her hair. "I'm sorry."

"Do not be," she said as he shifted her closer. "I wanted this."

"I love you, Adina." He brushed his mouth across her pale cheek.

"Aye, I know," she smiled and he rested his forehead against hers.

Val crouched beside him. "Faren? Will you live?"

"Yes." Faren looked around the forest. The mantorians were dead and the others were staring silently at him.

He stood and lifted Adina into his arms as Kane shifted to his human form. "Is everyone all right? Uncle?"

Asher shifted and touched his bleeding chest gingerly. "I'll live."

"Good," Kane clapped him on the back before turning to the others. "Come, let us go home."

"YOU'RE LOSING YOUR TOUCH, MY LOVE," ABBY said teasingly before striking at Val with her sword.

He parried the blow and yanked her into his embrace, kissing her on the mouth and sliding his tongue between her lips.

"No one wants to see that, leech!" Neil shouted from his spot by the fire. Sienna poked him in the stomach and he winked at her before kissing her and pulling her closer to him.

It was the next night and although it was late, the shifters showed no signs of retiring. Reese had insisted on a celebration for both the return of Kane and the others and their defeat over the mantorians, and the shifters were more than happy to oblige.

Val took Abby's hand and led her toward the large fire in the middle of the clearing. Michael was sitting on a fallen log, sharpening his sword. They sat down next to him as Meeka trotted by. Violet was sitting on top of his head with her tiny hands buried deep within his shaggy mane. She grinned cheekily at them as Abby laughed.

She gazed around the fire as Val put his arm around her waist and drew her closer. She rested her head on his shoulder and kissed his neck. "Did you know that Asher claimed Maria as his mate?"

"I did not," he said.

"I'm happy for her," Abby said. She watched as Asher handed Maria a small stone. Maria kissed him on the mouth and studied the stone before placing it carefully in her pocket.

"Where are Faren and Adina?" She asked suddenly.

"They have retired to Adina's cabin. Faren said it was because Adina needed more rest after he drank so much of her blood but she did not appear tired." Val grinned.

Abby laughed. "Did you ever think Faren could fall in love with a human?"

"I didn't think Faren could fall in love with anyone but himself," Val replied.

Abby laughed again as she relaxed again him.

"The young Sara seems to be happy," Val said.

"Yes. She told me this morning that Radek had claimed her as his mate. She was more than a little excited about it," Abby replied.

"He will be good to her," Val said.

"I know," Abby said. "I'm happy for her too. Hell, I'm happy for everyone."

"You know what would make me happy?" Val nuzzled her throat affectionately. "If you joined me in our cabin."

"You don't want to celebrate with our friends?" Abby said teasingly.

"What I want, little dove, is to have you underneath me while I make you come repeatedly," he murmured into her ear.

She shivered and took his hand before tugging him to his feet. "We can celebrate later. Good night, Michael."

Michael rolled his eyes good-naturedly, "Good night, Abigail."

They walked quickly towards their cabin as Kavine sat down next to Michael. "Hello, human."

"Hello, Kavine."

"Do you find me attractive?" She asked bluntly.

He stared at her and she raised her eyebrows. "Well, do you, human?"

"Yes."

"Good. We should try mating."

His jaw dropped and she smiled encouragingly at him as he cleared his throat. "Uh, aren't you in love with Radek?"

She shrugged. "I was. Now I am not. I find you handsome and would like to know what it's like to fuck a human. Are you willing?"

"We barely know each other," he said.

"Do we need to in order to fuck?" She gave him a curious look.

"I guess not."

"Good. Join me in my cabin." She took his hand and he cleared his throat again.

"Kavine, are you sure?"

"Aye, human. Very sure." She smiled again at him. "Are you worried I will hurt you? I promise I will be gentle with your cock. I know you are only a weak human."

"I'm stronger than I look," he said.

"Are you? Let's find out," she said sweetly.

RAINA GIGGLED AND RADEK STUDIED HER CURIOUSLY. "WHAT is it, Raina?"

She pointed to her left. Kavine was leading Michael to her cabin and Raina giggled again. "Kavine is taking the human back to her cabin. Earlier I overheard her telling Verna she

286

was going to find out what it was like to mate with a human. I hope she doesn't hurt him."

"Michael is very strong," Sara said. "I'm sure he can handle her."

Raina shrugged. "Aye, perhaps you are right." She reached across Radek and squeezed Sara's hand. "I'm so happy that Radek has claimed you and I have a sister now. Did I already tell you that?"

"Only about a dozen times, Raina," Radek said. "I'm starting to think you will enjoy having a sister more than a brother."

"Oh, I will," Raina said.

Sara laughed and Radek pulled her into his lap before pinching her ass. "Do not encourage her, sweet one."

"I am not," Sara said innocently. "But I have always wanted a sister as well."

Mia waved to Raina from across the fire. "Raina, come dance with us!"

She ran to join them as Radek nuzzled Sara's hair. "I love you, Sara."

"I love you too, Radek," she said.

He kissed her, his hands stroking her back before reaching under her to squeeze her ass, and Sara blushed when Kane's voice growled, "Perhaps you should take your mate back to your cabin, Radek."

"Hush, Kane." Reese squeezed his ass. "There's nothing wrong with showing affection for your mate."

She leaned down and kissed first Radek and then Sara. "Congratulations, you two. I haven't had the chance to tell you how happy I am that you're mated."

"Thank you, Reese," Sara said. She stroked Radek's hair affectionately as Kane led Reese to an empty spot by the fire.

He sat on the fallen log and tugged Reese into his lap.

"Are you happy, my love?"

"Very." She smiled at him. "Are you?"

"Aye." He glanced at his pack. "Our pack has grown substantially in the last two moons."

"It has," she said. "In a few months, it will grow again."

"What do you mean?" He asked.

She took his hand and rested it against her belly before smiling at him. He stared blankly at his hand and her grin grew when his eyes widened in understanding.

"You carry my pup in your belly?"

"Yep. As they say in my world, I'm knocked up."

He didn't reply and she stroked his face. "Kane? Are you still happy?"

He wrapped his arms around her and she made a breathless squeal of pain. "You're crushing me, Kane!"

"I'm sorry, my love." He released her immediately and rubbed her belly. "I'm sorry, little one."

She laughed. "I don't think he or she can hear you just yet."

"Perhaps not," he said.

"Are you still happy?" She asked again.

He cupped her face and kissed her before nodding. "Aye, Reese. I have never been happier. I cannot wait to hold our pup in my arms. I love you."

"I love you too, Kane."

END

Please keep reading for an excerpt from the next novel in the Other World Series, Claiming Quinn

CLAIMING QUINN EXCERPT

(OTHER WORLD SERIES BOOK FIVE)

Copyright © 2015 Ramona Gray

"Silas. Silas, wake up, man. C'mon, open your eyes."

Silas groaned and blinked rapidly. His head was aching and throbbing. He blinked again as Gage's worried face swam into focus.

"You okay, buddy?" Gage helped him sit up and Silas touched his hand to his temple. It came away wet and he stared in disbelief at the red liquid on his fingers.

"You must have hit your head on a rock. I've been trying to wake you up for five minutes." Gage squatted beside him and gripped his shoulder. "How do you feel?"

"Like I've been hit by a truck," Silas groaned. The rain was still falling steadily but the wind had died down. He took a cautious look around. "Where the hell are we?"

"I have no idea." Gage helped him to his feet, steadying him when he swayed a bit. "But I don't think we're in Kansas anymore, Toto."

Silas continued to look around as Angela joined them. The entire wet and shivering group was standing in the middle of a field. In front of them was a large forest with tall and impossibly thick trees. Behind them was more field. He squinted in the darkness, but it was impossible to tell how far the field went.

It was raining as hard as ever and thunder and lightning was crashing across the sky. It showed no sign of letting up as Steve pointed to the forest.

"C'mon, we should head for the trees."

"Are you sure that's smart?" Craig asked nervously. "We don't know what's in there."

"It's better than standing exposed in the middle of a field." Steve's brown skin was glistening with water. He shoved past him and started towards the trees. After a moment, the others followed.

It was even darker in the forest, but the trees were so dense and their branches so thick that the rain could barely penetrate the trees and was reduced to a light drizzle.

"God, I'm so cold," Veronica moaned. Silas shrugged out of his jacket and handed it to her. She took it with a nod of thanks and slipped into it.

They gathered under a large tree and stared blankly at each other.

"Anyone have any goddamn idea what's happening to us?" Gage asked.

"Isn't it obvious?" Kyle pushed his thick black hair off his forehead.

"Isn't what obvious?" Craig asked.

"Time travel." Kyle touched the tree behind them, rubbing his finger along the bark and then staring at the pad of his finger.

"Shut up, Kyle," Evan said testily.

Kyle shrugged. "Then you explain it."

"I can't and neither can you. But we didn't just fucking travel in time through a giant glowing orb."

"I think we did." Kyle stared solemnly at them. "Shit like this happens all the time."

"It does not!" Paula said indignantly.

"Sure it does. People disappear under mysterious circumstances. Their family and friends say it was aliens but what do you want to bet it's some type of time travel."

Lacey snorted. "Or maybe it is alien abduction. Maybe that orb is some kind of alien life force that sucked us into space and dumped us on its planet."

Kyle shrugged. "Maybe. Anything's possible."

Lacey rolled her eyes. "I wasn't being serious, Kyle."

Silas wiped the blood from his face as Gage took a few steps into the forest. "Gage, stay with the group."

Gage frowned. "Did you hear that, Silas?"

"Hear what?"

"It sounded like singing. Everyone be quiet for a minute."

Silas listened carefully. Although he heard nothing, Gage frowned and moved deeper into the forest.

"Gage!" He said.

Gage shook his head. "I heard it. Can't you hear it?"

"No. Just stay here. Don't -"

Silas cursed as Gage broke into a jog and disappeared into the forest. "Goddammit, Gage!"

He chased after his brother and after a moment the others followed.

"Gage! Wait up!" Silas held his hand to his aching head and jogged faster. The blood was really flowing now and he felt sick to his stomach and woozy. Great. He probably had a concussion.

Behind him, he could hear the girls grumbling and complaining as they struggled to keep up in their high heels.

He dodged around a tree and breathed a sigh of relief when he saw Gage standing motionless in front of him.

"Gage? Are you okay?" He stood next to his brother and peered anxiously at him.

"Yeah. Look." Gage pointed in front of him at the large pit in the ground. Silas frowned at the young woman who was standing in the pit, staring up at them.

"What the hell?"

"Please help me. Please." The woman's voice was soft and anxious.

Silas stared at her. Her blonde hair was long and wavy, and she was dressed in an ankle-length blue skirt and a form fitting halter top that left her trim stomach bare. The halter top was cut low and revealed the tops of her small breasts. Her skin was pale, and her light blue eyes stared pleadingly up at them.

"What are you doing in there?" Gage whispered as the others joined them at the edge of the pit.

"Please help me," the woman repeated. "I've been trapped in here for days."

"Did you – were you singing?" Gage couldn't stop staring at the woman and he paid no attention when Angela pulled on his arm.

The woman smiled. "You heard me?"

Gage nodded and Angela frowned a little at the look on his face before staring down at the woman. "What's your name?"

The woman ignored Angela completely. She was staring at Gage with a combination of delight and desire and Gage was returning her look unabashedly.

"Gage – knock it off." Silas shook his younger brother.

"We need to help her. We need to get her out of there."

Gage took a deep breath and tore his gaze from the woman's face. "We should find rope or -"

"Guys, is it just me or is the chick glowing?" Evan was peering into the pit and the rest of them followed his gaze.

"Holy shit. She is," Steve whispered.

Silas stepped back. The woman in the pit *was* glowing. Glowing so brightly that the entire bottom of the pit was illuminated and soft light was flowing up to wash over their faces.

"She's so beautiful," Gage whispered. He took another step forward as Angela gave Silas an alarmed look and tugged hard on Gage's arm.

"Gage, what's wrong with you?"

"Please help me. It's been days and I'm hungry and thirsty," the woman pleaded again.

Gage's eyes swept down her body, lingering on her breasts and then her hips. She began to glow even more brightly and her pale face reddened.

Silas frowned. Something didn't feel right. The woman looked too good - too clean - to have been in the pit for days. He took a few steps back, abandoning the group that was still gathered around the pit, and looked suspiciously into the trees. He squinted into the darkness that suddenly didn't seem as dark as it was before. There was a glow coming from the trees. He was sure of it. The hair on the back of his neck stood up and the throbbing in his head increased until it was a pulsing, blinding pain. He turned back to the group.

"Get away from there!" He suddenly yelled.

The group, except for Gage who was still staring transfixed at the girl in the pit, turned toward him.

"Get back now! It's a trap! Get -"

There was a soft whooshing noise. There were curses and startled screams as a large rope net hidden under the leaves that littered the forest floor swept the group off their feet and into the air.

"Gage!" Silas ran toward the gently swaying net. His foot hit something spongy and soft, something rough tightened around his ankle and the world was suddenly turned upside down. He swung back and forth, the tips of his fingers just brushing the ground as the others fought to escape the net.

"Silas! Silas – are you okay?" Gage stared at him, his face smashed up against the net. A foot rested against the side of his head.

"Just great," Silas groaned. The blood was rushing to his head and he could hear the blood from the cut on his temple dripping onto the ground in a steady patter.

Someone brushed by him. He caught a glimpse of long tanned legs and then a low voice was calling, "Kila! Kila – are you hurt?"

"No, Quinn. I'm perfectly fine. Get me out of here."

Silas watched as the dark-haired woman uncoiled a rope and dropped it into the pit. She wrapped one end around her arm and braced her feet. "Climb," she instructed.

He was rotated in the air by strong hands around his hips.

"Ooh, this one is big." A blonde, pale woman ran her hand down his chest. "Strong too. I'm going to claim him."

"Like hell you are, Fionn! I saw him first." Another blonde, she was shorter and curvier than the woman who was touching him came out of the trees and squeezed Silas' ass.

"You did not, Barkha! You're lucky he even got caught in the trap. He saw you glowing." Fionn glared at the woman.

Barkha shrugged and ran her hand up and down Silas' thick thigh. "I could not help it. You know I like the danens. Just thinking about having this one between my legs gets me going." Her pale skin began to glow and Fionn rolled her eyes.

"God, Barkha, you're such a tarnan."

Barkha scowled at her. "Take that back, Fionn. Take it back right now or so help me I'll - "

"Enough." Quinn's voice was quiet, but the two women immediately stopped their bickering and bowed.

"Forgive us, massina," Fionn murmured.

"There will be plenty of time to claim him later. Right now we need to chain them and go."

"Are we taking the females as well?" A fourth voice could be heard, and Silas strained to see around Barkha's ample hips.

"Yes, Akia, she wants them all." Quinn squatted beside him and poked at his blood-stained temple. "This one is injured."

Silas quickly grabbed her wrist and twisted hard. "Let us go, now."

Before he could twist again, two long and very sharp blades were pressed against his throat.

"Release her," Fionn snarled as Barkha pressed her blade deeper against his skin.

"Silas!" Gage yelled and struggled frantically in the net. There were grunts of pain and shouts of anger as his friends were kicked and jostled.

Silas released the dark-haired woman's wrist. She was staring at him with amusement in her dark grey eyes as she stood and indicated for the others to follow her, leaving him to swing helplessly. Working together, they released the net and it fell to the ground with a hard thump.

"You're on my hair!" Gemma screeched and Steve grunted as he was kicked in the stomach by Paula.

"Quinn, what of the danen?" Kila asked.

"We'll cut him down and chain him quickly," Quinn replied.

Akia was already scaling the tree. She reached the branch that the rope was tied to and sawed through the rope with a knife she pulled from her belt. Silas collapsed on to his back with a loud grunt, hitting the back of his aching head on the hard ground. Before he could rise, Barkha and Fionn had their knives to his throat.

"Stay steady, danen," Fionn warned as Quinn straddled him and dropped to her knees.

She sat firmly on his sternum. Barkha handed her a large, thick leather collar and she quickly buckled it around Silas' neck. She rose up a little and smacked him lightly on the chest. "Turn over."

He stared unblinkingly at her and her eyes narrowed. "Turn over."

"If I don't?" He challenged.

She leaned over him, her breath warm on his face. "I'll kill one of your females. But first, you'll watch me cut out her eyes."

He grunted and she leaned back, smiling with satisfaction when he turned onto his stomach and chest. She took his wrists and locked leather cuffs around them. The cuffs were linked with a piece of heavy chain that was just long enough to allow him to move his hands to his hips but no further.

She patted him on his back. "Turn over and lay on your back again. Don't move. Watch him, Barkha."

She moved off of him and joined the others who were opening the net. Silas stared at them. There were seven of them including Quinn. Correct that - eight. The one they called Akia had shimmied down the tree and joined the others.

With the exception of Kila, they were dressed similarly in short, blue cotton skirts that were cut into long strips so the fabric flowed easily around their legs. Their tops were leather bustiers with metal cups. On their upper arms they wore wide leather arm bands with metal studs hammered into them and leather wrist bands adorned each of their wrists. Knee-length leather boots completed their outfits.

They were of varying shapes and sizes with Kila being the smallest and Quinn the biggest. He guessed that she was around six feet tall and she had wide hips and large breasts. Exactly his type, he decided, if she hadn't just buckled a collar around his neck and chained his hands together.

"Listen to me!" Quinn stared at the squirming bodies in the net. "Quiet your tongues and listen."

Her tone brooked no refusal and they quieted as Akia and Fionn worked together to open the net.

"If you stay quiet and obey us, you will not be harmed. If you fight or if you try to run, I will kill you. Do you believe me?"

She squatted and stared at each of the prisoners. "Do you?"

"Yes." Craig cleared his throat. "We do."

"Good. We are going to open the net and each of you will lie still until you are collared and chained. For every unnecessary movement you make, I will cut off one of your fingers. Do you understand?"

"Yes," Craig replied again.

Akia and Fionn opened the net. All of them stayed perfectly still as one-by-one they were collared and chained. Kila helped Gage to his feet, her pale hands lingered around his waist and she smiled shyly at him. "Your name is Gage?"

"Yes." Gage swallowed as her fingers explored his chest through his t-shirt.

"My name is Kila." She pronounced it with a long e sound, and Gage repeated it. His hands were bound in leather cuffs and he clenched them tightly when she slipped her hands under his shirt and stroked the smooth skin of his chest.

"Get your hands off of him!" Angela glared at the blonde woman and Kila studied her carefully before looking at Gage once more.

"Is she your woman?" Her hands caressed his chest as Gage stared at her light blue eyes.

He hesitated and Angela scowled at him. "Gage!"

"No." Gage continued to look at Kila. "She isn't."

"You son of a bitch!" Angela tried to kick him and Fionn pulled her back and laughed.

"Quiet down, girl. It wouldn't matter anyway – we share the breeders."

"What do you mean breeders?" Gemma frowned. A woman with sandy brown hair and plump cheeks attached a chain to the metal hoop that was on the front of her collar.

"It will all be explained later." She smiled in a friendly way at Gemma, but Gemma gave her a look of suspicion.

Kila was smiling at Gage. Her white skin radiated a soft glow and Quinn spoke sharply to her. "Enough, Kila. Remember who you are."

Kila flushed. Her glow cut out abruptly and she removed her hands from under Gage's shirt. "I remember well enough, Quinn."

"Good." Quinn turned around and rolled her eyes. "For Garna's sake, Barkha! You *are* a tarnan."

Barkha was emitting her own soft glow as she cupped and caressed Silas' dick through his jeans. "What? I am only touching the fabric of his pants. They wear such strange clothing when they get here, do they not?"

She continued to rub Silas as she spoke, and Quinn stomped over and knocked her away. She fell hard onto her backside and glared up at Quinn.

"Garna! You don't have to be so rough, massina."

"Your orders were to watch him not fondle him." Quinn crouched over her and grabbed her chin. "Disobey me again and you'll find yourself working in the kitchens. Do you understand?"

"Yes, Quinn," Barkha said sullenly.

Quinn grabbed Silas' bound arms and heaved him to his feet.

Jesus, she's strong, Silas thought as he weaved a little in front of her.

"Garna, he's so big." Barkha stared up at him and glowed brightly.

"Barkha!" Quinn sighed with annoyance and Barkha cast her eyes to the ground, her glow dissipating immediately.

The darkness was still lit up and Quinn glanced around to see that everyone besides herself and Kila were staring at Silas and glowing brightly.

"Oh for the…" Quinn shook her head. "Have you all gone mad? He is only a man. If your queen were to see you this way – her own personal guard acting like wanton tarnans – she would have all of your heads."

She clipped a heavy short chain to the metal ring at the front of Silas' collar. "All of you are to stay away from him. No one touches him except for Naveen or myself."

"Who are you to make such rules?" Akia said. "Do you mean to claim him for yourself then?"

Quinn stared coolly at her. "I guess you'll have to wait until the claiming ceremony to find out. Until then – no one touches him. He's dangerous."

She gave the chain a hard yank and Silas had no choice but to follow her deeper into the trees.

ABOUT THE AUTHOR

Ramona Gray is a Canadian romance author. She currently lives in Alberta with her awesome husband and her super cute dog. She's addicted to home improvement shows, good coffee, and reading and writing about the steamier moments in life.

For more information about Ramona, check out her website at

www.ramonagray.ca

facebook.com/RamonaGrayBooks

twitter.com/RamonaGrayBooks

instagram.com/ramonagrayauthor

amazon.com/Ramona-Gray/e/B00OD26SAM

bookbub.com/profile/ramona-gray

The Welder

The Electrician

The Landscaper

The Firefighter

The Cop

The Paramedic

Working Men Series Bundles

Working Men Series Books One to Three

Working Men Series Books Four to Six

Working Men Series Books Seven to Nine

Other World Series

The Vampire's Kiss (Book One)

The Vampire's Love (Book Two)

The Shifter's Mate (Book Three)

Rescued By The Wolf (Book Four)

Claiming Quinn (Book Five)

Choosing Rose (Book Six)

Elena Unbound (Book Seven)

Other World Series Box Sets

Other World Series Books One to Three

Other World Series Books Four to Six